Far From Glory

Printed in the United States of America. For information, address Finns Way Books™, 360 Grand Avenue, Suite 204, Oakland, California, 94610; or contact www.finnswaybooks. com

For information on Finns Way Reading Group Guides, please contact Finns Way Books™ by electronic mail at readinggroupguides@finnswaybooks.com

The poem by Horne, Frank. "Kid Stuff,"(1942), from Christmas Gif': An Anthology of Christmas Poems, Songs, and Stories, Written by and about Negroes, Compiled by Charlemae Rollins, Chicago: Follett Publishing Co., 1963.

Section and Cover photos -
Part I: Courtesy National Archives, photo no. 26-G-27-015-001
Part II and cover: from the personal collection of the author
Part III: by the author

ISBN 978-0-9985288-2-3

November 15, 2018

from the author of

The Glory Road

Far From Glory

BRUCE COYLE

Far From Glory

A NOVEL

BY

BRUCE COYLE

Part I

1

Three days ago, the seagulls fled inland. Coots and mudhens still paddled around near the shore, but the coming storm had driven the seabirds toward higher ground. They were good barometers, and the rains started soon after they left, pounding the coast and sending the river out of its banks. But the bigger storm was yet to come.

Jack Moon studied the dark clouds rolling in from the sea. It was just dark, and the wind blew inland up the coast where the river emptied into the ocean. The river formed a lagoon at its mouth, but the storm had opened the river to the sea, and huge waves surged into the breach. "Big storm coming soon – you watch."

I sat beside him on the steps of the low barracks building. I couldn't disagree. Indian Jack had lived on this stretch of the Pacific coast all his life. This was his land before the Coasties came. He'd raised sheep in the oak openings in the hills above the river. His face was well-worn leather, mostly unlined, and his gray hair hung in a single braid down his back. His calloused hands were scarred from hard work. Jack's eyes, creased at the corners, had a distant look that said he had seen much and forgotten little in his time. That look was about the long ago and the far away, of memory stretched back in time. When he looked at you, he looked deep–studied you in a way that unnerved some and led to his being called Mad Jack by some of the men in the beach patrol.

That night the waves pounded the beach, and the wind carried the spray and the sound of the booming surf inshore. Water ran off the eaves of the barracks, dripped on the ground, and collected in long puddles at each side of the building.

"Crossing that river now makes no sense. Your lieutenant's a fool. Japs got more sense than him."

We had only been on patrol for a few months now. There had been other storms before this, but we had still managed. My friend Wiley and I had never seen the ocean before we arrived at this new Coast Guard station on the California coast. Our heads were filled with notions of bold adventures that lay just ahead, but it didn't turn out the way we expected. The ocean was just an endless gray line that separated the sky from the sand. And there was a lot of sand. The coastline was rugged in some places, steep bluffs rising up from the beach. Big rocks, some with trees growing on top, stuck up out of the water. These were called sea stacks, they said. At night, they looked like ships just offshore.

Our job was to patrol the beaches. We looked for aircraft, for ships, for anyone who might be a threat to our shores. People worried about an invasion, about planes launched from submarines–any sign that the Japs were headed our way. Our beach was as isolated as any spot along the coast could be. It was possible someone could try to sneak ashore, but even on shore, they would be a long way from anything important.

We had thought it would be exciting, but it wasn't. When we first arrived, patrolling an unknown beach in the dark at night gave us the shivers. Every sound gave us pause, made us worry. After repeated outings where nothing happened, we relaxed, complained about the cold and the damp and the long walks–but we donned our heavy weather gear and kept at it. It was what we were there for. They called us "sand pounders," not very glamorous, maybe, but important, they said. We were the first line of defense.

Not that we had much to defend anyone with at first. Most of our patrols were made up of two men with a Very pistol and a .38 between them. We weren't supposed to "engage the enemy"—only to observe and report. But so far Wiley and I hadn't seen much and had reported less.

We thought things would improve some when the dogs came, but it didn't turn out that way. Wiley and I usually managed to be on patrol together. It was reassuring to have him by my side on the dark beach at night, even if we only had one pistol between us. But after we got the dogs, it was just me and Jig, a big black and tan German shepherd, alone on the beach at night. His nose was better than Wiley's and his eyes and ears, too, I was told, but it took me a while to warm to the idea of being alone on the dark beach at night, with just Jig at my side. Like the others, I had been issued a Springfield rifle, too–a heavy ten-pounder with a leather sling that dug into my shoulder as I slogged along in the sand.

Wiley ended up with Doc, another shepherd, and Wiley and he took to each other like they had been raised in the same litter. I don't know what it was, but there was something between them from the beginning. Doc was Wiley's dog as sure as if he had signed a loyalty oath. He was bigger than Jig, eighty-five pounds of pure muscle under black and brown fur. I couldn't get near him, but Wiley could get him to do almost anything. One of Wiley's favorite tricks was to bend over at the waist, brace his hands on his thighs, and then signal to Doc, who would jump onto his back and stand there until Wiley signaled him to get down.

Once Wiley had gotten Jack's daughter Lucy to save him a big bone from the mess, and he was taking it down to Doc's kennel when he realized that he had left his hat behind. He'd already let Doc out of the kennel and didn't want to lock him up again, so he just put the bone on the ground in front of Doc and told him to wait. Twenty minutes later when he got back with his hat–and a cup of coffee–Doc was still sitting there in front of that bone, guarding it. When other men and their dogs passed by, the dogs would look at Doc and his bone, then turn away when Doc growled. If anticipation counted for anything, that must have been the best bone ever.

At night, the beach south of the river was a long, unrelieved stretch of endless sand. Under clear skies, with the moon out, it was a nice walk, even though my boots sank in the sand, and my legs turned to jelly by the end of my tour. Civilians weren't allowed on the beaches at night, and fishing boats had to run with blacked-out lights. When I was alone on the beach at night, I was really alone. Sounds carried from far off. The pounding surf was constantly at my side, but sometimes I heard other sounds I couldn't identify. Sometimes a skunk or raccoon rustled through the bushes that grew on the crest of the ridge just above the sand. At other times I heard man-made sounds from far off, maybe engine noise carried on the wind from a blacked-out boat at sea. Jig's ears always perked up, and then he'd stick his nose in the air, snuffling loudly to test the wind. Sometimes he heard things I hadn't, and that really gave me goosebumps. Jig raised his hackles, and growled softly, making a low sound in his throat. But he rarely barked. I was assured he knew what he was doing, but it took me a while to put my trust in him.

North of the river was a different story altogether. The river rolled out to sea against a giant bluff. In summer, the river formed a lagoon, and the spit below the bluff was a continuous stretch of sand. But when winter storms began, the river broke out into the sea, the water swirled along at the base of the bluff, and you couldn't go north unless you crossed the river in a boat, climbed over the bluff, and hiked down the other side. There was a rocky landing at the base, and a steep, winding trail that climbed to the top. Fog sat on top of the bluff sometimes, making it hard to keep your bearings, especially at night. Once, when it was like that, I nearly walked off the edge, but Jig had stopped in front of me and refused to go any further. I pulled on his lead like crazy, but he wouldn't budge. My heart leaped when I realized he had just saved my life.

Once over the top, the trail wound down to another long stretch of sandy beach, but it was tough going through scrub brush that tore at my leggings and roots that caught my boots and tried to trip me every other step. Jig had little canvas boots to protect his feet, mostly from the broken shells that littered the beach. He didn't like it when I tried to put them on him, but once he was wearing them, he kept them on and didn't complain.

It was a relief to finally set foot on the beach. Telephone lines strung on poles led to a shack at the end of the spit. When everything was working right, you could call in from there, then rest for a bit before heading back.

Lieutenant Peake had a thing about the north side. The bluff blocked our view up the coast, and he was convinced that made it a perfect place for the enemy to land. The attack on the *Emidio* and other ships along the Pacific coast last year had convinced some more than others that the threat was real. Peake didn't want to be caught with his pants down, I guess.

Most of the men got along with each other just fine. We had all signed up for this, and if it hadn't turned out to be what we'd thought, we were still doing our part. But Peake was a pain in the ass, hard on everyone most of the time, even when he needn't be. Another officer, Ensign Tyler, was Peake's junior officer. Tyler was older than Peake. He had been a lieutenant himself once, but he'd gotten in trouble and been busted back to ensign. Nobody knew for sure what the trouble was, but he had somehow managed to keep his commission in spite of it. Tyler had an easy manner that inspired cooperation without resentment and made him popular with most of the men. Tyler knew his stuff. His authority was clear, but he saw us as men, and we respected him for it.   Peake, on the other hand, was a ninety-day wonder who seemed like he always had something to prove, and he was a hardass about everything he did. He seldom listened to suggestions, even from Tyler. The men followed Peake's orders no matter how unreasonable they seemed because he was their commanding officer, but they weren't always happy about it.

This was my night off, and I was sitting on the porch with Jack Moon outside the mess. His daughter Lucy worked in the kitchen, and she had just brought us two steaming mugs of coffee. I was as happy for the warmth of the thick white mug in my hands as I was for the strong brew it contained.

"Wiley's got north side duty tonight," I told Jack. "As bad as this storm is shaping up, I was thinking Peake might call it off."

"Peake don't take nobody's counsel but his own. I told him myself. No way to cross when the water's like that. Ocean rolling into the river, pushing those big waves in, but he don't want to hear all that–got his mind already made up. He thinks I'm just a crazy old Indi'n. But I've watched that river my whole life. Can't cross when the water's like that."

He stood up then, drank the last of his coffee, tossed

the dregs, and turned to go inside. When Lucy finished her work, they would get in Jack's old green pickup and drive back to their house on the hill. "G'night, Justin. Keep your powder dry, son."

"You too, Jack."

2

Later that night, I was lying on my bunk, thinking about writing a letter home and what I could say to make things here seem interesting. There were half a dozen others in the barracks, too. Tommy Rainwater and Red Morgan had dragged a footlocker between their bunks and were playing cribbage for a penny a point. Tommy squinted at the cards in his hand through the smoke from the cigarette between his lips. Since it wasn't too long after payday, he was still smoking tailor-mades–Luckies. By the end of the month, he'd be rolling his own from a five-cent bag of Bull Durham.

Nick Walsh had his face stuck in a book as always. We called him Professor 'cause he was always reading. Just started college, then quit to join up after Pearl Harbor. He was a little stuffy, but he got along okay with everybody. Anybody who wanted to know about something usually asked the Professor first, unless it had something to do with the service. For that kind of thing, we all looked to Ensign Tyler for advice.

"Mac" McDonald was snoring on his bunk, and a couple others were sitting on their bunks just passing the time. Suddenly there was a commotion at the door, and it was flung open, the doorknob slamming into the wall. Wiley burst through the door, soaked to the bone, dripping water that puddled on the floor around him. He looked up at me, white as a sheet, his hair plastered to his forehead, his eyes wide. "They're all gone, Justin."

Everybody stopped what they were doing and looked up at Wiley. I grabbed a blanket and pulled it around his shoulders. "What do you mean? Who's gone?" The other men left their bunks and gathered around Wiley and me.

"Billy, Tony, Swede–they're all gone. We were about halfway across. The swells coming in were huge. We were loaded down, with only about eight inches of freeboard, and water kept lapping over the gunwales. We were trying to keep the boat headed a little upriver as we crossed, knowing we would drift down toward the beach, but a big one caught us broadside, and the boat heaved up and tossed us all into the drink. I didn't see what happened to the others. I went under right away. My gear dragged me down. Somehow I managed to get out of my coat, but my boots were pulling me under, and I couldn't shed them. Everything was happening too fast. I looked around for something to grab onto and caught the end of one of the oars as it drifted past, but it didn't help much. I knew I wouldn't make it back. I just drifted a bit, those big rollers lifting me up and down.

"Then I heard a chuffing, snorting sound nearby, and here comes Doc paddling toward me for all he's worth. He clamped his jaws on that oar and started paddling toward shore. I paddled along with him as hard as I could. We drifted a long way, but we made it to shore. I latched onto a tree root sticking out of the bank and just hung there, but Doc grabbed my sleeve and kept pulling until I finally managed to sit up. We just sat there together for a while." Wiley shivered and pulled the blanket tighter. "I will love that dog as long as I live."

They had made the crossing in a surfboat with four men and two dogs. The men were all wearing heavy gear–boots, heavy waterproof jackets, and rain hats with wide brims. Wiley sat at the first of the three banks of oars, Doc and another dog named Maisie in the bow behind him.   Billy Randall and Tony Benzonelli manned the other oars, and Stieg Alvarsson sat in the stern with the equipment. Stieg was a stocky, barrel-chested fellow everybody called Swede. He was known to speak his mind, often without considering who he was talking to. Wiley told me he and Peake had gotten into it before the men shoved off in the surfboat.

"Swede tried to talk nice at first–said the crossing wasn't safe. Said if we couldn't cross the river, the Japs weren't going to be landing on the north side of the bluff, either. We knew Tyler had figured it out, too. Swede asked him to talk to Peake, and I guess he tried–the two of them walked along the bank a ways and had a chat, but you could tell it wasn't going our way.

"We could see Tyler talking, pointing to the river and then the sea, but Peake just stood there with his arms folded and didn't seem to say much. You know Peake don't like to be challenged."

"You're right about that. The man thinks he'll lose face if he changes his mind. Too bad Tyler isn't in charge. Peake could learn a few things about command from him."

"If Tyler was in charge, they'd still be alive. All of them– Maisie, too."

The next day, the storm passed and the weather cleared. The skies were still gray, but the wind had died. By afternoon, the sea had calmed as well. The river was still muddy and swollen, but the big rollers had subsided. The men gathered in front of Peake's office. Wiley and I stood in the back with Jack Moon. After a few minutes, Peake stepped out onto the porch.

"What's this about, men?"

"We want to go look for the other boys," one of the men said. It was Ted Sturgis, "Reverend" Ted we called him. He was a quiet man who always carried a little Bible in a watertight case in his pocket. He was friendly enough when you spoke to him, but he kept to himself most of the time. "We owe it to them."

Peake looked at the men, studying their faces for a moment before he spoke.

"Those bodies have all washed out to sea by now. But go look if you want. I don't think you'll find anything. Ensign Tyler will lead you." With that, he turned back and went into his office.

Jack Moon had heard what Peake said. "Those men are still in the river, most likely. Those big waves pushed in toward land last night. There's a big shelf comes out underwater from the bluff. Got a deep hole right below it. Those bodies sank with all that gear on them. The ocean pushed in, and the river swirled underneath 'cause it couldn't make it out to sea. Look just off that shelf–see what you find there."

Wiley stayed behind with Jack and watched from the shore as four of us set out to search the river. We had a hundred feet of line, and Jack had given us a set of big treble hooks he used to snag logs that came downriver in the winter. We tied the hooks at intervals on the line and headed out across the river. It was tough rowing upstream, but three of us pulling hard made enough headway to get across to the area where Jack said we should look. Tyler sat in the stern with the line looped at his feet.

We were upstream from the rocky landing at the base of the bluff, and we let the boat drift until we were opposite the rocks. Ensign Tyler dropped the line overboard from the stern, and we set to rowing upstream as hard as we could. When we had gone a couple hundred yards upstream, we moved closer to the bank where the current wasn't so strong, and pulled in the line. We made three passes like that, but didn't find anything. I was beginning to think Jack had been wrong.

Sometimes the hooks seemed to catch on something, but the only thing we brought up was a chunk of wood from a submerged log. On the fourth pass, the line straightened out behind us, and we started hauling something in. "Probably just another log," Tyler said. "Keep pulling."

The line held tight, and Tyler gathered it in, coiling it in the bottom of the boat as we went. As we neared the end of the line, Tyler shouted "I see something!"

When we drew the line in closer, we all saw what he was looking at. An arm, with a wristwatch on it, broke through the surface. When we brought the body up to the boat, we saw it was Swede. We hoisted him in over the side and headed back to shore, exhausted. Swede's watch was still ticking. We never found the others.

3

The next morning, Wiley and I had breakfast together and walked down to the kennel to feed the dogs and give ourselves and them a little exercise. Wiley was still shaken up, I could tell. He was usually talkative, making jokes, kidding me about one thing or another, but he'd hardly said anything at all during the meal. When we got to the kennel, he let Doc out, knelt down and hugged him, made little "good boy" talk in the dog's ear, and snapped on his lead. Then he turned his head and looked up at me. "Don't tell Annie what happened. She'll tell Agnes, and I don't want her to hear about it."

"What do you mean? It's the biggest thing that's happened since we got here."

"I know, but Agnes told me she'd never forgive me if I got myself killed, and I came pretty close. I don't want her to know. You know how she is. She just thinks we're walking along the beach, looking for spies. I'd like her to keep on thinking that."

Wiley and I were the same age. We met when I started school in Glory, and we hit it off right away. There weren't many of us in the little one-room community school, but we had a good teacher, Mr. Phillips, who tried hard to help us learn. Some of the kids were old enough to shave, and some were little ones who were antsy in their seats and pestered each other constantly, testing Mr. Phillips' patience. Wiley and I stayed over at each other's houses and tramped around the countryside together, doing the foolish things boys will do if left to their own devices. Wiley had a reckless streak that rose in him sometimes and got us in trouble on more than one occasion.

Agnes had toned down Wiley's reckless impulses somewhat. His girlfriend lived out in the country on the other side of town and rode her horse to school every day. Agnes was smart and really good at school. She was headstrong in a way that annoyed me at times, but she knew her own mind and didn't put up with foolishness from others she met. Her long red hair and her cowgirl figure were the flames that lit Wiley's candle, and she soon had him roped and tied.

Wiley's father was a farrier. He traveled around the countryside shoeing horses and trimming hoofs and such. He had promised to teach Wiley to drive a car, but had given Wiley a horse for Christmas one year instead. Agnes had taught Wiley to ride, and after that he was a goner. It wasn't hard to tell who was holding the reins with those two.

When we got back to the barracks, some of the men were gathered outside. Red Morgan and Tommy Rainwater were talking. "It ain't right," Red said. "Peake should be strung up for sending those boys out in that storm, sent them to die, sure as hell."

"Yeah, he's got it coming, for sure. But I bet it don't happen. Guys like him never get what's comin' to 'em, seems like."

There was a lot of grumbling among the men. Then Reverend Ted spoke up: "Most of us are as good as God made us, but some of us are a lot worse. We all know what kind of man Peake is. But nothing's gonna happen to him."

"Professor" Nick jumped in then. He pushed his glasses up on his nose and looked around at everybody. "Ted's right. You know about the blackouts, hear the cars crawling through the hills at night, going slow with barely enough light to see twenty feet ahead. You hear fishing boats putting along at night, not showing enough light to be seen except when the moon is full. Well, there's a news blackout, too. Nothing gets out, gets in the papers or on the radio. They don't want the locals to panic. None of those boys were from around here. They'll just make up some story to tell their folks, but it'll be kept quiet, you can bet on it."

I wouldn't say anything to Annie about what happened. I knew she would tell Agnes, and no matter how tough she talked, Agnes would worry. I didn't want to give her more to worry about. Before this war was over, there would be plenty more things we didn't want to talk about.

I liked to sit outside the mess with Jack in the evenings when I wasn't on duty. Sometimes we just sat there on the porch steps and watched the sun go down, but usually we found something to talk about. I talked more than he did. Jack was comfortable with silence, content to just sit and be, to take in the sounds of the surf and the river nearby, and watch the arrows of ducks making their way across the sun as it sank into the sea.

I interrupted some of those quiet evenings by telling Jack about how I had lived in a little lumber camp called Cooper's Gulch before we moved to Glory. My daddy and his best friend, a Negro man called Waters, had grown up together on nearby farms in Oklahoma and traveled out here, working their way along till they ended up at the mill. I told him how Daddy and Momma had met there and gotten married. But Daddy got killed in a logging accident when I was almost fifteen. Waters had always spent Saturday evenings with Momma and Daddy and me, and he still came by after Daddy died.

The other men who worked in the woods were a pretty rough lot who carried tins of snoose that wore holes in their back pockets and spat when they felt the urge, timber tramps and short stakers with colorful language that seemed to need at least two cuss words to make a sentence, men who seldom shaved or bathed more than once a week, who spent most of their pay on gambling and drink. But they were white, and they didn't take kindly to Waters spending time with Momma and me, and one night a tough named Brady and some of his cronies caught Waters out and tried to drown him in the log pond.

"Momma's Uncle Hal was the foreman at the mill, and he knew trouble was brewing. Caught up to those toughs just in time to save Waters."

Jack turned and looked at me. "Sounds like a good man—stood up for your momma like that."

"He was afraid for Momma—and Waters, too—took us sixty miles away to a ranch he owned at the end of the Glory Road, pretty much in the middle of nowhere. But he was still worried those men might come back, so he took Momma away and wouldn't tell anyone where she was, even me and Waters."

"Must have been tough on you. First your daddy, then your momma's gone, too."

"Yeah, but he was right. Those men did come back and beat up Uncle Hal pretty bad. Cracked some ribs and broke his leg so that even after it healed he had a permanent hitch in his getalong. Some of the folks in town helped the sheriff stop them before they could get to Waters, and the men got sent off to take up rooms in the stony lonesome."

"Seems like the good men turn out when there's a need—like you boys here. But the bad ones are easier to find, seems like. Don't have to look too far to find trouble. Good thing to remember, Justin."

Momma had come back after things settled down,

surprising us all by bringing me a baby sister. It was her and Waters' baby. Rebecca was cute as hell and hard not to love, but the color lines were clearly drawn. White shoes smudge easily, and Momma and Waters had kicked up a lot of dust. Lots of folks were unhappy about that. I didn't understand how it could matter so much to them. I had known Waters every day of my life. He and Uncle Hal had watched over me all the time Momma was gone. I had learned a lot from both of them, but mostly it was Waters. He was a good man, and those who knew him soon realized that. But I guess that's the problem. People are afraid of what they don't know, and so they make up things, or they make themselves out to be better than others so they won't be afraid. It was tough on Momma and Waters–and on Rebecca and me.

I told Jack about the tough times in Glory after Momma came back and how people had treated her and Rebecca, too.

"Used to be, long time ago," Jack said, "a white man might take up with a Indi'n woman. Not a lot of white women in some places. Sometimes they found each other and took a liking. Most of them men got hard treatment from their own kind. Told the man he had the smell of the blanket on him, made fun in a hurtful way, sometimes beat 'em up. 'Course the Indi'ns didn't exactly welcome him either."

"That still happen?" I asked.

"Not so much. Lot more white women–not so many Indi'ns." He laughed a little at his own joke. "Your momma kind of got the smell of the blanket on her, too, when she come back with Rebecca. Hard for mean people to see a white woman with a black baby and keep their mouths shut, act like it don't mean nothing to them. I don't understand all that nonsense. People good or bad–don't matter how they come into the world."

I liked talking with Jack. He reminded me some of Waters. He was a good listener, didn't always say much, but there was wisdom in his words, and a sense of humor so delicate it was easy to miss. Like Waters, he'd had some "hard treatment" from white folks. He had stayed on his ranch, not far from the old tribal lands, but the villages of his people were long gone, and there weren't many of them left. With the war and the arrival of the Coasties, his little world was changed. He had accepted this, knowing that there was a larger enemy to be fought, but he knew that most of the men never thought about whose land they were camped on, never thought much about him at all, except to dismiss him as "Mad Jack, that old Indian."

Uncle Hal hadn't thought much of Waters at first, but he'd stepped in to save him because it was the right thing to do, and he'd sworn to take care of Momma. After he took her away, it was just him and me and Waters on the ranch, and the two of them had made a kind of truce, with me in the middle. I didn't know what to do with myself most of the time. And then I met Annie.

Annie was small, with dark hair and a little spritz of freckles on her face. She had a smile that always made me melt when it was aimed at me. Annie had a good heart, and I could talk to her in ways that I couldn't with Uncle Hal and Waters. I told her about Daddy getting killed and Momma going away and how much I missed both of them, especially Momma. After school I stopped by Sadler's Market, her parents' store, before I went home to the ranch. I'd help out in the store if there was something that needed to be done, but I was really there to see Annie. She'd find time to sit with me on the bench behind the store, and we'd talk for a while before I had to go. Talking with Annie always made me feel better.

Annie was the one I'd given my heart to hold. She had saved me when I was lost, and I would never forget that. When she put her arms around me and looked into my eyes, we could push back the rest of the world and its troubles for a moment, and it always made me feel that no matter what happened, things would work out somehow. I didn't know how I could keep the news from her, but I had promised Wiley.

I think Annie was mostly right about things working out, but it wasn't easy the way we thought it would be when we were kids. "Hard times make folks strong," Annie's father used to say when we were growing up during the Depression. Those days were behind us—and now we had a war to win. It seemed to me that the hard times wouldn't leave us alone.

4

When Momma came home, she and Rebecca stayed in Waters' cabin on the hill. The cabin and the barn had been there before Uncle Hal bought the ranch. He'd had big plans for the place. His wife Orla was in Ireland, and he had come over before her. He'd worked hard, saved his money, and bought the ranch, building a catalogue house for Orla while he lived in the cabin. It was a nice little house, and he and Orla were happy there for a while.

But happy endings only seem to take place in stories, and misery seems to creep in when nobody's looking. Orla died not long after she and Hal had settled in, and he was knocked sideways for a long time. He closed up the house, rented out the ranch to a tenant farmer who stayed in the cabin, and traveled around, taking jobs as they came. Eventually, he ended up in Cooper's Gulch and worked his way up to become a foreman at the mill. He was a good man, but Orla's death had soured him on life, and he was gruff with everyone and kept to himself most of the time.

But after we left the mill and Hal took Momma away, I had spent a lot of time with him, living in the house he had built for Orla, and he'd softened considerably. He and Waters reached an accommodation of sorts. Waters pulled his own weight and revived an old orchard on top of the hill behind his cabin. He pruned back the old trees and gave them new life. He and I built an apple house that we cut into the hillside to store apples in the winter, and I helped him create a special tree he called the All-American that had shoots from most all the other trees grafted onto the old stock and eventually grew all kinds of apples on the same tree. Waters sold apples and cider and made applejack that proved popular with people along the Glory Road.

But Rebecca changed everything. If it had just been Momma that finally came home, everyone would have been happy for me. Annie and her parents knew how much I missed her. Wiley's mom and Sully, our mailman–everybody in Glory knew, I'm sure, especially after the trouble with Brady and his boys. Waters' applejack customers had grown to know him and accepted him, had stepped in with Sheriff Max to save Hal and him. But Rebecca was a different story. Seeing her stirred up fires long banked, and there was a lot of talk about Momma and Waters and me.

People I didn't even know stopped me on the street in Glory, asked me how I liked my pickaninny sister. Al, who owned the gas station where I had bought gas for the Model A I drove to school every week, invited me into his office for coffee one afternoon, something he'd never done before. He poured some hot coffee around the rim of a dirty cup that lay on the counter beside a little sink and filled it, handing it to me with grease-stained hands. I just stood there, wondering why he wanted to talk to me.

"Your momma didn't need to do that, you know."

"What do you mean?" I asked, though I was pretty sure where he was headed.

"You know, bringing that baby back with her like she done. Most folks don't think much about that kind of thing. Ain't no Negroes around here to give them cause. That man Waters stirred things up a little when he showed up with you and Hal, but most folks got over it when Sully sold them on that applejack he was making. But nobody knew what him and your momma been up to till she come back. She shoulda left that tar baby wherever she was. She didn't need to do what she done."

I'd had enough of this. I set the dirty cup down on a map that was unfolded on the countertop, spilling a little 'cause my hand was shaking. "Try this on, Al," I said, looking him straight in the eye. "Maybe the folks in Glory'd be happier if your momma had left *you* on a doorstep somewhere." I turned my back on him and walked out of his office, thinking how different it was going to be next time I had to buy gas.

5

The storms had passed. The seagulls returned, wheeling overhead. The sky was overcast and the fog pushed out to sea, at least until night came when it would crawl back to cover the beach like a blanket at bedtime. Jack had dropped Lucy off by the barracks, and I heard his pickup grinding slowly up the hill behind us. I was on my way to the kennel to get Jig and start my daytime patrol.

Lucy saw me and waved. She was short and pleasantly round. She wore a faded blue jacket over a kind of shapeless dress that she favored. Most of the men just ignored her. Peake, in particular, treated her like dirt, but she never complained. She didn't usually say much, but like Jack, she was interesting to talk to. "Good morning, Justin. You're out early today."

"Just getting ready to go on patrol. How are you doing?"

"Okay, I guess. Nice to have a break in the weather. I hoped I'd run into you. I brought you something. My father said to give it to you." She reached into her pocket, pulled out a package wrapped in tinfoil, and handed it to me. "It's just Indi'n candy. Y'know, salmon, smoked with honey and other spices. Take it with you, give some to your friend later."

"Thanks," I said, taking the package from her. Her eyes had a questioning look. "You heard about what happened?"

"Yeah–terrible thing. Your friend gonna be all right?"

"I think so–he just got scared. Barely made it back, you know?"

"Yeah. The sea and the river can be unfriendly if the water don't know you." She put her hands in her pockets, and looked out toward the ocean. "My father tells me stories passed down from the old ones. The water watches you, he says, takes your measure, decides what to think about you. If you've been to the same spot many times, the water is used to you and don't mind you looking at it. He's heard all the old stories. He says old men can talk in the presence of the water because they have been around so long. But the water can be very rough if you talk in its presence or look at it too long."

"You believe all that?"

She looked at me and smiled. "Not so much. Some of them ideas seem sorta silly. He says you shouldn't talk right before a wave breaks. I don't think my father believes it all, either. But I think he don't want to take a chance, just in case the old stories have truth in them. He knows the river, knows how dangerous it can be. He knew that crossing was a mistake—told me so."

"We all knew it, too. Peake was the only one couldn't figure it out."

"Man's got shit for brains, Swede told me once. I never saw nothin' to prove he was wrong about that. I liked Swede. He was nice to me, not like some of the others."

"Yeah," I said. "Swede was a good guy."

I'd never met Lucy when she had so much to say. It wasn't hard to tell she was upset. Her gift wasn't just a treat. It was comfort food, the kind folks bring to the house after a funeral. I held up the tinfoil package. "Thanks for the salmon. I'll make sure Wiley gets some." She started up the steps to the mess hall, and I turned and headed down to the kennel to get Jig.

When we got to the beach, I let Jig off his lead, and we started down the south spit. The storm had tossed a lot of stuff up on the beach. The smaller waves played with a driftwood log caught in the surf, pushing it onto the beach and pulling it back as the waves rolled in and out. Long strings of seaweed were everywhere. Fingers of white foam crept in with each wave and scrubbed at the sand as we walked along. The high tides had pushed waves of gravel ashore and left them in fan-shaped drifts here and there.

The Professor liked to collect rocks he found in those gravel beds. He kept a jar in his locker filled with agates and pieces of jade. One time he showed me some odd-looking little speckled brown stones that looked brittle and broken. I asked him what they were, and he said. "Those? Oh, those are just pieces of Paul Bunyan's crockery."

I looked at him like he had rocks in his head and not in the jar, but he just looked at me and laughed. "Went to the beach with my folks when I was little. Dad was tossing driftwood into the surf for the dog to fetch, and Mom and I were sitting on the sand, sifting a patch of gravel the sea had washed up, looking for agates. I saw a bunch of these little speckled rocks and asked her what they were. She laughed and said, 'Those are just pieces of Paul Bunyan's crockery', told me how Paul and his wife had a big fight over something or other and how Paul's wife had gotten mad at him and pulled all their dishes off the shelf and thrown them at him. She said those little speckled rocks are all that was left of Paul Bunyan's crockery."

For all his airs, the Professor was just like most of us. We were old enough to be here, doing this job, but we missed our families, and we missed the kids we used to be.

Further ahead two seagulls were fighting over a crab shell that had washed up, but they gave up and flew off as we got closer. Jig's ears perked up, but he decided they weren't worthy of his attention. He trotted ahead, swept back and forth between the water and the edge of the hill above. The wind was behind us, and he turned back frequently, looking at me, nose in the air. We didn't always take the dogs out during the daytime, but Peake was on edge and covering all the bases. I didn't mind; it wasn't like I had anything else to do. And it was a lot better than stumbling around in the dark, worrying about what I couldn't see. It gave me time to think.

When I was alone on the beach with Jig, my mind always drifted back to Annie and the situation at home. Things had settled down somewhat since Momma came home. When she first got back, Hal hardly spoke to her. She hadn't told him about Rebecca, and the news had thrown him for a loop. He was happy she was back, safe and sound. He had kept her safe until the trouble was over, but he knew she had brought new troubles that were more than he could deal with. He wouldn't talk to her for weeks. I had stayed in the house with him, helped with the chores as usual, and generally tried to stay out of the way while he and Momma worked it out between themselves.

One morning I had been in the barn, helping Hal feed his cows, when Momma walked down the hill from the cabin. We had split the bale and tossed the hay over the fence to the cows, who were chewing happily, long wisps hanging from their mouths. The new calves were feeding, too, butting their heads against their mothers' udders as they nursed. I had gone back inside to get oats and barley to spread on the hay. I dipped the coffee can into the sack and filled it up, intending to take it out to the cows when I heard Momma and Hal talking.

I felt awkward standing there in the shadows. I could hear what they were saying, but I was out of sight, and I couldn't help listening in. This was the first time Momma had come down to talk to Hal, and I didn't want to get in the way.

"Lovely cows, these. You've made a fine start, Hal."

Hal didn't say anything at first. I peeked out to see what he was doing. He just leaned both arms on the fence, staring ahead at the cows and, beyond them, to the cabin on the hill. Momma stood next to him, put her forearms on the fence, too. After a while, Hal turned to Momma.

"I don't know what to say, Molly. I've given it a lot of thought since you came back with the baby."

"Her name's Rebecca."

"I know—it's just… You've always been a strong girl, held your own with those men at the mill. I know you've got iron in you, but things will be tough for you and Waters, for Justin and Rebecca, too. I'm getting too old to keep trying to change the world."

Momma put her hand on his shoulder, looking up at him. "We can't change the world, Hal, but we can push it back when we must. We will make a way for ourselves and for Justin and Rebecca–you'll see."

"I don't know about that, but I hope you're right. I only know what I think, and I know I won't have any children of my own, or grandchildren, either. You and your children, Rebecca included, are as close as I will ever come to that.

"The house was filled with sad memories for me. Justin was a big help to me when I got hurt. Got used to being here with him. Last Christmas was the best thing that happened in years. Justin and Annie and her parents–Waters, too. They all made me believe that good times might yet come. When you came back with Rebecca, I didn't know what to do. I was glad—I am glad that you're back safe, but I knew there would be trouble. I don't care about you and Waters taking up with each other. You've made up your minds on your own about that, but it won't be easy." He looked up at her then and smiled. "I reckon I'll stick around to see what happens."

He tipped his head in my direction and said, "Justin and that girl are pretty sweet on each other, you can tell."

"I know – and won't it be great to see what happens with them?"

My cheeks got hot when I heard them talking about me and Annie. I made some noise slamming the lid on the trunk Hal kept his oats in before I stepped out to join them.

Jig and I made our way to the little shack at the end of the spit. I called in and reported that everything was okay— the coast was clear, no spies today—and put a fire under the coffee pot. I leaned my rifle against the wall and sat down on the doorstep. I unwrapped the tinfoil package and broke off a piece of the salmon Lucy had given me. I held it in my mouth, chewing slowly, savoring the honeyed taste of it.

Jig and I watched the tide come in as the water heated in the coffee pot. The sea had calmed after the storm passed, but smaller waves steadily rolled in. Every wave was different, yet the same. I thought about the water and what Jack had told Lucy. The people came and went. They fought wars and moved on. The villages of Jack's people were gone, destroyed by other people in another war, but the sea rolled on. Maybe she was right, and the water was getting to know me. I would get to know it well in the months to come.

6

When I got back to the station, I checked in at the office. I logged my return time on the chalkboard beside the door. Peake was in the day room outside his office, putting up a new poster on the wall. I'd seen others he'd put up before, pictures of Japanese soldiers made into monsters with bulging teeth like fangs, wild eyes behind horn-rimmed glasses, holding knives that dripped blood. They were lurid images that made the enemy look as evil as possible. This one said, "Open trap make happy Jap" and showed a grinning Japanese soldier listening at a keyhole. It was pretty tame compared to some I'd seen before. I knew what those posters were for, but they always took me by surprise. I'd never even seen a Japanese person, but I knew for sure they didn't look like that.

Whenever I saw one of those posters, they always reminded me of the way people drew pictures of Negroes. Annie's father got sent all kinds of advertising to put up in his store, ads for stuff like Ivory and Palmolive soap, for Postum, Cream of Wheat, and Jell-0. One day Annie and I were sitting together on the bench behind the store, just holding hands and talking. As we were talking, the back door opened, and Mr. Sadler came outside, pushing a trash bin on a little rolling cart.

"Need any help with that?" I said, getting up from the bench and walking over to see if he needed a hand.

"Just help me lift it off the cart." He wheeled it over beside the wall, and the two of us, one on each side, set it down on the ground.

There was a long, rolled-up paper sticking out of the top

of the can. "What's this?" I asked, pulling it out.

"Advertisers—send me all kinds of stuff to sell their products. It's a poster—but not one I care to use."

When I unrolled it, I saw why he was throwing it out. It was an advertising poster for Bull Durham. It showed two "happy darkies" dressed for hunting, holding shotguns. They had huge lips painted bright red, and one man was letting the other light his pipe from his own. Below the men was the slogan "without a match," apparently a comment about the tobacco as well as the men. On the side, it said "Standard of the World for Three Generations."

"I'm not putting that up in my store. It's a stupid picture. Most folks don't even think about stuff like that, think it's old-timey and quaint, but it's not. It might be the 'Standard of the World for Three Generations', but maybe the world needs some new standards. Aunt Jemima and the fellow on the Cream of Wheat box aren't quite as bad, but that picture is ridiculous." He turned and walked back into the store, wiping his hands on his green apron and shaking his head.

"I never gave much thought to that kind of thing before I met Waters," Annie said. "But I know what Daddy means. Waters is a real man, not a cartoon. Stuff like that is shameful, and Daddy's right to keep it out of the store, but there's plenty of people around that wouldn't see anything wrong about it at all."

Annie and her parents had their hearts in the right place. They were good souls, and I knew what Annie was saying. Waters was always there when I was growing up, and he had come to mean the world to me, but some folks still had some growing to do. It was okay to make the enemy into a monster in wartime, but there were monsters of another sort at home, and it was sometimes hard to tell who they were.

It was the week before Christmas. It was 1942, and I was

twenty-one. Everybody around me was thinking about other Christmases at home, and the people they had left behind. The mail came on an irregular schedule, but usually about once a week, we'd hear a supply truck grinding down the hill in second gear, brakes squealing, and those of us who weren't on patrol would all step outside as the driver sounded his horn.

We helped him unload the supplies while Eddie Purdue, the company clerk, took charge of the mail. Sometimes there wasn't much, and some of the guys walked away disappointed, but as Christmas got nearer, the mail had gotten heavier, and the mailbags were full now, stuffed with packages from home. The clerk would sort the mail while we unloaded the supplies. After dinner, the men strolled down to the office and gathered at the bottom of the steps, eager to get word from home.

Wiley and I joined the crowd, waiting for Eddie to come out with the mail, and call out our names. As we stood there I thought about Agnes and Wiley, about Annie and me and what we meant to each other. Wiley and I had been writing letters home pretty regularly, and Agnes and Annie and our folks had been keeping us in the know about everyone in Glory. Wiley still kept mum on the drowning, and found things to say about our days on the coast. Agnes wouldn't marry him when he asked her before we left. She said she loved him but wasn't going to be a war widow, even for him. She told him if he could get back without getting himself killed, she'd be happy to toss the bouquet and make some babies, but not until it was over and he came back in one piece.

Annie'd had my heart from our first kiss, and I knew I would be lost without her. When Momma was gone and I was stuck on the ranch with just Uncle Hal and Waters, my life had turned into a mystery that I couldn't figure out by myself. Waters helped me a lot, but it was Annie who came along when I was at the end of my rope. She had tied the knot that gave me something to hold onto. We had moved on from a few stolen kisses behind her daddy's store, but Annie was smart enough to tell me to stop when we got carried away. I always felt kinda bad when that happened, but when my head cleared, I knew she was right. There were good things to come, but the war would make us wait.

When Eddie stepped out on the porch, he had two big bins of mail. We all looked up expectantly, waiting for him to call our names. Sometimes he dragged it out to torment us, pretending he couldn't read the name on a letter, holding it up to the light and twisting it back and forth, but there was a lot of mail now, and everybody was impatient to see if there was anything for them.

"Sturgis, Ted."

The "reverend" stepped up, and Eddie flipped the envelope, saying "air mail!" as he tossed it in the air to Ted.

"Knock it off, Eddie," Red said. "Just give us our mail."

"Ooh, get a whiff of this," Eddie said, drawing a letter back and forth under his nose. "Looks like the Professor's got a sweetie. Must be from his mother."

Nick stepped up and snatched the letter from Eddie's hand. The other men yelled at Eddie, telling him to cut it out. Ensign Tyler came outside when he heard the commotion. "Cut the crap, Eddie. One of these nights, these boys are going to throw you a blanket party. You better start sleeping with one eye open. Just pass out the mail."

After that, Eddie stopped fooling around and got down to business. The men stepped up when they heard their names and walked off with a letter or two, sometimes with a package. Wiley and I each got a box, wrapped up in brown paper and tied with twine. Leaving the others behind, we tucked our treasures under our arms and headed back to the barracks.

We sat on our bunks and opened the packages. Wiley's mom had sent him a fruitcake she'd made, wrapped in waxed paper and tinfoil. She had also enclosed a letter from Agnes and one of her own. "Lot of people don't like fruitcake, but Mom's is the best. Wait'll we finish the letters—you gotta try it." He set it back in the box, took out the letters, and laid down on his bunk to read them. Wiley's mom was a good cook. I'd tasted her home-baked bread and pies before. The fruitcake was bound to please.

I cut the string and unwrapped my package. Annie had sent me snickerdoodles, my favorite cookies, wrapped in waxed paper and packed carefully in a round Quaker Oats tube tucked inside the larger box. They had traveled well and were mostly whole. There was another smaller package inside. It was from Momma, with a note from her and Waters. Rebecca had drawn me a picture on the back of the envelope. In the picture, she was standing in front of a tree with different colored apples on it. Momma and Waters were standing on either side of her, holding her hands. Of course, they were stick figures that looked like scarecrows, but I knew who they were right away. It was a family picture. I wished I was in the picture, too.

I untied the ribbon on Momma's package. When I unwrapped the paper, there was a little box inside. I opened the box and found Momma's medal that she had worn when she went away. It had a picture of a man with a walking stick, carrying a child, and crossing a stream. Momma's note said, "This is Saint Christopher, who will carry you across the water and bring you home safely. Keep him with you, and remember us always." Waters had added his own note, "Trouble is never very far away, Justin. But look for the joy—it's there waiting for you, just like we wait for you at home. Annie loves you and is keeping the home fires burning–don't let that girl down."

There was a letter from Annie in the package, too, and I waited a long time before I opened it. I held it in my hands and looked at it, thinking of how much I missed Annie and what she meant to me. Finally, I opened the envelope, took out the letter, and unfolded it.

My Dearest Justin,

It's only been a few months since you left, but it seems like such a long time. I'm beginning to really understand how you felt when your momma was gone so long, When the bell rings above the shop door, I look up, expecting to see you coming in. Sometimes I walk over to the school and just sit on the steps in the afternoon like we used to and think about our time together. Whenever Agnes comes into town, we go over to the Bon Ton and sit at the counter drinking cherry Cokes, and we talk about how we miss you and Wiley. Agnes wouldn't say it out loud, but I know she misses him more than she lets on. She needs something to do. Her brother, his friend Curt, all the older boys are gone now, sent who knows where, and things are so different. Blue star flags hang in a lot of windows, and everybody is a little on edge.

Gas rationing started this month. Hal got an A sticker for his windshield. He told me four gallons a week was only enough for two trips to town. I don't know how you would have been able to go to school on four gallons a week. I hope you enjoy the snickerdoodles. Sugar is being rationed and butter is sure to follow, so be sure to enjoy them while you can. Daddy's worried about what will happen with the store as things get worse. We will just have to see.

Hal and Waters brought your momma and Rebecca over to visit. We talked about that first Christmas together before she came back and what a special time that was. Hal talked about how you took care of him when he was laid up after those men caused all the trouble, and I could tell how proud he is of you. I don't know if he ever said that to you, but it's the truth. People still talk about your momma and Waters, but things have settled down some. Sometimes people give me a look from time to time, and I know what they're thinking, but I don't pay them much mind. We all put this package together for you. Christmas is a special time. The last few years haven't all been what they should have, but the good times will come. Keep a good heart, protect our shore, I know we will be together again one day. I hope it's soon.

Love,
Annie

p.s. Daddy took the picture when everybody came to visit. I hope you like it–keep us close in your heart.

Inside the envelope Annie had enclosed a small snapshot. She was holding Rebecca on her lap, and Momma and Waters were standing behind her. Everybody was smiling. It was perfect.

7

Our Christmas celebration did little to lift our spirits. Reverend Ted cut a little pine tree on the hill above the beach, and he and some of the others decorated it with little pinecones and some shells and tiny starfish. Lucy had given us some tinfoil from the mess hall, and we cut out some stars and hung them on the tree, too. It was pretty sad, but it was enough to remind us of Christmas at home.

We put the tree up in the day room, and we tuned in to the Armed Forces Network and listened to Christmas songs. We heard the new Bing Crosby song, "White Christmas." It was a nice song, I guess, but I'd never lived where it snowed, so that part didn't mean much to me. When he got to the part that talked about the Christmases we used to know, I think most of us were sad to think of what we were missing at home. I liked it when he whistled in the second chorus. The guy could sure whistle nice. It kind of reminded me of Waters when he played his mouth harp, sort of wistful and far away.

Reverend Ted wanted us all to sing "Silent Night." The Professor said it started out as a German song, which, of course, none of us knew before. I didn't know where he learned all the things he claimed to know. Sometimes he was handy to have around, but sometimes he was kind of a pain in the ass.

Tommy and Red had downed quite a few beers as we sat listening to the radio. Red's face was a little flushed, and he swayed a bit when he stood, but he looked down at Tommy and said, "What the hell–let's give it a whirl." Then Tommy stood up, and the two of them sang together. Red's whiskey tenor blended with Tommy's baritone in a pleasing way none us expected. All was calm, all was bright–for the moment.

The winter storms that pounded the coast eased off when spring came along, and we just had rain–lots of rain. The river was up, but behaving itself, a steady flow of muddy brown that merged into the gray sea. Crossing the river was a chore, but it wasn't like it was the night Wiley and Doc almost drowned. We were getting to know the water—maybe it was getting used to us, too.

Patrolling the beach was no fun, either. Slogging along, boots sinking in the sand, wrapped up in foul weather gear and carrying a heavy rifle, it was slow going, and we plodded along under gray skies that seemed to press down on us. It made me think of Ethel Waters singing that "Stormy Weather" song. She was singing about her man who went away and how lonesome she felt. I thought about how I was the one who'd gone away and how lonesome I felt, but it was just the same thing. Dark days and bad weather put me in a mood, and I couldn't wait for the sun to come out.

Most of the time it was just that nothing ever seemed to happen. We didn't capture any spies, no ships tried to put troops ashore, and it made everybody restless. A couple of times we caught a fishing boat running at night that forgot to black out its lights, and sometimes we caught some kids trying to sneak onto the beach after dark, looking to fool around, but the bad weather had finally kept them away, too.

We did have some excitement when a skunk decided to take up residence under the mess hall, where it was warm and cozy, and we spent a lot of time trying to get rid of it. Peake seemed to take it personally, and it sure put his shorts in a twist. He sent some men to try to chase it out from under, but that ended badly when one of them got sprayed and had to spend an afternoon in the shower. Even after all that hot water and soap, nobody would sit next to him for days. We sealed the trash barrels with tight covers, but the building was open underneath, and that skunk was free to go in and out as it pleased. Ensign Tyler headed up a detail to enclose the underside with plywood, but the skunk stayed put.

To tell the truth, most of the men found Peake's frustration kind of entertaining. But finally Wiley came up with the idea that saved the day.

"We had skunks at home, came after the chickens and their eggs at night. They only come out at night and hole up during the day. We should just post a guard on each side of the building at night. When he comes out, we can seal up the place so he can't get back in."

It sounded good to me. Wiley and I went to talk with Ensign Tyler. "The other thing we used to do," Wiley said when we met up with him, "was leave a light on at night. Used to do that in the garden to keep the coons out of the corn. They wouldn't bother the garden if we left that light on all night."

Tyler picked four volunteers and posted one on each side of the building. They pulled away the plywood on one corner and waited. The guard on that side kept a close watch, but the others kept a lookout too, just in case there was another way out. Sure enough, about ten o'clock that night, the little devil came out, looked around for a few seconds, and wandered off in the direction of the river. Wiley had borrowed a long cord with a little lamp wired onto the end, and he shoved it in under the building, and the others closed up the opening. We left that light on every night for a week and never had any more trouble. Sometimes we saw our friend poking around the trash barrels, but we had learned to keep them sealed tight, and eventually he left us alone. Peake seemed to relax a little when the striped critter departed, but it was hard to tell. He wasn't generous with praise.

One morning in May the supply truck made its way down the hill. As it rolled to a stop in the turnaround outside the barracks, those of us inside turned out to help with the supplies and the mail. The driver was Stub Martin. He was short and sturdy, built like a fireplug, but he got his name from the pencil stub he always had tucked behind his ear. I never saw him without it. And it was always just a stub, never a whole pencil.

"Maybe his ear ain't big enough for a whole pencil," Wiley said one time. "Probably cuts 'em in half to fit."

I didn't know about that, but Stub was a character. He stepped down out of the truck, clipboard in hand, pulled the pencil stub from his ear, licked the point, and started checking off items as they were unloaded.

Stub hauled supplies and mail to some of the other stations, and he was in the know about what was going on up and down the coast. He was a constant source of rumor and gossip, but he was often right. Wiley said, "I don't know how he keeps his eyes on the road with his ear to the ground all the time—amazing he don't lose that pencil."

When our mail and all the supplies had been unloaded, Red came out of the mess hall with a coffee mug in each hand. When he got to the truck, he held out one of the cups to Stub. "Black, two sugars, right?"

"Just like my women, hot and sweet – thanks, Red."

As Stub perched on the bumper with the coffee, Red asked, "Heard any news lately?"

Stub took a sip, made like he was trying to think of what to say, then squinted up at Red. "Word is, you won't be pounding sand much longer. I'll prob'ly still be driving a truck somewhere, but you boys are going to get your feet wet a little ways offshore. They're takin' the war into the Pacific, gonna push them Japs back to where they come from."

We'd heard some talk before, but nobody really knew anything before Stub let us in on what he'd heard. If Peake knew what was in the works, he was keeping it to himself. I suspected we'd find out soon enough. We were all tired and ready for a change.

As the weather brightened, so did our spirits. There were blue skies overhead, and the sea lost the gray color it had worn all winter. When the sky was clear, we were treated to some fine sunsets. The river cleared up and dwindled down until it just sort of sank in the sand as it flowed into the sea. A sandbar connected the north and south beaches, and the patrol no longer had to row across the river and climb over the bluff. Our lot had improved. But the world was still at war, and we waited to hear what was coming next.

Letters from home helped us through the gloomy months. The folks on the home front weren't sitting on their hands. They had been very busy, and the letters kept us up on what was happening. Wiley got a letter from Agnes that set him back a bit.

"Jesus, Justin—Agnes has joined the Marines!"

"What do you mean?"

He waved the letter at me. "Just what I said. Pearl put a recruiting poster up on the wall in the post office. Showed a woman in uniform standing in front of an airplane. It said, 'Be a Marine—free a Marine to fight.' Agnes says she looked at that picture every time she stopped at the store and went in back to say hi to Pearl." Wiley looked at the letter. "'All the boys've gone off—Jesse, Curt, most of the others we know. I don't just want to sit around and wait. I want to do something.' Says she's going to be an airplane mechanic."

"Well, that sounds like Agnes to me. I wouldn't be surprised if she was going to fly planes, too." If any girl we knew would want to join the Marines, it would be Agnes.

That girl never lacked for confidence. She always seemed to know what she wanted. If anybody could keep 'em flying, I'd put my money on her.

"I don't know, Justin. What if something happens to her? What if she goes off somewhere and meets someone she likes better than me?"

"I'm pretty sure Agnes loves you, but you know what she's like. She wants to be in the thick of things—make a difference by being who she is. Don't worry so much. Probably the only people she'll meet are other women like her and some flat-footed old farts who couldn't get into the service."

"Maybe so, but I need something to count on, and I've been counting on her to see me through whatever happens. "

"Tell her, then. Write her a letter and tell her how you feel. Tell her what you just told me. But don't worry too much. If she flies off with someone else, you've still got me."

"Thanks a bunch, pal."

Annie wasn't like Agnes, but she'd been busy at home, too. She had been helping her daddy keep track of the new rationing regulations. Everyone was trying to learn how to use their ration coupons. Some people didn't know they expired and tried to save them up, only to learn that they were worthless when they went to use them. The government wanted to prevent hoarding. It started with gasoline and the thirty-five mile an hour speed limit to save tires, but this spring, the list had grown to include everything from shoes to Spam. Mr. Sadler and the folks in Glory were having a hard time keeping up.

Annie said she was organizing a scrap metal drive. She got Mr. Phillips to get the kids at school to bring in their tin cans from home, and Annie had put out a bin in front of the store where the people in town could drop off their cans as well. Mr. Phillips sent a note out to the parents asking them to send in victory keys. Most people had a coffee can or two filled with old keys that no longer fit anything, and he asked them to give them to the kids to turn in at school. They collected two big buckets full of keys and small metal pieces.

Momma had been coming to town with Hal and Rebecca and always stopped in at the store. Momma had become good friends with Annie's family. They'd helped keep the tide of public opinion about her and Waters from overwhelming her, and she loved them for it. I think it was easier for them because of me and Annie, but they were the sort that had their heads screwed on right, good people who made up their own minds. They had accepted Waters even before Momma came home, and they took Rebecca in as well. Sometimes Momma would leave Rebecca with the Sadlers if she went to the Rexall or had an errand to run in town. It gave Momma a chance to keep Rebecca from having to hear the nasty things some people still said about her and Waters and Rebecca.

Waters wasn't exactly hiding in the shadows, either. He mostly stayed on the ranch, but the war effort meant as much to him as to anyone else. He and Hal and Momma had been working on a plan to do something they could be proud of, something that would really count for something. Mr. McManus at the feed store had put up a poster from the John Deere Company that said "Sink a Sub from Your Farm. Bring in Your Scrap." On one of his trips to the feed store, Hal had seen the poster, and it gave him an idea.

Hal remembered the time Wiley and I had wandered off to explore an abandoned mine not too far from the ranch. The place was littered with all kinds of old metal junk, and he and Waters and Momma hatched a plan to gather a lot of it for a scrap drive. Hal talked to Mr. McManus, asked him if he was serious about a scrap drive or just liked to put up posters. McManus asked him what he meant, and Hal told him if he would lend them his flatbed truck, they would bring in scrap from the old mine.

Apparently McManus rose to the occasion when Hal challenged his patriotism. He told Hal he could borrow the truck, but since he was short-handed at the feed store they'd have to load it themselves. Momma and Waters and Hal drove the old Model A down to the mine and spent two days gathering up whatever they could carry—pulleys and gears, chunks of wire rope, some short rail sections, an old metal tank they found behind one of the buildings–too heavy to carry– they had to roll it along till they got to the road – all kinds of stuff. They stacked it in a big pile, Annie said. Then they drove to town to get the truck from Mr. McManus.

When they drove up in the Model A, Momma took Rebecca across the street to stay with Annie's parents while they went back to load the truck. Annie had taken Rebecca's hand in hers and handed Momma a rolled-up paper that she tucked under her arm as she walked back to the truck. According to Annie, they got the usual stares from folks on the street, but they were getting used to that and paid them no mind. I bet those folks were even more surprised to see Waters and Momma climb into the truck with Hal and drive off.

I wished I'd been part of all that. I could imagine them loading the truck–Waters with his easy grace making the work seem like fun, Hal carrying what he could, limping along on his bum leg, Momma with her dark hair pinned up under a scarf. It would have been something to see. Annie said they had stopped just outside of town on the way back and unrolled that paper Annie had given her and tacked it onto the stake sides of the truck. Annie had used some butcher paper to make a banner that said, "Doing our Part to Win the War." She had painted a red border and added blue stars around the words so it looked like the service flags people were hanging in their windows. As they drove into town, Momma and Waters stood on the running boards, holding onto the truck's big mirrors. Hal blew the horn as they pulled up in front of the feed store.

Customers poured out of the stores to see what the commotion was all about. Annie and her parents, with Rebecca in tow, Billie and the cook from the Bon Ton, Sully, the mailman, even Sheriff Max came out from his office around the corner to take a look. George Babcock rushed out of the drugstore and snapped a few pictures with his Kodak Brownie. Al leaned against his gas pump, looking unimpressed, and some of the toughs outside the bar called the Snug looked on as well. There was a long pause, Annie said, and then McManus, standing on the loading dock, tucked his tote board under his arm and started clapping. Pretty soon, other people got the idea and started clapping, too. Annie said there were even a few cheers and whistles. There was progress on the home front, in more ways than one. I wished I was there to help.

8

Stub's predictions turned out to be true. Word spread that the beach patrols were being reduced and would eventually be disbanded. The threat of invasion hadn't panned out, and America was pushing back. Our troops were fighting bloody battles in the South Pacific, and they didn't need us to walk our dogs on the beach. Lt. Peake made it official. Our stretch of the coast wasn't ever a likely target. We weren't close to anything important—not a major seaport, not a factory, not a refinery, not even a military base. Ours might have been a good spot for a sneaky invasion, but that never happened, either, so we were going to be among the first to leave the beach.

Peake made the announcement during formation one morning. We were lined up outside his office, standing at attention. Eddie Purdue ran up the flag as we all saluted. When Eddie was done, Peake said, "At ease," and we all relaxed in place.

"Good morning, men."

"Good morning, Sir!" we all answered.

"Most of you have heard rumors by now that the beach patrols are coming to an end. Well, those rumors have finally been confirmed. I've received notice that we are to close this station. We've been given thirty days to prepare, after which time you will all be reassigned. We are in this for the duration, and every man is an important weapon in this fight.

"We've a ways to go yet to win this war. To that end, everyone will be retrained for assignments in the Pacific Theater. We will beat the Japs and send them packing, I'm sure of that. Personally, I can't wait. You've all done what was asked of you, but you're going to be asked to do more. Whatever you're asked to do will be important, even if it doesn't seem so at the time. All of you will save lives by your service, the lives of those we hold dear. Some of you will have to take lives to do this. Some of you may give your lives in the effort.

"Spend your remaining time here with the friends you've made. Write letters home and tell them you won't be coming back for a while longer. They hear the news at home. They watch the newsreels. They know what's going on in the world. They will understand.

"Ensign Tyler will answer whatever questions he can."

Tyler called us to attention, said "Present arms," and we all saluted. Peake returned the salute. Tyler gave the command, "Order arms," and we all remained at attention as Peake left the formation and returned to his office. Tyler gave us the "At ease," and we all relaxed.

Mac McDonald was standing behind me. I heard him muttering to Tommy. "Nice speech. Might have meant something if Peake hadn't said it. Wonder where he read it."

In his gravelly baritone Tommy said, "I know what you mean. The man's an ass. Says he can't wait—probably thinks he can win the war by himself."

Just then Ensign Tyler spoke up. "I'm sure you boys have a lot of questions. I'm not sure I have many answers just yet, but I'll try to let you in on what I know. Feel free to fire away."

There was a rumble among the men, and I could tell everybody was knocked sideways at the announcement, even though we knew it was coming. Red Morgan spoke up first. "Do you know where we're gonna be sent, sir?"

"No. You're all going to be retrained for sea duty, but I don't know where. I expect you will be sent to different locations, depending on your assignments. You may have some choice in your duty assignments. Some of you probably have civilian skills that can be put to use. I don't really know."

Most of the questions were about the when and where of things, but finally Wiley spoke up. "What about the dogs, sir? What will happen to the dogs?"

Leave it to Wiley to worry about Doc. I think that dog meant almost as much to him as Agnes did. I was fond of Jig, too. He had been a good companion on patrol, kept me from walking off the cliff in the fog. I would surely miss him. But I knew Wiley would be sunk low if Doc were taken away from him.

"The dogs were donated to the service. Some of them came from kennels. Some came from private donors. Some will be returned to their original owners. Some will be sold. They all have service numbers, so their records can be located. But I don't know all the details. Spend some time with them while you can."

Wiley nodded, looking down at his feet. He scuffed his toe in the dirt, and looked up at me. "You know I love that dog, Justin. I don't know what I'll do without him."

"Well, you've still got me," I said. He punched me in the shoulder as we left the formation and headed back to the barracks.

With Peake's permission and Tyler's help, the boys put together a big party the night before we were to leave. Everybody showed up at the mess hall for the send-off. Tyler had sent Eddie over with the radio from the day room, and there was music playing. Peake had sprung for a few cases of beer, and there was a lot of food laid out on tables. The professor had made a big banner that said "Semper Paratus – Always Prepared" and put it up on the wall. Underneath the words some wag had written "For a Party!" I thought it kind of looked like Wiley's writing, but I wasn't sure. There was a lot of cheerful talk, some backslapping, and a few dirty jokes being told. The uncertainty of what came next was in the air, but most of the boys didn't think about it if they could help it.

Everybody wrote their names and addresses in a log book Tyler brought over from the day room and wrote notes about their time at the station together. Reverend Ted made a speech, saying he prayed God would bring us together again one day. He asked for a moment of silence to honor Billy and Tony and Stieg—and Maisie, too. He said we should plan to have a reunion when the war was over.

There was enough alcohol to get some of the boats floating, and some of the boys got a little teary. Tommy Rainwater and Red Morgan got up, held up their beer bottles in an attempt at a toast and began to sing that Vera Lynn song "We'll Meet Again." It was hopeful and kind of sad at the same time. We all looked forward to the sunny day that would bring happier times, even if we didn't know where or when.

Tommy and Red really weren't half bad. Vera Lynn wouldn't have to worry, but they could carry a tune. Swaying a little, Red said, "Come on, you bums, you all know this. Let's hear the hooligan navy sing!" And then we all did just that.

It was goofy and a little sad, but it was nice. We had bitched about the weather, cussed the cold and damp, complained about Peake and his hard-headedness, and pounded the sand searching for things that weren't there. But we *had* found something in each other. Our time together had meant something. We just weren't sure what was ahead.

The next morning, Wiley and I ate a quick breakfast and headed down to the kennels to say goodbye to Doc and Jig. We fed the dogs and walked along the beach for a while. It was a gray morning that didn't do much for our spirits. We sat on a driftwood log and looked out at the sea. As I sat with Jig, I wondered what was waiting out there for us, but I knew Wiley's thoughts didn't go beyond the end of the leash he held in his hand.

"I don't how to say goodbye, Justin. Doc's been the best thing about being here. He kept me from drowning with Stieg and the others. What will he think when I just go away?"

"I know what you mean. Jig's been good for me, too. I'll really miss him when we leave this place. Tell you what—I'm going to walk down the beach a ways with Jig. You have a talk with Doc while I'm gone. When I get back, we'll drop them off at the kennels and get our stuff together. The trucks are coming in a couple of hours."

And that's what we did. I let Jig off his lead, and we trotted together down the beach, just running alongside one another on the sand. After a while, we sat and looked out at the sea. I sat beside him with my arm around him. He sniffed the air and looked up at me, his tongue hanging out. He looked happy.

When I caught up with Wiley, he was sitting in the grass at the edge of the sand with Doc lying beside him. He looked up at me, and his eyes were shining. "Time to go, I guess."

"Yeah, I expect so."

Wiley wiped his nose on his sleeve, patted Doc on the head, and stood. He snapped on the lead, and we walked back to the kennel.

We had our sea bags piled outside the barracks, and most of the boys were just sitting around, smoking, drinking coffee, waiting for the trucks to arrive. Tommy and Red were a little green around the gills, nursing hangovers from the party. I told Wiley to keep an eye on my bag while I hiked up the road to Jack's place. I couldn't leave without saying goodbye to Jack and Lucy.

Jack's house was a mile up the road. It was a small whitewashed house set among some trees. It had been there a long time and looked its age. The paint was faded, gone in some places. A brick chimney with a rusty metal cap poked out of the middle of the roof, and a little smoke drifted out, flattening on the wind. Pine needles littered one end where a limb hung over the roof. Jack's truck stood in the open shed behind the house.

As I walked up from the road, the gravel in the driveway crunched beneath my boots. The smell of the sea carried on the wind, and I could hear the gulls crying. Jack was sitting on the porch steps. He wore an old leather jacket over a gray work shirt that looked like it had been washed too many times. Brown boots peeked out from the frayed cuffs of his jeans. He looked up when he heard me coming.

"Hey Justin, how you doing?"

"I'm okay. We're getting ready to leave today. I didn't want to go without saying goodbye."

"I'm glad you came by. Not something most of the others would think of. Sure will be different when you're gone. Pretty quiet around here, you know." He had that faraway look again as he turned toward the sea, just visible through the trees.

I sat on the porch with him and tried to think of what to say. I enjoyed Jack's company. I would miss him when we left this place. Without my knowing, spending time with him had taught me some things. He had taught me to respect the silence, to listen to the world around me and see a little of what he saw when he looked at the river and the waves lapping at the shore.

"Know where you're going yet?"

"Not really. We're going to be retrained for sea duty.

Then we'll ship out. Probably end up out in the Pacific somewhere."

"You boys in the Coast Guard. Looks like the coast is further away than we thought." He gave a little laugh, looked at me, and said, "Might have to change your name."

"Yeah, maybe so."

We sat on the porch for a while, not saying much. The sun came out and drove away the gray overcast that had hung over us earlier. Sunbeams through the trees lit the ground in bright patches, and somewhere behind the house, blue jays were having a raucous argument. An acorn fell from an oak tree and rattled down the tin roof of the shed. Even this far up the road, we could hear the sound of the surf as the waves rolled up on the shore.

"I don't know how to say what I'm thinking, Jack. I never knew this place existed till they brought us here. And we didn't particularly like being here. Bad things happened to some of us. But we stuck with it. And now we're leaving. You showed me some things I didn't know were important. I think I know what you meant about the water. But it's more than that. You taught me how to listen to this place, to see and hear what's around me, to see that we're all part of something bigger than ourselves. I hope I can take that with me when I go."

"If you've learned that, you've learned a lot, and it will stay with you. But it will be hard to remember sometimes."

"Seems like I'm always leaving one place for another. Don't really think about what I have till I don't have it anymore. Then I end up wishing I could get it back. Ever feel like that?"

Jack looked at me with just a hint of a smile. "Not a good question to ask an old man, Justin. But you've hooked a big one, for sure. You're still figuring life out, learning how everything works. You get old and there'll be a lot you wish you could have again. Keep the people and places that helped you write the story in your heart. Those are the things that make you who you are. But looking back all the time will make you sad.   Listen to what the day tells you."

Lucy brought out two mugs of coffee for us, and we sat together a while longer until I heard the whine of the trucks coming from further up the hill. I held out my hand to Jack, and he took it in his own calloused hand and looked me in the eye. He held me in that solemn gaze for a long moment. "Good luck, Justin. Keep us in your thoughts."

When Jack released his grip, Lucy surprised me by stepping up and throwing her arms around me in a big hug. She pulled me down to whisper in my ear, "You're a good man, Justin. We'll miss you." She let me go and stepped back to stand next to her father. "The war can't last forever. Come back to see us when you can." I could have sworn there was a tear in her eye.

The trucks were coming closer now. I thanked them both again and turned and ran back to the road. When I got to the end of the driveway, I turned back to wave. Lucy and Jack were standing beside each other, looking my way. She had her arm around his waist, her head leaning on his shoulder. That was the way I would always remember them.

Part II

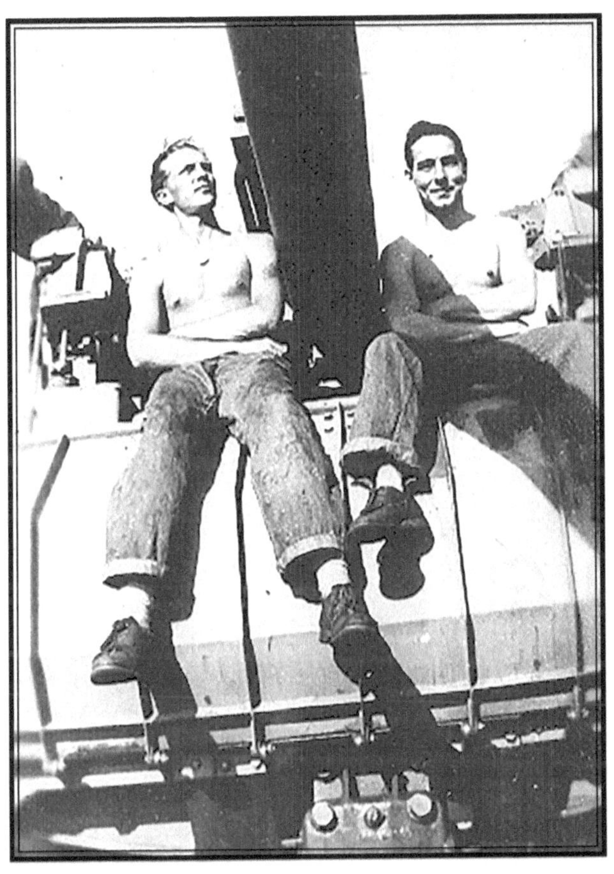

9

Wiley and I stood on the boat deck, white steaming mugs in hand, taking a look at the morning. There wasn't much to look at. Everything had been painted with the same brush, dipped in the same bucket of gray paint. The few clouds looked like the smudges left behind on the page when the words have been erased, and the morning sky met the sea at the dark gray line of the horizon. In the distance, the other ships in our convoy were darker silhouettes, comforting in their presence. Otherwise, the *Mintaka* would be alone in the middle of the empty expanse that was the Pacific Ocean.

The *Mintaka* had the other ships for company, and Wiley and I had plenty of company ourselves aboard the ship. We had joined the crew as gunner's mates two weeks before the ship sailed from San Francisco, barely enough time to learn our way around. We'd been given a brief tour of the ship and a rundown on its short history. Our ship had been laid down in Los Angeles at the California Shipbuilding yard in February 1943 and launched in March, only a month later.

She was a Liberty ship, one of Roosevelt's "ugly ducklings" built in a hurry to meet wartime demands. Before we came on board, she had sailed to the South Pacific and up to the Aleutians, hauling cargo. After returning to Seattle, she had sailed to Portland and been refitted to transport troops as well as cargo. The troops were billeted on the tween deck above the cargo holds. The crew numbered 206, including the eight other sailors who came on with Wiley and me. We settled in quickly, learning our way around the ship. It wasn't long before we embarked over a thousand troops and headed out to sea. We passed through the Golden Gate, leaving San

Francisco. The orange towers of the bridge rose out of the low lingering fog, lit by the morning sun at our backs, and that was the postcard of home I carried with me now.

We had been steaming for almost two weeks now, heading southwest toward Noumea, New Caledonia, a name that meant nothing to Wiley and me. Our tour of the ship had given us a look at the bridge, and we'd taken a gander at the big map on the wall. Our guide had pointed out our destination, but it was just a spot on a map. I knew all the potholes on the Glory Road, the place where the creek pushed against the big rock that I sat on to collect my thoughts, the stump that lay alongside the pool where Waters and I fished, but there was nothing to see in the middle of the ocean. We were in the middle of nowhere, halfway between Glory and Australia, pushing along at a steady eleven and a half knots with no landmarks to guide us.

Looking out from the boat deck, Wiley and I watched the soldiers crowded on the main deck below us. They stood in little groups, talking together, smoking, looking out to sea. Two men were puking over the side. A few men were gathered around one of the hatch covers where three men were playing acey-deucey. A roar erupted from the group as the dealer tossed out a card and one of the boys dragged in his winnings. Four or five men sat alone, reading or writing letters.

"God, Justin—look at them. All those guys with nothing to do, waiting around for weeks to land six thousand miles from home. At least we have jobs to do. You know what it's like down below? Bunks stacked five high, only two feet between them. You have to slide in like a letter in an envelope. Can't even sit up once you're in the rack. That little squall we had last week, people were puking from the top bunk all over the guys below. Couldn't get out fast enough to keep from making a mess. No wonder they like to come up top–air's a lot better up here."

What Wiley called a little squall had turned into a storm that had tossed us about pretty good. We were forced to remain belowdecks as the ship rode out the storm. The bow rose as the wave crested beneath it, and everything tilted upward. There was a sickening moment when the ship seemed to hang in the air before it slammed back down into the trough with a loud thump and a metallic groaning that was audible even over the steady throbbing of the steam engine pushing us forward into the next one. I hoped the yardbirds in Los Angeles and Portland really knew how to weld. We tied ourselves into our bunks and waited out the storm with the other men.

It had taken us a while to get our own sea legs in the beginning. For a couple of days crackers and a little soup were the only things I could keep down. Our duties as gunner's mates kept us busy. It was mostly a lot of maintenance and drills, and sometimes we got sent on errands to other parts of the ship. All of that helped us get acclimated and kept our minds occupied. Though that storm had laid us low, we were making headway toward becoming sailors. It was a work in progress.

"Some of them take their meals in the galley, come outside for a smoke, walk around a little, and then get back in the chow line. Takes so long to feed them all, some of 'em have to wait hours. Guess they figure they might just as well get back in the line."

Wiley chuckled. "Lot to look forward to, these guys. Sea cruise to a tropic isle, then jump off the boat and get your ass shot off."

"Think about that a lot, do you?

"The thought has occurred to me. But I'm more worried about keeping my own ass afloat till we get home."

"Let's go with that. I like that idea."

We were a little later than some joining the war in the Pacific. It was February, 1944, and the bloody victory at Guadalcanal had been won a year ago. There were more battles raging where we were headed. We were sure of that, and we were on our way, bringing supplies and our human cargo to add to the effort.

When the skies cleared and the sun came out, spirits brightened as the sea around us changed from gray to blue. Wiley and I had drawn galley duty and were busy trying to keep up with the cooks who were putting supper together. Wiley was taking orders from the spud coxswain, Arne Swensen, who was showing him how to operate the machine that knocked the peel off the potatoes. It had a big tub with a drum inside that whirled around and tossed the spuds against the rough inside of the tub to rub off the peel.

"Watch what you're doing, Travers. Leave 'em in there too long, and it'll grind 'em down to the size of marbles. When they're peeled, take 'em out and look 'em over. Don't just dump 'em in the pot. Take the paring knife and cut out the deep eyes and the bad spots that didn't come off in the machine. You can put another load in the peeler while you're doing that, but keep your eye on the machine, understand? I don't wanta haf' to tell the chief you wasted a load of spuds."

I watched as Wiley tried to keep up. When he opened the doors and emptied out the peeled potatoes, I dug through them, put the good ones in a big pot and cut out the eyes and bad spots I found in the others and then tossed them in. When we had been at it for a while, we had filled several pots, and Swensen sent us out to dump the trash.

"Cubby's outside, taking a break. Get him to tell you where that garbage belongs. You can take a short break yourselves. Smoke 'em if you got 'em, hit the head—whatever. Just don't be all day at it—and don't disappear!"

Wiley and I dragged the big trash bins outside. Cubby Buckman was leaning back, one foot braced against the wall behind him, smoking a cigarette and studying the view beyond the railing.

"Where do we dump this stuff?" I asked.

He looked at us then, abandoning whatever thoughts had occupied him. "Usually goes over the side, off the stern. Fish food, you know. But not today. Head back there, you'll see a big pile under some canvas. Peel back the canvas and dump it on the pile. They saving it for the party next week."

"We're having a party?" Wiley said. "What kind of party needs a pile of garbage?"

Cubby let out a throaty chuckle, coughed, and flipped the cigarette butt over the rail. "You polliwogs in for a surprise. We 'bout to cross the line, and the shellbacks who been there before going to throw you a party. Only thing you need to know is, you the ones providing the entertainment. Be lots of fun for everyone, 'cept maybe you." His eyes had a twinkle as he said that, and he chuckled again. "Just put that trash on the pile."

Wiley and I found the garbage pile and added our load to the rest.

"Whew," Wiley gasped when he pulled back the canvas. This shit is pretty ripe."

"Wait till next week. Should be even worse by then. You know what Cubby was talking about, don't you?"

"Not really, something about a party, he said."

"You need to pay more attention. We'll be crossing the equator next week. They make a big deal out of it. I don't really understand why. It's just a line on the map. It's not like the water's gonna change color or something. But they always throw a big party. I think because we're out in the middle of nowhere, and it gives the crew something to do. The old-timers are apparently looking forward to giving us polliwogs a hard time – part of the fun, I guess."

"They're saving up garbage for our party—don't sound like fun to me."

"Me, either. We'll find out what they have in mind soon enough."

We dragged the empty bins back to the galley and stood outside on the deck, hoping to catch our breath for a bit. Wiley made a break for the head.

Cubby was standing at the rail, looking out to sea, lost in his own thoughts, it seemed to me. I don't think he even noticed I'd come back. He was a smallish, slim Negro a little older than Wiley or me. He had a boxer's build, broad in the shoulders and narrow at the waist, with a lot of upper body muscle. He never said much, but he looked like he could handle trouble if it came his way.

Cubby was a steward in the captain's mess, mostly. I had seen him before, spoken to him a couple of times. He was a cook striker, assigned to learn his way around the galley when he wasn't tending to the officers. He told me they had him working to learn how to be a baker.

"Hey, Cubby," I said, "How you doing with the baking?"

"Not so hot, according to the Old Man. Never happy with my biscuits. Always find something to complain about. He say they too soggy, too hard, too soft, too pale, too dark, too crumbly—always something. Ain't like makin' biscuits at home. My momma taught me how to do that just fine. Whole lotta diff'rence between makin' a dozen and makin' five hundred." Never gonna make cook the way I'm goin', Justin."

"Gotta keep at it. My momma worked in a cookhouse at the lumber camp when I was growing up. Used to make lots of biscuits for the men. She let me help her when I got old enough. Let me roll out the dough on this big table in the cookhouse kitchen. Spread flour on the tabletop, roll out the dough till it was about three-quarters of an inch thick, then cut out the biscuits. I always liked doing that—couldn't wait till they came out of the oven and I could take one for myself. I'd spread butter on it and go sit on the porch and eat it while it was still warm. She had a big recipe book she kept on a shelf in the kitchen. Acted like it was her Bible. You got something like that, Cubby?"

"Yeah, we got one, too. Big old thing." He looked at me then, an odd expression on his face.

"What's wrong. Did I say something I shouldn't have?"

"No, Justin—you okay. I like talkin' to you. Lot of men on this ship. Everybody need someone he can talk to. Can't talk to the captain. He just talk *at* me, all about how the table set, what the biscuits like, never really talk to *me* at all.

"You wanna know something? I don't wanna just be the captain's boy. It's why I'm strikin' for cook. I could learn somethin' to take home with me if we outlast the Japs. But I don't think I can do it. It's a lot to learn about food storage and safety and taking care of all the equipment. Other things, too."

"Give it time. You can study all those things, read up on them when you're not working in the kitchen."

"I could do that, I suppose." He hesitated, looked down at his feet. "Only one problem with that—I don't read so good. Cookbook's got pictures, and I can learn a recipe if I practice it enough, but it's slow going."

"I'm sorry, Cubby, I didn't know. Truth be told, a lotta these guys can't read, either. GI was on deck the other day, writing a letter to a buddy's girl. His buddy would tell him what he wanted to say, and the GI would write it down for him. Hope she had someone at home to read it to her."

I liked Cubby. It meant something that he was able to open up to me. "I won't let on—maybe we could look at that cookbook together."

"Maybe so. Thanks, Justin."

Wiley came back just then, said "Hey, Cubby," and we headed back into the galley to find Swensen scowling at us.

"You get lost or something? I said a short break, not shore leave. Grab a bucket and a couple of mops—this deck's a mess."

10

We were sitting on the deck in front of the five-inch gun mount, leaning back against the base. The barrel above cast its shadow in front of us as we looked out to sea. The weather had changed as we neared the equator. Blue skies were the order of the day, and Wiley and I were catching some morning sun.

"Seasons are upside down out here," Wiley said, peeling off his shirt. "Folks back home are decked out in stocking caps and trying to figure out where they left their mittens. Middle of February—must be eighty degrees today."

We were birds flying south for the winter, and the warm weather was a pleasant change. The troops shed the heavy gear they wore when they came aboard and were strolling the deck in tee shirts and fatigues, dog tags hanging from their necks.

"Let's enjoy it while we can. One of the deck apes told me it's gonna be hot and steamy where we're headed. Said we'd have something new to complain about when we cross the line and push further south."

Wiley took off his hat, wiped his forehead with his shirt, and put the hat back, pulling it down over his eyes. "At least we get a little breeze once in a while up here. Those hole snipes down in the engine room—hot as hell down there now. Imagine what it will be like for them when it gets hotter."

"Yeah, I don't know how they do it, hardly ever come up for air. They look pretty bad when they show up in the galley for meals. They're supposed to wash up, but they've still got dirt under their fingernails and oil and grease on their dungarees. Cubby says they have to sit in a special area –

makes it easier to clean up, wipe off the greasy handprints they leave behind."

Wiley and I had been down below a couple of times. That steam engine was three stories high, and the big connecting rods constantly pumped up and down, turning the prop that pushed us through the sea. I had never seen a machine that big. It was fascinating to watch, but the noise from the engine, the generators, and the other machinery made you want to clamp your hands over your ears.

"I heard they don't even come up to use the head if they don't have to, just take a leak in the bilge and keep working. That's not the life for me," I said. "At least we'll know when somebody's shooting at us. We get hit by a torpedo, I guess they'll be the first to know."

"Jesus, Justin, you're just a bundle of fun, ain't you? Just enjoy the sunshine. Nobody's shootin' at us yet." He pushed his hat back and threw me a serious look. "You know what's really naggin' me?   I keep wondering what's going on at home."

"Me, too. There's supposed to be mail when we get to New Caledonia. Folks at home are supposed to be using that new V-mail. Hope it works like they say. I've been writing a little every day, but it's worrisome not knowing."

"Hope Agnes don't forget my name, think about twisting some other guy's prop down at the airplane factory."

"You worry too much, Wiley. Agnes is hard-headed sometimes, but she's loyal as the day is long. When she makes her mind up, she's in it to win, and she set her cap for you a long time ago. Never could figure out how you charmed her so, but there it is. Like folks say, there's a lid to fit every skillet.

"I worry about Annie and my folks—Momma and Waters and Rebecca. Not knowing what's going on with them is hard. Annie's folks've been great. Yours too, I expect. But not everybody's like that. Can't win 'em all over just like that. Rebecca should be going to school in the fall—how's that gonna work out?"

"Could be some trouble there, for sure. But it's a ways off. Let's see what's in the mail when we get to Noumea. In the meantime, we got that party Cubby was talking about. Always something, isn't it?"

Cubby knew what he was talking about when he told us we were the polliwogs who would provide the entertainment for the rest of the crew. Rumors had been flying for days, and the ones who'd made the crossing before, the shellbacks, they called them, started giving us looks when they passed by us on deck, met us in the head, or sat across from us in the galley.

Three days before the scheduled crossing, all of us polliwogs got called out on the main deck by a bosun's mate named Harper. He was a beefy guy, with arms like Popeye, who always went around with a big marlinspike in a holster that hung from his belt. Most of the deck apes he worked with called him Spike. He was a pretty scary guy, with a lot of tattoos and a gold tooth that flashed when he spoke. Wiley and I hadn't had much to do with him up to now.

Some of the soldiers lounging about on deck drew in closer to get a look at what was going on. Old Spike gave us a once-over, looking at each of us in turn, and then smiled. "Look like a sad bunch of slimy polliwogs to me. Ol' King Neptune gonna be hard on you boys, if you don't put on a good show for 'im tomorrow night. You boys better work hard. It ain't good to piss off the king."

Harper then explained that it was the custom for the polliwogs to put on a show for King Neptune and his court the night before the crossing. We had to make up something that would please him. Then the next day we would get a summons from Davy Jones to stand before the court and answer to the charges the shellbacks dreamed up against us. It reminded me of Mr. Phillips' Thanksgiving pageant back in school, but there was a threatening undertone in Harper's comment about pleasing the king and answering charges. I gave Wiley a look, thought he looked like I felt—a little scared and worried about where we were headed with this.

Harper told us from now on we were supposed to wear our clothes inside out and backwards, showing proper respect to the shellbacks. I figured it just made us easier to pick out for torment, and would create some laughs for the other guys when we tried to use the head with our pants on backwards.

He opened a locker next to the ladder that led up to the boat deck. "Take a look in here. You can use anything in here to put together your show. If it ain't in here and you need something else, you're on your own. Steal it, borrow it, I don't wanta know. Just make it good—the king ain't easy to please."

Wiley threw me a worried look. "What are we gonna do, Justin? I don't like the sound of this at all."

"Me neither. I have a feeling Neptune won't be happy no matter what we do. I think Spike and the others are looking forward to making fools out of all of us, probably push us around, whatever they can get away with."

Rex Lambert, another polliwog, spoke up. "I heard about these crossing the line shindigs before. Guy in boot camp said his old man told him all about the shit they put you through."

"What'd he tell y'all?" drawled Dilly Brown, a skinny kid from Alabama.

"Said they make you crawl through some garbage, beat

you with sticks, kiss the royal baby's belly—whatever they can think up. Ends when you get baptized, whatever that means. After that you get to be shellbacks—torment the next batch yourself."

"What about this show we got to put on? I ain't never done nothing like that," Dilly said.

"Look in the locker," Rex said, "see what's inside."

We opened the double doors on the locker and took a look. It seemed more like a storage closet than anything else. There were the usual brooms and mops, some buckets stacked inside one another, a set of shelves with cleaning supplies lined up along the top. A couple of wooden boxes with hinged lids were shoved underneath. Wiley and Rex had leaned in, peering into the back corners. Rex told Wiley, "Pull those boxes out. Might be something in there."

Wiley grabbed a rope handle on the end of the box and dragged it out into the light. He flipped up the hasp and raised the lid.

Rex started going through the contents of the box, pulling things out and laying them on the deck. "Well, lookee here. This must be what Spike was hinting at." He pulled out a grass skirt, held it up to his waist, and said, "Not exactly my size. Looks like it might fit Dilly, though, skinny as he is. Look here." He reached in and pulled out a coconut shell that was split in half and tied together with boot laces. "Here, Dilly. It's the rest of your costume."

"I ain't wearin' that," Dilly snorted. "It's plain ridiculous."

"With that southern accent of yours, I think you'd be a real charmer. See here, there's even some flowers for your hair," and he pulled out a kind of woven hat thing that had fake flowers stuck to it. He plopped it on Dilly's head. "That's perfect."

There was lot of groaning and grumbling on the part of

the men. Dilly was blushing and shaking his head. But Rex was unstoppable. I could tell he had an idea for the show.

"Where's Opar? Get that Polack over here."

Frank Oparowski was a tall, dark-haired fellow with a heavy beard and a deep voice. I had heard him in the shower, and I thought I knew where Rex was heading. The man knew more songs than anyone I ever met. He could sing church songs like "Amazing Grace" and "Leaning on the Everlasting Arms," popular ones like "Night and Day" and "Stardust." But what he liked most were the novelty songs, and he knew a bunch. He sang "Mairzy Doats" and "Mr. Five by Five" and "Nobody Knows What a Red Head Mama Can Do."

"C'mere, Frank. I've got an idea."

Frank stepped away from the railing, and walked over to Rex.

"Let's have some fun with this, Frank. It don't really matter what we do. They're saving all the real fun for the next day. Those soldiers'll be watchin' us take our licks—that's the crew's idea of showing them a good time, anyway. Let's show 'em some real fun without worrying too much about what's gonna happen later."

"Sing some songs, put together a skit or two. Goofin' around a little—we could do that," Frank said.

And that's what they did. Frank and Rex put together a quartet that included Sam Benson and another guy named Bobby Carco. I didn't know them very well, but we would get to know each other in the next few days.

Wiley and I were on our own, with the others for support, but Rex wasn't the only one to come up with a plan. We'd just have to wait and see how it would work out. We gathered some more things from the boxes and got to work.

Since the polliwogs were the only ones wearing their clothes inside out and backwards, we were pretty easy to spot and easy targets for the shellbacks. The GIs watched us going about the ship, hoping to get a laugh at our expense when some of the shellbacks started pulling their pranks on us. I learned to watch them, too—hoping for an early warning to avoid trouble. Wiley and I had been doing maintenance with the gun crew on one of the three-inch guns and were headed back to put our gear away when some of the GIs saw us coming and moved aside to let us pass. One of them looked up over our heads as the others scattered a little more rapidly than seemed right to me. We were about to step out from under the overhang of the deck above us. I grabbed Wiley's elbow, said "Hold on!" and pulled him back just as a bucketful of water splashed on the deck in front of us. When we stepped out, a voice rang out from above: "Sorry about that—musta slipped." Of course, it was only a voice. The guy was long gone when we looked to see who had tried to douse us. The GIs laughed and cheered. Whenever the troops saw us getting the treatment, they cracked up. We were providing some distraction from the boredom. They had to give us that, at least.

11

When our big night came, we reported to the mess deck to put on our show. Even though the galley and the dining area had been enlarged when the ship was converted to a troop transport, the room wasn't nearly big enough to hold the entire crew. The soldiers and the crew still had to take their meals in shifts because there wasn't enough room. Besides, that many meals couldn't be served at one time. Tonight, some of the tables had been taken up at one end of the room, and a kind of makeshift stage had been created, with a big canvas curtain hung to separate it from the rest of the room. The ten of us polliwogs entered the galley through the door we usually used to exit after a meal and found ourselves behind the curtain. We were all wearing our dress whites, carrying the costumes and props for the show in our arms.

Spike Harper, dressed in khakis, entered behind us. He gave us a look that started out as his usual scowl, but the corners of his mouth twitched a little, and I thought he was about to break into a grin, but the moment passed, and he went back to his old self. I thought, *he's really enjoying this.* "Stow that gear wherever you want," he said. He held up the bosun's pipe that dangled from a chain around his thick neck. "When you hear me call, you come out from behind here and line up in front of the curtain. The king and his court are waiting. You got three minutes." He gave us another look, turned, and left the way he had come.

We could hear the crowd on the other side of the curtain. There was a lot of shuffling, scraping chairs, people talking loud to be heard over the conversations of others. Our audience would be made up of "Neptune and his court" —

whatever that meant—all the officers and chiefs, and anyone else with enough rank to squeeze his way in. The room wasn't big enough for everyone, but it sounded like it was packed.

I looked over at Wiley and saw the same panicked expression on his face I had seen the night he nearly drowned. Beads of sweat trickled out under the brim of his dixie cup hat. My own heart was pounding, and I felt a little light-headed. I looked at the other guys. Opar and Rex managed to look bored, but Dilly looked a little flushed, and I hoped he could get through his part without fainting. He'd never hear the end of it if that happened. The rest of the guys leaned against the bulkhead, trying to imitate Opar and Rex, but not quite carrying it off. I just wanted to get it over with.

The crowd suddenly went quiet, and I heard footsteps on the other side of the curtain. Spike blew his whistle, and we all trooped out. We lined up beside each other in front of the curtain and got our first look at the crowd. The king and his court were sitting on a raised platform at the far end of the room. The rest of the space was jammed with the officers and chiefs, all dressed in khakis.

Neptune sat on his throne. He wore a long robe and held a trident in his right hand. He wore a crown on his head that had shells and starfish and what looked like seaweed woven through it. He had on a long gray-green wig that hung down past his shoulders. Sitting a little below him on his right was Davy Jones, wearing a three-cornered hat and a patch over his left eye. A gold earring hung from his left earlobe. He had a big cutlass in his right hand and rested the long blade against his shoulder. He held a rolled-up scroll in his left hand. Neptune's queen sat on his left, a big guy stuffed into a long white gown with long white gloves that didn't quite hide his hairy arms. He had a long string mop wig that hung down below his chin. His lips were painted red, and his eyes were rimmed with some kind of black stuff that made them look like burned holes in a blanket. He was the scariest woman I'd ever seen.

Chief Harper called everyone to attention. Everyone stood and turned toward Neptune and his court. "Your Majesty, it is my duty to introduce to you, her Highness, and Captain Jones this pitiful group of polliwogs you see before you. They wish to become shellbacks and hope to seek your favor by offering entertainment that will please you."

Neptune stood, pounded the end of his trident on the deck, and said in a rumbling voice, "Let's see what they have brought. Let the entertainment begin."

After the shock of standing there wore off, I started to figure out Neptune and his court. I recognized that booming voice as the captain's. We had met Captain Briggs when we came aboard, but didn't have any reason to see him after that. But that voice was something else. Wiley said the captain could probably whisper during a hurricane and be heard at both ends of the ship. He was rumored to be a good guy, fair enough unless somebody crossed him, and he must have a sense of humor, too, if he was willing to dress up like that and take part in this foolishness.

Davy Jones looked a lot like the ensign we always saw following the captain around like a puppy dog. Ensign Weems had beady little eyes that made him look shifty to me, and Wiley had him pegged as a suck-up who could get us in trouble if he thought he could make it work to his advantage. I didn't know who the queen was, but he kind of looked like one of the engine room chiefs I had seen before, a beefy older guy with gray at the temples and busted knuckles that looked like they'd healed badly.

Neptune settled onto his throne, and everyone in the room took their seats. Chief Harper hustled us back behind the curtain and we got ready. Rex turned out to be quite the organizer. He got everyone into their costumes, lined up his quartet, and marched them out in front of the curtain. They waited till the room quieted down, and then started singing one of Opar's many novelty songs, a little ditty called "Lalapaluza Lu." It was about the girl everybody wants to win the war for, a kind of musical pinup girl, like the ones they painted on bombers sometimes.

Wiley and I pulled the curtain apart, and Dilly stumbled out, wearing the grass skirt and the coconut shell bra with that silly hat on his head. He was blushing so hard his ears turned red, but he was trying to hold up his end. He grabbed his left elbow with his right hand and put his left hand on his cheek, trying to make his hips sway as he sashayed back and forth in front of Rex and his boys.

The audience erupted in whistles and catcalls and some of the verses got lost in the hubbub. Dilly did his best to look seductive, but he was pretty hopeless. I had to admit, it was really funny. When the song ended, Dilly made a mad dash between the curtains.

Wiley and I were up next. We'd come up with a skit based on "That Harlem Goat," an old camp song that Opar taught us. Wiley was playing the part of the goat, with paper horns taped on his forehead and white socks tied to his ears and hanging down. He had some mop strings tied under his chin for a beard. His dress whites had a bunch of string mops tied to the back so when he crawled out on his hands and knees, they hung off his sides. It was pitiful, but it got the idea across.

Rex and the boys started singing. Opar's booming voice took the lead. After each line, the other fellows echoed what he said in higher tones:

That Harlem goat
--That Harlem goat –

Was feeling fine
--Was feeling fine—

Here the curtain parted to reveal a clothesline that had some red machinist's rags cut into little tee shirt shapes pinned on it.

Ate three red shirts
--Ate three red shirts—
Right off the line
Right—off—the—line

Wiley raised up on his hind legs and plucked the shirts from the line and stuffed them into the blouse of his uniform, trying to look smug about it.

Along came Bill
--Along came Bill—

That was my cue, and I came out carrying a broom handle and a coil of rope, trying to look angry at the goat who ate my shirts.

Gave him a whack
--Gave him a whack—

Here I gave Wiley a good one with the stick. He didn't look pleased.

And tied him to
--And tied him to—
The railroad track
The—railroad—track

Wiley collapsed on the deck, and I wrapped the rope

around his feet and hands, pretending to hogtie him to an imaginary railroad track.

He gave three groans
--He gave three groans—
Of awful pain
--Of awful pain—

Wiley made some gagging sounds and did his best to look sick.

Coughed up the shirts
--Coughed up the shirts—

Wiley pulled the shirts out and threw them up in the air.

And flagged the train
And—flagged—the –train

Wiley and I took a bow to some applause, then scrambled through the opening in the curtain and pulled it closed behind us.

There were a couple of other acts. A guy named Sticks Bentley and another guy, Artie Gates, grabbed a stack of buckets and came out from behind the curtain. I'd been on galley duty with Sticks once before. He was a nervous type, always in motion, even when he was standing still. He'd been a drummer in a band and constantly tapped and fiddled with stuff, tapping out rhythms and beats till it made you crazy. It was hard to be around him for very long. I didn't know Artie at all, but I had seen the two of them together sometimes.

Rex and his crew separated into two pairs with one on each side as Sticks and Artie took center stage. They took some things out of the buckets and then turned them over and sat on them, with another bucket between them. Sticks had two long-handled wooden spoons. He turned them around and used the ends like drumsticks, starting a steady beat on the bucket in front of him. Artie had a pair of metal tablespoons in each hand, and he picked up the beat from Sticks, rapping the paired spoons on his knees. Soon they had a rhythm going between them that was fascinating to watch. Sticks managed to get different notes from the bucket by drumming in the center of the bucket bottom or on the outer edge, sometimes rapping the rim or the side of the bucket. Artie made those spoons sing, crossing his wrists to show off a little, creating a kind of melody line while Sticks hammered out a beat. They kept at it for a few minutes and finally led up to a big rattling and thumping finish that seemed to delight the crowd. There were a lot of cheers and whistles for those two when they bowed, grabbed the buckets, and disappeared behind the curtain.

Rex had saved the best act for last. A little guy named Andy Feltzer came out on stage. He had on an army shirt and a garrison cap borrowed from one of the GIs. The shirt was way too big for him and hung down almost to his knees. He didn't appear to be wearing anything else. He was blond and very fair-skinned and had slim legs and stood barefoot in front of the crowd. As Rex and the gang hummed along in the background, Andy Feltzer sang "You Can't Say No to a Soldier." He had a high, but pleasing voice that was strangely compelling.

The song told the "little lady" to put on her makeup and do her patriotic duty. There was a call to arms that had nothing to do with guns. She couldn't turn down a soldier or a sailor if she wanted them to win the war for her.

There were several verses. Andy did his best to look flirty, while Rex and his gang did a little humming interlude in the middle of the song. When the song was over, Andy turned sideways, looking at the audience over his shoulder. He gave them a sassy wink, kicked up one heel, and scampered off the stage, vanishing behind the curtain. The crowd went wild. It made me wonder how long it would take him to live that down.

When it was all over, Harper led us up to the throne and made us stand before the court. Davy Jones stood up and scowled at us one at a time. He unrolled a scroll and read from it. "You are hereby summoned to appear before the court of His Majesty Neptunus Rex at 0900 hours tomorrow. You are to answer the charges against you, after which you will be initiated into the solemn mysteries of the ancient deep." He handed Chief Harper a bundle of pages. Harper bowed before the king, then turned and gave each of us a sheet from the bundle. After that he had us bow and do an about face, then marched us through the crowd to a chorus of catcalls, hisses, and whistles.

When we left the galley, Wiley looked at me and said, "Wonder what they'll cook up for us tomorrow?"

I looked at the Davy Jones' paper in my hand. It said *Subpoena* at the top and had a *List of Charges* with a lot of *Whereases* and *Therefores* underneath. "I think they already know—and I'm sure it won't have anything to do with how well they liked our show."

12

Spike Harper banged his marlinspike on an iron skillet, "Get up, shitheads!" He rousted us out of our bunks at 0700. "You wanta eat before the fun starts, get your asses up and dressed now."

We staggered into the head with our ears ringing, enjoyed another saltwater shower, and got dressed in our turned-out clothes. Wiley and I headed down to the galley with the others.

Cubby Buckman stood outside, leaning against the open hatch, smoking a cigarette. He watched as the polliwogs paraded past him. As I headed inside, he gave me a funny look. "Careful what you eat. Biscuits and gravy ain't always what they seem."

I nodded and ducked inside the galley with the others, wondering what he was trying to tell me. Wiley and I grabbed a metal tray and got in line with the others. We looked down the serving line to see what they had to offer.

"Looks like the usual stuff – Spam, SOS, powdered eggs again," Wiley observed.

"Any of your chickens ever lay powdered eggs?"

Wiley chuckled, "Not that I ever saw. We had Anconas that laid white eggs, and Rhode Island Reds that always laid brown eggs. We had a couple of Araucanas once that laid blue eggs, but the coons got in at night and killed 'em. Hard to figure what kind of chicken could lay a powdered egg."

"Probably not one we'd want to see. Move up, it's your turn."

Wiley slid his tray along, and the server loaded it up with the things Wiley pointed to. A couple of toast triangles topped with a ladle of creamed chipped beef affectionately known to all of us as shit on a shingle, a scoop of scrambled eggs, and a slab of Spam filled the indentations in the tray. Wiley got a bowl of hot cereal to add to his pile.

Breakfast was my favorite meal, mostly because it was the one I was best at cooking, but I had never warmed up to SOS, and I preferred Cream of Wheat to the galley's thick, lumpy oatmeal that looked like it could be used to patch plaster if you let it dry long enough. I got toast, a slab of Spam, and convinced my server to double up on the powdered eggs. They looked pretty much like scrambled eggs, but just seemed to have all the character left out.

All the polliwogs had to sit at two tables by the exit door. We got our coffee from the big urns on the side table, took cream and sugar if we wanted, grabbed our silverware, and toted our trays to the table.

Rex was still charged up from last night's show. He looked around the table and grinned, "You guys were great last night. How do you think it went?" He stirred the cream and sugar he'd put in his mug as he talked.

Dilly drawled, "Puttin' me in a grass skirt didn't make much of a lady. Just don't ask me to do it again."

Artie beat out a little rhythm on the back of his hand with a couple of spoons. "I don't really think it matters much. They already decided what's gonna happen. Like Rex said, it's a tradition, and you know how the service is big on that stuff."

Rex took a swig of the coffee. A horrified expression appeared on his face, and he spit it back in the mug. He started coughing, wiping his mouth on a napkin. When he had recovered, he said, "I think the fun has already started."

The cream was soured, and some wise guy had put salt in the sugar shaker. For once I was glad I took my coffee black. I studied my cup carefully. It looked okay to me, just a little greasy shine on the top. I tasted it, and it wasn't that bad. Probably strong enough to burn a hole through the deck, but it was like that most days, reminding me of Uncle Hal's brew at home.

Wiley sliced up the Spam, brought a forkful to his mouth and studied it, cocking his head to one side, looking at it like a chicken studying a bug. "Looks okay to me. What could they do to Spam?'

He shoved in the Spam and started to chew. After a few seconds, he pulled it back out, and launched into a coughing fit. When he came up for air, he wheezed, "Red pepper, lots of it." When he had recovered, he dabbed at his watering eyes, "Still tastes like Spam, though." He dipped it in his coffee cup, then tried it again. "Better this way," he said, chewing slowly.

I looked at the eggs. Powdered or not, they were usually edible. Flavor wasn't everything, after all, and I usually doctored them with salt and pepper. The color was a little off, it seemed to me. I wouldn't usually have thought much about it. I liked to put the eggs between two pieces of toast like a sandwich, but after Wiley's discovery, I decided to try a bite before I spoiled the toast. I took a big bite and rolled it around in my mouth. It didn't take long for my mouth to catch fire, and I tried to put it out with a couple swallows of coffee. "Tabasco," I gasped.

Dilly Brown heard me gasping, said, "Pass that shit over here. I like Tabasco on my eggs."

I slid my eggs over onto his tray and contemplated my toast. It was a little too dark, but looked otherwise like its natural self. I decided to make do with toast and coffee, although I did think about laundering my Spam if I could wangle a second cup.

Andy Feltzer, who last night couldn't say no to a soldier, had to say no to the SOS when he patted it with his spoon, and saw a puddle of grease form on top. Opar pronounced his fit to eat, but he was a big guy who was rumored to have a cast iron stomach. The rest of us just watched him put it away, shaking our heads.

Carco gave up on the oatmeal while Wiley was still giving the Spam a bath. I was a little late on the uptake, but I finally realized what Cubby was trying to tell me. Wiley wasn't the only one who needed to pay more attention to what people told him.

Chief Harper got our attention when he appeared in the hatchway and blew his pipe. "You ain't done yet? Dump that shit and line up outside."

We got up together, tossed our breakfast in the garbage bin, and headed out after him.

Wiley whispered, "Better to toss it out now than toss it up later."

Spike led us out onto the main deck. The GIs had gotten the word by now, and there were more of them on deck than I'd ever seen before. They were lined up along the railings on both sides, standing in a mob on the boat deck, hanging out over the rail like bunches of grapes. Knots of men filled the gun tubs where the Bofors and Oerlikon guns were mounted. We were greeted with hoots and cheers as Harper marched us along the starboard side of the deck.

Neptune and his court were lined up beside each other like last night–Davy Jones on the King's right and the Queen on the left. On the Queen's left was a guy I'd never seen before. He was dressed in what looked like a diaper. He was the fattest guy I'd seen aboard the ship. I don't know where they found him. I thought maybe he was a hole snipe, brought up from some dark corner of the engine room, but I couldn't picture him making it up the ladder without help. He had a huge, floppy belly that hung over the top of the diaper. He stuck his thumb in his mouth, and I figured it out soon enough. He had to be the royal baby.

Davy Jones stood up, gave us a look like he'd stepped in something he couldn't get off his shoe, and said, "What are these creatures that come before the King?"

Harper gave us his own disgusted look and turned to face Davy Jones. "Slimy Polliwogs, one and all."

"Their mere presence offends the King and his court. They must be held to account. Prepare them to approach the court. Peel the slime. See that they are presentable to His Majesty."

Harper grabbed Bobby Carco, who was closest to hand, and dragged him over to a chair where the ship's barber was waiting. "What do you think, Chief," the barber said, "landing strip or victory?"

"Landing strip. Peel off some of that slime."

The barber took up his clippers in one hand, clamped Bobby's shoulder with the other, and mowed a strip from front to back, peeling his head to the scalp. One more pass and Bobby's curly black hair fell away, leaving a wide white strip down the middle that gleamed in the sunlight.

Bobby got up, rubbing his scalp, as Harper dragged another victim to the chair and plopped him down. "Victory for this wog, I think."

Rex leaned back in the chair, resigned to his fate. The barber expertly carved a v-shape that started near each temple and ran back to a point, leaving a triangular tuft in the middle. It was goofy-looking, for sure, but the GIs found our misery delightful and whooped and hollered each time a new victim rose from the chair.

Wiley got the victory cut, and I was treated to the landing strip. Wiley looked as silly as Rex. I felt the skin on top of my head and thought my next look in the mirror would be interesting. Maybe I could wear my hat in the shower.

Harper marched us toward the stern where two rows of men were lined up facing each other. Each of them stood at parade rest, feet apart, hands behind their backs. Beyond them was a long tube made of canvas that stretched out along the deck, up against the side of the cargo hatch.

"On your knees, wogs! Crawl through the tube and be reborn."

We all hit the deck then and started crawling toward the tube. As we passed between the men, we discovered that they each had a length of fire hose that they used to beat on us as we crawled between them. It stung like crazy, and it made me want to go faster to get away, but the deck was rough, and the guys in front couldn't go fast enough to keep ahead of the ones coming along behind. We ended up bunched together, nose to butt, as the sailors kept pummeling us with the hoses.

As we neared the tube, we could smell what had become of that pile of garbage. The tube was filled with it, and we had to crawl through it to get away from those bastards beating us with the hoses.

Dilly was in front, with Rex behind him. "Dammit, Dilly, just hold your breath and go before they beat the crap out of us."

Dilly had a panicky look on his face. "Don't y'all push me. I'm going!" He took a deep breath and plunged into the mess spilling out of the tube.

I heard Wiley say, "Tube's too long to make it in one breath. Hope he don't pass out in there, plug it up."

Rex crawled in behind Dilly, not waiting for him to come out the other end. The rest of us were hoping to see somebody come out before we had to go in. Just before it was my turn, Dilly popped out, covered in slime, looking green as a gourd.

When it was my turn, I forged ahead, trying to hold my breath as long as I could. There was just a little light making its way through the canvas, and I could only imagine what

I was crawling through. It was deep enough that my hands plunged into the muck halfway to my elbows. I tried to go as fast as I could, but it was slicker than snot and hard to get a purchase. Here and there were big lumps of stuff I was glad I couldn't see. I slipped once and fell onto my side, flailing to keep my head above it all. When I was about halfway, I ran out of air and had to take a breath. The garbage reeked, but there was a vomity smell laid on top that almost made me puke, and I wished I hadn't given Dilly my eggs. I took another breath and plowed on toward the light that finally appeared ahead. I slid out of the end into the sunshine and stood up, slimy goo sliding off me, plopping onto the deck. I rushed over to the rail, coughed up a load, and sent it over the side.

It took a while, but everyone made it through. I hoped Dilly was the only one who puked inside. I was really glad I didn't have to go last.

When Sam Benson finally appeared, one of the deck apes opened the big red valve on a fire hose and washed us down. He hit us hard with the spray, but I think we were all happy to blow the stink off.

The GIs laughed and pointed at us, cheering as Spike paraded us along the deck to present the polliwogs to His Majesty. Harper was actually grinning, that gold tooth catching the light as he bowed and spoke to the King. "These polliwogs have been prepared to come before the royal court. They bow before your greatness, hoping to become shellbacks who will serve you proudly."

Neptune rose from his throne and looked us over. "Before you can become shellbacks, you must show your respect for my Queen and kiss the Royal Baby. Then you may be baptized if you are found worthy. Step forward and kneel before the Queen. You may kiss her foot, and then the Royal Baby's belly."

I thought we were coming to the end of this, but I should have known better. The GIs close enough to see leaned in to get a better look as we took turns showing our respect. When I was growing up, saying "Kiss my foot," was a mixed company substitute for "Kiss my ass." I was glad we weren't just being polite now, 'cause kissing the Queen's hairy foot was bad enough. We all took our turns with the queen and the baby. I didn't think kissing the queen's foot would amount to much, but it was a hot day and Her Highness was a big guy who clearly hadn't found time for a shower before the ceremony. That hairy foot had been a long time in the boot and mixed its flavor with what floated down from up above. I knelt on the deck, gave her a big smacker, and moved down the line.

The Royal Baby was another story altogether. While we were enjoying ourselves in the garbage, somebody had smeared that big belly with grease and mixed it with something that made it change color from the black stuff that was used everywhere on the ship. It was what Uncle Hal would have called shit brindle, or calf turd sorrel, depending on the exact shade. Just the thought of smooching that bundle of blubber made me queasy, but thinking about what that stuff was made me shuddery inside.

Spike grabbed Artie Gates and towed him toward the baby. He grabbed Artie by the scruff of the neck and pushed down hard. Artie collapsed to his knees and leaned forward, looking at that jiggling smear in front of him. He stretched his head out a little further, trying to work up enough nerve for a peck-and-go, but the baby grabbed him by the ears and squashed Artie's face into his belly, smearing his head around in the goop. When the baby finally let go, Artie tottered to his feet, wiping his mouth with the back of his hand. Then he licked his lips, which was a big mistake. He shook his head and shoulders like a wet dog, and made a sad face that looked like Emmett Kelly's Weary Willie. It was a mistake I didn't want to repeat.

When it was my turn, I was determined to keep my mouth closed, but the baby grabbed the back of my head with one meaty hand, caught my jaw with the other, and squeezed my cheeks till my lips popped open. Then he rubbed my face all over his belly, coating my front teeth with the nasty stuff. I spit out what I could, but there was a greasy aftertaste of mustard and Tabasco that lingered, burning my tongue.

The deck ape who'd doused us with the firehose stepped up, grabbed Artie by the arm, and led him over to a cargo hatch that had been lined with waterproof canvas and filled with sea water. Spike prodded the rest of us along behind Artie. All the garbage hadn't been wasted in the tube. Some was floating on the top of the pool. Davy Jones stood beside a plank that was fastened to one side, resting that cutlass on his shoulder.

"Polliwogs still, I see," he said, trying to look grim and not quite carrying it off. "Before you can be shellbacks, polliwogs must be baptized in the briny depths, steeped in the mysteries of the ancient deep." The deck ape grabbed Artie by both arms and lifted him onto the plank and gave him a shove. He teetered on the edge, and Davy Jones smacked him on the butt with the flat of his sword, tipping him headfirst into the pool. Artie came up sputtering, puked up some sea water he had swallowed, and paddled to the other side. He climbed out and stood dripping on the deck.

The rest of us got the idea pretty quick. We stepped out on the plank and fell into the pool one-by-one without getting manhandled. Davy Jones tried to smack each of us on the butt with that stupid sword, but some of us were quicker and got in and out of the pool without help from either of them.

Harper and his assistant marched us back in front of the King and his court. We stood together in a line and bowed to His Majesty. Water dripped off us, making little puddles on the deck.

Neptune rose to his feet. He looked us over carefully as a silence settled on sailors and GIs alike. Everyone waited to hear him speak. After a long pause, he raised his arms toward us. "You have been tested, and you are deemed worthy. Welcome shellbacks!"

Everybody cheered and hooted. Clearly everyone had enjoyed the ceremony more than we had. But it was over. We were shellbacks. Maybe the rest of the crew would leave us alone–after our hair grew back.

Wiley looked at me, patted me on the head, running his hand over the bare scalp. "Pretty pale up there–needs a little sun," he said. He didn't look happy. "I've about had it. It's time to pee on the fire and put out the dogs. Let's get out of here."

We dragged our soggy selves away from the party, hoping to hit the head, take a shower, maybe see how bad our haircuts looked. On the way we saw Cubby standing outside the galley in his cook's whites, apron tied around his waist.

"Have a good time out there?" He chuckled, "You look like you been rode hard and put away wet."

"I've had fun before," Wiley said, "and this ain't it."

"Jes' let it go," Cubby said. "Tomorrow's a new day, and it ain't been touched yet."

13

On the map New Caledonia looked like a chunk of land that broke off from Australia and drifted out to sea. It turned out to be a lot bigger than that little dab on the map— two hundred miles long and forty wide, with green hills that rose beyond the beaches and turned into shadowy peaks in the distance.

It was late morning, hot and humid, with a few cloudy streaks painting the mountaintops. After three weeks at sea, it was a comfort to see our destination poking up out of the sea before us. We had sailed past a few smaller islands in the last week, but this was bigger by far than the others. It was February 23rd, almost exactly a year after Guadalcanal had been won, and Noumea was an important base for army and navy operations in the South Pacific.

Everyone who wasn't on duty gathered on the main deck to get a look. The GIs had finished breakfast and were eager to put their boots on dry land. They'd been ordered to pack their gear the night before, and they didn't need to be told twice. Their officers were corralling them into manageable groups before disembarking.

Wiley and I stood on the boat deck as the *Mintaka* and the other ships in the convoy threaded their way between smaller islands and steamed into the harbor. The ships drifted apart, each headed for its own berth. As we neared the docks, a tugboat came alongside, nudging us toward the pier, white water churning from her stern. The deck apes cast mooring lines ashore, and men on the dock looped them around the bollards, making the ship fast. We had arrived.

The deck crew swung the gangway out and lowered it to the dock. A jeep pulled up and three army officers got out, leaving the driver to wait. The one who rode in front had captain's bars. He looked up at the ship, then led his lieutenants up the gangway.

Captain Briggs was waiting on the bridge. The officers exchanged salutes and had a little talk, but we were too far away to hear. They shook hands all around, and Captain Briggs pointed to the GIs clustered fore and aft.

The lieutenants headed down to opposite ends of the main deck. The army officers that sailed with us called their men to attention, turned, and saluted the new guys. The captain stayed on the bridge deck, chewing the fat with Captain Briggs.

A couple of trucks showed up on the dock. Two GIs stepped down and unloaded boxes from the back. They set up a row of tables beside the trucks and began unpacking. A sergeant got down from the cab of the truck with a clipboard in hand. He took a folding chair from the back of the truck and set it up beside the table. The three of them stood there, waiting.

Our GIs marched off the ship, reduced to single file as they headed down the gangway, duffel bags perched on their shoulders. Some of the ones we knew gave us a wink and a wave as they passed. A few looked up at the bridge and snapped off a respectful salute in Captain Briggs' direction. The line slowed when they hit the dock. Each man tossed his duffel into the back of the truck, got his name checked off by the sergeant with the clipboard, and was handed a shiny new mess kit by the guys with the boxes.

They stood around, getting the feel of solid ground again, waiting around for the rest coming off the ship behind them. Finally, the junior officers who arrived in the jeep gave their instructions to the GI officers who'd sailed with us. The soldiers fell into formation quickly and began marching away, their new mess kits glinting in the sun as their arms swung back and forth.

"Where you think they're taking them?" Wiley said.

"One of our guys who'd been here before said there's rows of Quonset huts just over the hill. All those mess kits–looks like they'll be taking their meals in a field kitchen out there somewhere."

"Our food wasn't that bad–even Cubby's biscuits are gettin' better. Always so much to look forward to, these guys. Makes bein' on ship seem like traveling in style."

"Yeah, check out your stylish haircut in the mirror."

The rest of the GIs disembarked, following the same routine. When the last of them had left, Captain Briggs and the army captain exchanged salutes. The captain trotted down the gangway, got into the jeep with his lieutenants, nodded to his driver, and the jeep putted away. The trucks trailed after them, disappearing over the hill in the distance.

The bosun's mates opened the hatches to start pulling cargo from the holds. Ensign Weems came down from the bridge deck. He rounded up Wiley and me and the rest of the new shellbacks, and sent us down in the hold to help. "Can't have you men just sitting around, admiring the view. You need to turn to and lend a hand, learn your way around the ship like the rest of the crew. Report to Chief Braddock in cargo hold number 2. You'll recognize him when you see him."

The cargo winches were poised over the open hatches, cables dangling down inside. We made our way to the hatch that led down to the hold.

"What'd he mean," Wiley said, 'You'll recognize him when you see him'?"

"Beats me," I said. "Never been down there before."

Rex took the lead, and we dropped down the hatch after

him. When we stepped off the ladder at the bottom and looked around, the first thing that hit us was the heat. We were inside a soup can somebody had left on the stove. The place was packed with cargo of all kinds: a lot of jeeps, some small trucks, machinery I didn't recognize strapped onto pallets. Drums filled with grease, tires, wooden spools of wire cable and rope, all shoved in cheek-by-jowl with hardly any room between.   It was noisy, too–mostly from the machinery powering the winches and the men shouting to be heard.

As we stood there gawking, a sweaty guy in a t-shirt and dungarees saw us and came over. "Nice haircuts—must be the new guys. Today you're honorary deck apes. You gotta see Chief Braddock–he's in charge down here." He jerked his thumbed over his right shoulder. "Over there."

When I looked in that direction, I knew what Ensign Weems meant. Chief Braddock was the Royal Baby–but he wasn't sucking his thumb today. He was barking orders as men wrestled the cables from the cargo winch and secured them to the lift rings on a jeep. He looked different without the diaper. His belly still flopped over his belt, but his barrel chest and beefy arms looked like they'd be sure winners in a wrestling contest.

When he saw us, he waved us over. "Get your asses back behind those jeeps and lend a hand." He pointed toward the forward end, where some men were already struggling to untangle vehicles and roll them out under the hatch to be winched out of the hold. The whole place was packed tight, with barely enough room to squeeze between the vehicles and the equipment stacked around them.

We joined two sailors struggling to free one of the jeeps. When the way was clear, we got in behind. One of the men hopped in, released the brake, and we pushed as he steered it over to where the cable hung down. Wiley and I watched as men attached lines to lift rings front and rear. When the cables were secured, the winch took up the slack and the jeep started to rise up toward the main deck.

Chief Braddock yelled at us, "It's just a jeep, dammit. Don't just stand there lookin' up like it's died and going up to heaven. Get back there and roll out another."

We worked most of the afternoon with the Royal Baby yelling at us. There was a lot more cargo aboard, but most of it was headed for other places. Noumea got a dozen or so jeeps, some drums of grease and motor oil, pallets of kitchen gear and canned goods, and other stuff hauled up in cargo nets. As each load was raised, the boom swung around and the cargo was lowered down to the crew on the dock below.

When Braddock finally let us go, we climbed the ladder topside. The breeze washed over our sweaty bodies, a welcome relief from the heat belowdecks. We looked over the side and watched the men loading the cargo onto trucks lined up on the dock. The jeeps were gone, fueled up and driven off to replace some of the ones already driven to death by the motorized cavalry that patrolled the island.

Beside the sailors on the dock were some native laborers. I heard someone behind me, and turned to see Cubby, looking fresh in a clean set of cook's whites. Wiley looked up at Cubby, then turned back to watch the men on the dock.

"Don't have to say it, Travers. I know what you thinking. They 'bout the same shade as me, but they ain't my kind."

Wiley seldom missed an opportunity to step on his tongue. "He's making progress, Cubby," I said, "But it's slow going. He doesn't mean to offend."

"No offense taken, Justin. I've heard it before. I guess it's a logical question."

"Who are those guys?" Wiley said. "Just asking, you know."

"They're Kanaks – natives. Saw them on our first cruise

out this way, before we went up to the Aleutians. Hundred years or so ago, the French took over, sent their convicts out here to the prison they built. Put the natives to work in the mines–copper, nickel, chromium–I don't know what all. The Japs wanted that stuff, too. That's why they were here.

"I think the Kanaks are happy we're here, better than the Japs, for sure. I think they had enough time to get used to the French by now. Most speak some French, at least. Not so much English. Just say 'bula' when you meet 'em. Or 'bula vinaka' – just means hello. I think it's more to it than that, but 'bula' will get you by."

Captain Briggs showed his good side when the work was done for the day. Not long after we finished, the hatches were closed, the winches were shut down, and the crew drifted up from down below, taking in the breeze with the rest who had finished earlier. A big box truck pulled up beside the ship, and the sailors started down the gangway.

I asked one of them, "What's going on?"

"Captain's treat," he said brushing past me. "Come on."

We trooped down the gangway and gathered by the truck. The driver and his partner got out and went to the back. They opened the big doors and started shoving out crates. Most of the guys knew what was happening, but we were in the dark till one of the guys opened a crate and started passing out cans of beer to the others.

Cubby explained, "You know alcohol ain't allowed on board the ship. This just three-two beer, but that truck refrigerated, and the captain know a cold beer do a lot for a man's spirits. Seen him do this before. Don't hurt his popularity none."

We grabbed a beer in each hand and strolled down near the end of the pier, Cubby in his clean whites looking like he'd found two derelicts to make friends with. Wiley and I were pretty sorry to look at. We were sweaty and grimy and our dungarees were smeared with grease. The breeze wasn't enough to dry our sweat-stained shirts, but the beer was cold, and we made do. We sat on some crates, looked out on the harbor, and enjoyed each other's company.

After a while, Wiley spoke up, poking his nose in again. "How come they call you Cubby? That your real name?"

I could have smacked him. Sometimes Wiley forgot to put his brain in gear before he let out the clutch. I cringed a little, but Cubby didn't seem to mind. Maybe the cold beer helped.

"You ask a lot of questions," Cubby said, taking his eyes off the view and turning to look Wiley in the eye. I saw Wiley's shoulders stiffen.

"Shit like that used to bother me. Always thought guys were looking for trouble, trying to push me around. Guys like me get a lot of that. I used to always want to fight 'em. Didn't really matter what they said. I always knew what was behind it." He smiled then, and Wiley seemed to relax a little. "I know you okay, though. You Justin's friend."

Cubby opened his second can of beer and looked out over the harbor again. "Use to get in a lot of fights, thought if somebody called me a name I had to try to kill 'em. Turned out I was too mad to fight. Couldn't keep my head on straight. Came home one day, all tore up from fightin'. Daddy took one look at me, broke out laughin', then pulled me up and hugged me till I thought I'd bust. Said I looked just like him when he was a kid.

"Daddy taught me what he knew, told me names were just words, and when I let the words make me crazy mad, I'd already lost the fight. Taught me how to keep my head and how to box. Didn't need to fight so much after that, but when I did, I usually came out on top.

"Daddy's name was Baron, but folks mostly called him Bear. Momma called him her big ol' brown bear, so naturally I got to be Cubby. Real name's Lucius, but everybody calls me Cubby. "

Wiley was looking a little sheepish, but I thought he'd get over it. "Thanks for telling us about your name. Justin says I'm too nosy, but I was just curious."

"It's okay," Cubby said. "Justin told me you never met a Negro till you came to his place and saw his momma's friend Waters. Just remember, we all sailin' on the same boat."

We heard brakes squealing and turned to see a truck pulled up alongside the *Mintaka*.

A sailor got out and went around to the back of the truck. He pulled aside the cover that hung down to the tailgate and took out two big canvas sacks, lumbering up the gangway and ducking through the hatch that led into the boat deck. After a few minutes, he jogged down the gangway again, but now the sacks he carried were empty. He hopped into the truck, tossing the sacks into the back. The driver put it in gear, popped the clutch, and they putted away down the pier.

"Looks like the mail just came," Cubby said.

14

Nobody had to be told twice to get up the next morning. We all rolled out, hit the showers, and dressed in a hurry. Mail was passed out to each division after breakfast, so we trooped into the galley and joined the others in line. Rex, Opar, Dilly, and the other new shellbacks were up ahead of us.

"Glad to see breakfast is back to normal," Wiley said. "I'm tired of studying the food after the tricks they played on us before."

"That fun's over," I said. "Two things they won't mess with, and that's the food and the mail. Food's not always great, but they do what they can. I'm looking forward to hearing from home myself."

"Me, too. We haven't had any news in almost a month. I hope Agnes is still lighting a candle for me and not burning it at both ends."

"You gotta give those worries a rest. Everything's probably fine."

"How can you be so sure?"

"I'm not, but we're too far from home to do anything about what's going on in Glory."

"I'm not worried about Glory. Agnes ain't in Glory. There's probably a lotta guys more interesting than me where she is."

"Lotta guys more interesting than you everywhere we go," I said, punching him in the arm. Wiley didn't seem to think that was very funny. "Look, temptation might come along, but that girl's got too much goodness in her to get her head turned easily. Your charm'll take longer than this to wear off. We haven't been gone that long."

Wiley looked at me, frowning, "Ma says it ain't goodness till it's been tested."

"This war's put a strain on the whole world. We just have to ride it out, see what comes next. Right now, it's breakfast."

We filled our trays with the usual fare, added fresh fruit that had been brought on board since we landed, and settled in with the others.

The gunner's mates gathered to get their mail near the five-inch gun mounted on the stern. There was no joking around like Eddie Purdue had done when we were on the coast. The chief gunner's mate stood by while the clerk who brought the mail read off our names. Men hollered "Yo" or "Here" when their names were called, stepping forward to collect their letters. Some walked away then, but most just hung back, hoping there was more for them in the sack. Wiley got a letter from Agnes and another from his folks. When I heard my name, I stepped up and got a letter. It was from Momma. I stood there waiting for more. The clerk passed out more letters, rummaging around in the sack. Finally he looked in the sack and came up with one last letter—for me. It was from Annie. I breathed a sigh. The other men who were still waiting turned away then, their shoulders sagging a little.

"Travers and Coulter—hang on a sec. You got something else. It's from the captain." He took two mailing tubes the chief had been holding and handed them to us. Someone had written our names on the tubes.

Wiley unscrewed the metal cap on the end, pulled out a big sheet of heavy paper from inside and unrolled it to take a look.

The chief said, "All the new shellbacks get one of those. Take a look, then mail it home. There's no place to keep it here. Makes a nice souvenir."

It was a big certificate, kind of like a poster. It said "Imperium Neptuni Regis" on a banner at the top with a picture of Neptune rising up out of the sea with his right arm raised and his left arm holding a trident. A pair of horses were rising out of the sea on each side of him. Mermaids rode scaly sea creatures down the left and right sides. It said USS Mintaka (AK-94) in the middle. Spaces below that were filled in with the date and the longitude and latitude of our crossing. There was a big space in the middle with Wiley's name, and the words underneath said he had been "found worthy to be numbered as one of our Trusty Shellbacks" and "duly initiated into the SOLEMN MYSTERIES OF THE ANCIENT ORDER OF THE DEEP." Near the bottom were printed signatures of "Neptunus Rex, Ruler of the Raging Main" and "Davy Jones, His Majesty's Scribe."

"Pretty classy-looking, don't you think?" I asked.

"I guess so. Probably not worth what we had to go through. I think I'd rather just kept my hair the way it was."

"Your hair'll grow back. This will be something to show your kids someday. Put it back in that tube, and let's go see what's in the letters."

We found a spot in the shade below the boat deck on the edge of the number four hold. Wiley looked at the letters in his hand. Funny-looking, these letters. Kinda small."

I looked at my own letter. The envelope was only about four by five inches, with a window where my name and address peeked through. It said "U.S." in the upper left corner with a big pair of wings spread out underneath the letters and the word "Mail" below that stamped on top of a giant letter V. There was an official-looking stamp with somebody's initials written over it in the lower left corner. "This must be the new v-mail they told us about. I don't know how you could put much in a letter this small."

"Did you notice the three dots and the dash under the

wings? Looks like Morse code."

"Yeah—V for victory. How about that?"

"Still looks too small to me. Let's crack 'em open."

Wiley peeled up the flap on one of his letters. I picked up Annie's letter to me and opened it carefully.

My Dearest Justin,

Got my v-mail kit from Pearl at the post office. It's hard to believe someone will actually read our private mail, but you'll see the space for the censor's stamp on the envelope, so I guess we have to watch what we say. Pearl says there's only room for about 250 words, and we can't just write smaller because they're only half as big when they print them for you. They tell us to write happy and newsy thoughts so you won't worry. "Is it fit to be read in a foxhole?" it says. Well, I'm glad you're not in a foxhole, but I'll try to be happy and newsy.

Things are fine in Glory, though everyone misses those who've left to fight. We're getting used to doing without. The rest of us are catching up to the ones who were always poor. Folks are still enjoying the fruits and vegetables they put up last summer, and even if it's cold and rainy now, they're already planning new victory gardens for the spring. Hal's cows are keeping them in milk and butter, and he is selling some on the side. Waters is fussing with his apple trees, and your mom is teaching Rebecca her letters and numbers so she can be ready for school.

I'm running out of room this time, but I'll just have to write another letter. You know I love you – always remember that wherever you go. You are my hero no matter what happens.

Love,
Annie

I was glad to get Annie's letter, but it left me wishing for more. I hoped another would come soon. It was hardly enough to keep me going, but it would have to do for now.

Momma's letter was kind of the same, but it was good to hear from them, too. She said Uncle Hal was getting along okay, but the damp weather bothered his bad leg, said he wished I was around to help milk the cows. Waters reminded me to keep my head above water and my eyes open for trouble. Rebecca wrote all the letters in the alphabet in two rows across the bottom of the page and printed her name, too. Momma said she was a handful, especially when the weather kept them inside, and she had been teaching her to keep her entertained when she couldn't follow Waters around in the orchard. Momma had apparently decided that "happy and newsy" was the way to go, too. I'm sure they would have told me if something more was going on.

I asked Wiley what Agnes had to say.

"Seems okay, I think. She likes her work, but she found out they got women pilots called WASPS in some Army program now, and she sounds really jealous." He looked at the letter again. "'Women Airforce Service Pilots', she says. They let them fly bombers cross country from the factories to wherever they're going, so the guys can fly combat missions instead. They have to have a pilot's license and pay their own way to a training program in Texas. I hope they keep her in the Marines. I could just see her saving her pay to take lessons and buy a bus ticket to Texas."

"That girl is a pistol, for sure. Maybe the war'll be over before she gets a chance. She say anything else?"

"Yeah. She managed to squeeze in a line or two about how she missed me and couldn't wait to see me again. I hope she means it. I feel her tugging at my heart all the time."

"I know. I miss Annie just as much. Sometimes it's all I think about. What we're doing doesn't seem like so much, but somebody's gotta do it so we can all go home. What'd your folks have to say?"

"Seems like they're all right. Dad got his foot stepped on when he was shoeing Mose Randall's mare, mashed some toes, but Mom says he's gonna be okay. Happened once before, I remember. Hurts like hell, I expect, but he'll manage. Part of the job when you're a farrier."

In three days, we were supposed to start shuttle runs between the islands, moving men and cargo, but today we had some time to ourselves. It was hot and muggy under an overcast sky that threatened a warm afternoon shower. Some of the crew, including Wiley and me and some of the new shellbacks, decided to see what Noumea was like.

It put Glory to shame for size. Somebody said the population was around fifteen thousand, and I don't think they were including the troops. The main street was lined with buildings—shops, a post office, and some important-looking buildings separated from the street by low stone walls topped with wrought iron fences. One had a fancy gate between tall pillars. A sign over the top said Palais de Justice. The tall spires of a church rose behind it. The buildings all had French names. Some like the Hotel de Ville with its tall palms shading the front were easy to figure out, but some of them were harder to decipher.

Shoppers haggled with vendors who sold fish and fruit and vegetables in open stalls. Other stands held handmade goods—clothing and jewelry and such. Lots of people were moving about, some hurrying like they had important business, others just strolling along, shopping. Soldiers and sailors moved through the crowd as well.

Rex and Opar headed off in one direction with Dilly and a couple of crew members. Wiley and I stopped to look at the goods on display in the stalls. One of the sellers had all kinds of shells and things she had gathered along the beach. She had necklaces and bracelets with bits of coral and jade. But the shells were what caught my eye. I'd never seen anything like them when I'd patrolled the beach with Jig at my side. Fan-shaped shells in orange and purple, spiral shapes, speckled green or tipped with blue, spiky white shells with pink inside—a glittering rainbow of colors laid out on her tables. I thought Annie would like them and decided to buy something to send her. We were going to send our certificates from the crossing ceremony home in those tubes, and I thought I could stuff some little thing inside for her.

"What d'ya think, Wiley? Let's get the girls something."

"Sure, why not?"

We'd gotten paid before we left San Francisco. We hadn't had a chance to spend our pay while we were at sea, though other guys had managed to gamble away quite a bit. They would be headed to the bars to spend the rest, I was pretty sure. It would be nice to send something home instead of frittering our money away.

I had picked out a cowrie shell bracelet and Wiley was looking at a pink coral necklace when someone tapped me on the shoulder. I heard Cubby say, "Never pay what they asking right away. They expect you to haggle a little."

He was with some other fellows, one of them a Negro named Jenkins. I'd seen him with Cubby on other occasions. Darker-skinned and taller than Cubby, he always looked like he could bite a ten-penny nail in two. Cubby had a temper, but he knew how to laugh, too. He had learned to take things as they came, find the joy hidden behind life's troubles. This fellow was just plain scary. He didn't seem to know we were on the same side. When Cubby stopped to talk, the others kept on down the street. Jenkins turned to look at Cubby, then walked ahead without him.

"Your friend's not waiting for you," I said. "Don't you want to catch up to him?"

"It's okay. He just ain't ready for *you*. I know where he

going. I'll see him later."

Cubby helped us bargain for the jewelry. The dealer was a shrewd-looking French woman, with deep-set wrinkles around her eyes. Even with the broad-brimmed hat she wore, she looked like she'd spent a lot of time in the sun. When we showed her the things we wanted, she named a price, but I didn't know anything about francs. I'd seen some of their colorful banknotes as we walked past the other stalls. They said, "Nouvelle Caledonie" at the top with pictures underneath. One had a picture that showed a deer head with big horns.

Cubby jumped in to help. The dealer didn't know much English, but "dollars" was a word she understood. Counting on fingers and hands, she and Cubby finally settled on a price. We ended up spending ten dollars, which seemed like quite a bit, but the jewelry was nice, and it was for our girls anyway.

Cubby showed us around, walking along the streets. There were meat markets, tailors' shops, places that sold island souvenirs, a bicycle repair shop, places that sold fabrics and something Cubby called tapa, a kind of cloth made from tree bark.

After we had been walking a while, we came to a corner where an alley led off to the left. It was a long narrow lane with a lot of seedy-looking bars and joints that reminded me of the Snug back in Glory. There were trees lining the street and a lot of sailors and GIs hanging out in twos and threes, smoking and laughing together. A few tough-looking local men leaned against the walls next to open doors that led to stairways just visible inside. Women stood in the doorways and the sailors and GIs were talking with some of them. One woman took a soldier's arm, and leaned into his shoulder as they turned into the doorway and started up the stairs.

"Sailors' Alley," Cubby said, pointing down the street,

"probably not the best place for you two. Lot of round-heeled women and rough types waiting to take your money. Jenkins gone down there, I know. I gotta go find him, keep him outta trouble. He get a few drinks in him, be likely to pick a fight with the first guy looks at him cross-eyed. Stay out of trouble. I'll see you later." He turned and headed down the street, looking for his friend.

Wiley watched him go, taking in the busy scene. "A lot going on down there. You wanta take a look? Might be something to see."

Wiley was my best friend, but his impulsiveness worried me sometimes. "Let's not test your virtue just yet," I said. Warm raindrops began to fall, giving us just a few minutes before it started to pour. "Cubby can take care of himself. Let's find somewhere else, grab some lunch, have a beer."

15

During the next few weeks the *Mintaka* was assigned to make shuttle runs to New Zealand and back to New Caledonia, hauling troops and cargo. We steamed along under blue skies with an occasional afternoon rain shower. The temperatures were in the seventies during the day, and as we got further south, the air lost some of the tropical mugginess we had known further north.

We had embarked several hundred battle-weary troops that had landed in New Caledonia and were taking them to New Zealand for some needed rest. They were a rough-looking bunch who had been through a lot in recent months. A few had been wounded in some minor way, the more seriously hurt having been sent somewhere else to recover. More than anything, they just looked tired, bone-tired. They sat in little groups on deck, smoking, talking quietly among themselves. Some just sat alone, staring hollow-eyed at the sea around us.

Our gun crews mostly conducted drills, maintained equipment, and helped out on other ship duties. When he wasn't worrying about Agnes, Wiley griped about having nothing important to do. "Look at those guys," he said, pointing to the GIs on deck. "They've seen a lot where they've been, I bet. Makes me wish we'd see some action. I'd like to fire those weapons sometime. I'm tired of running drills and greasing gun wheels."

"We'll probably get our chance. Don't be in a hurry," I said. "We've got a job to do, too. From the looks of those guys, I'm glad I don't have theirs. Just think about the ones they left behind, the bodies that washed up on the beach, the badly wounded ones all shot to hell lying in a hospital. These are the lucky ones."

When we arrived in Wellington and the troops disembarked, there was a band to greet them, a contingent of American nurses from the Red Cross, and trucks and other vehicles to carry them to a nearby camp at Anderson's Park, where Kiwi boys had played cricket before the war. I was told that there weren't as many American soldiers as there had been earlier in the war, but there were still thousands in camps spread across the two main islands.

The GIs' spirits perked up considerably when they saw what was waiting for them ashore. They smiled and cheered, waving at those on the dock as the gangway was swung out and lowered. It didn't take them long to hoist their duffel bags and make their way down to the dock. There was a bounce in their step that we hadn't seen before.

Turk, our chief gunner's mate told us, "This is a good place for them. Chance to get back to themselves. Folks here sent a lot of their own boys off to fight. They know how to treat our guys. Lot of them invite the GIs into their homes for dinner. Eat too much lamb for my taste—goddam greasy mountain goat—but a home-cooked meal just the same. Red Cross puts on dances, invites "nice" girls to come.

'Course there's the other kind, too—hang out not too far from the camps. Milk bars, two percent beer, and pubs that close early, but the ones lookin' for it will find hooch somewhere. GIs got money to spend, can afford to show a girl a good time. Makes some of the men here get pissed off when a girl develops a taste for Coca-Cola and Glenn Miller tunes. Be some fights in the streets once in a while, but it's nice here. I wish we could stay a while before we shove off."

We spent the rest of the day unloading cargo and taking on provisions for the return trip. It was a routine we had become accustomed to by now. We offloaded the supplies we had taken on before we left, helping out in the holds, shifting pallets and crates that were wrapped in cargo nets and hoisted topside and lowered to the dock.

Several trucks arrived later in the afternoon, bringing fresh fruits and vegetables in big wooden crates and fresh meat packed in ice. It was quickly brought aboard and put in the ship's reefers. From the labels on the crates, it looked like we were going to get to try that "greasy mountain goat" without having to go ashore. Hopefully Cubby and the other cooks could transform the lamb into something we'd enjoy eating.

Cubby and I had pored over the ship's manual, a big black book that said *Cooking and Baking on Shipboard* in big red letters on the cover. It turned out Cubby knew a lot about cooking, just not so much about reading. We learned that the biscuit problem was about "old dough" and "young dough." It turned out there was a lot of science involved in baking, something I'd never even thought about. Momma cooked and baked and made it look easy while she was doing it. As far as the biscuit problem went, the difference seemed to be in what the cookbook called "proofing" the dough. Apparently it made a difference whether the dough was "young" or "old." I didn't really understand it when I read it, but Cubby seemed to get it right away. Like I said, he knew a lot about cooking. The biscuits got better after that, putting a smile on Captain Briggs' face and adding promise to Cubby's progress as a cook striker.

I sort of envied those GIs who were happily ashore, looking to have a good time. They had certainly earned it. We were supposed to take on fresh troops and head back to New Caledonia in two days. It was supposed to be a quick turnaround, but I still hoped we'd have a little time off before we set out again.

I met Wiley in the galley the next morning for breakfast. As we moved along in the chow line, Wiley said, "Chief Turk thought we'd probably have some mail when we got here. I hope he's right."

"Me, too," I said. "Amazing how they can find us out here. I wonder how they can keep track like that."

"I'm just happy somebody knows where we are. I don't really know myself. I tried to tell Agnes, but she said when she got my letter, the censor had cut out all the names I put in to tell her where we'd been."

"Yeah, I don't think we're supposed to do that. They worry the enemy might find out something they shouldn't know. They're just being careful. Leave out names and places, make more room to tell Agnes you love her."

"I know, keep it light," he chuckled, "I'll tell her how much we're getting to like Spam."

After breakfast we went down to the main deck to see if the mail had come. The other gunner's mates were there waiting. Some were sitting by the gun mount. A couple others leaned against the rail, smoking and looking out over the dock. Chief Turk arrived with the mail clerk a few minutes after Wiley and I got there. The men scrambled to their feet and the guys at the rail took a last drag and flipped the butts over the side. We all gathered in front of the clerk as he dipped into the sack, pulled out a handful of letters, and started calling out names.

We both got letters. Wiley got two, one from Agnes and one from his folks. I just got one, from Annie. We walked over to sit on the closed hatch and read them over by ourselves.

Annie's letter was full of news from home, but it was not the happy kind:

My Dearest Justin,

I'm sorry to have bad news to tell you. The war has come home to Glory, I'm afraid. We just received word that Curt Spencer has been killed in Europe. The Spencers are devastated. Mrs. Spencer has a big wreath on the door, and cars have been stopping by their house, people offering their condolences and dropping off gifts of food like they always do. The minister is coming on Saturday, and there will be a service in the church. A long while back, Mr. Phillips put up a banner with a blue star for each of the men in Glory who are in the service. He will present Mrs. Spencer with a gold star, to be placed over the blue one, as is the custom.

No one has heard from Agnes' brother Jesse in a long while. He and Curt were together at first in Europe, but seemed to have lost track of each other over time. We heard that some who served in Europe are being sent to fight against Japan since things have improved in Europe, but we just don't know. All are praying he is safe somewhere.

I only have the vaguest idea where you are, but I pray for you every day and hope you are safe, too. I loved the cowrie bracelet. It is beautiful. I'm glad to know you think of me and can't wait till you come home to stay.

Love,
Annie

Curt Spencer... I didn't know what to think. I thought about the men who drowned crossing the river when we were on the beach patrol: Stieg Alvarsson. Tony Benzonelli, and Billy Randall. Their needless deaths had been a shock that washed over us like the wave that sank them, a tragic accident caused by Lt. Peake's inept command. Until now, I didn't really know anyone who had been killed in combat, though

I knew we had lost thousands of men. Curt was best friends with Agnes' brother Jesse. The two of them were older boys who tormented me and Wiley when I first went to school in Glory. Mr. Phillips let them come to school even though they were really too old. He hoped to help them learn, but they really didn't fit in. They used to give us the stinkeye, and I remembered that first day in school when Wiley told me to watch out for them. Curt wasn't so bad by himself, but when he and Jesse were together, they were pretty scary, and all the kids steered clear of them.

When Wiley and Agnes took a liking to each other, Jesse tried to give Wiley a hard time, but Agnes knew her own mind and soon put Jesse in his place. Curt and Jesse quit giving us trouble and not long after that, they stopped coming to school. After Pearl Harbor, they were the first ones to enlist and left Glory to save the world.

So now Curt was gone, and no one knew where Jesse was. Annie was right. Curt's death had brought the war to Glory in a way that made it real. Victory gardens and scrap metal drives gave folks at home something to do while their boys were away, but always with the expectation that they would all come home one day. This was a different story altogether.

I looked over at Wiley, then, and I could tell he'd gotten the news, too. There was a dewy look in his eye as he glanced at the letter in his hand.

"Does Agnes know yet?" I asked.

Wiley looked at me then, wiping his nose with the back of his hand, "Yeah. Mom told her. I think Annie probably sent her a letter, too." He didn't say anything for a minute or two, looking out toward the open sea. "You know, I really used to hate that guy. Him and Jesse both. But only 'cause they always wanted to pick on us. After Jesse let me and Agnes alone, I just didn't think about him anymore. So why do I feel so bad about Curt?"

I thought about it for a moment before I said anything. "Yeah, I used to feel the same way. But this is a different thing. Curt and Jesse were older, bigger, embarrassed to be at school with little kids who could read better than they could, so they acted tough and gave us a hard time. It was something they did so they could feel better about themselves. School came too late to help them. The world's a big place with room in it for everybody. I hope Curt found that out before he died."

"Listen to you talk. Kind of sound like Waters—all philosophical and everything. I guess I know where that came from. Well, I'm sad, too, even if I don't know why. Curt was a bully, but he was my bully, and I'll miss him. I hope Jesse is out there finding out the world's big enough for him to share with me and Agnes and that he's safe and gets back to Glory in one piece."

Later that day, GIs began showing up at the dock. Some rode in the backs of trucks, crowded in with others, piling out with duffel bags and stacking them on the deck beside the gangway. They stood together in groups, talking spiritedly, looking up at the *Mintaka* and the sailors they could see shifting cargo and going about their duties. They weren't in a hurry to board ship and appeared to be in good spirits, laughing and joking among themselves. These were the replacement troops who had been here on leave, enjoying some time off before returning to battle.

Cubby said some of them were new troops who had been training on long marches to toughen them up; some had practiced beach landings at points along the shore; others had gone on scouting missions in the mountains, practicing for jungle warfare to come. After we shuttled them back to New Caledonia, they would board other ships that would take them to dangerous places where their skill would be put to the test.

In the afternoon, several private cars showed up carrying GIs and their Kiwi girlfriends, much to the delight of the soldiers standing on the dock, who cheered and whistled. There were some lingering kisses that would make movie stars blush, but their enthusiasm was contagious and entertaining to watch. Some couples' farewells were tearful, like two hearts torn from each other while we looked on, and it made me sad to see that, thinking how much I missed Annie. One couple sat together in a little blue roadster, just holding on to each other for dear life.

Finally officers drove up in a pair of jeeps and began organizing a formation. When the troops were lined up, a group of Maori women in colorful dresses danced and sang a farewell song. A late-arriving GI rushing down the street joined the dancers, awkwardly imitating their graceful, swaying movements and hand gestures, which delighted the crowd but drew frowns from the officers. When the dancers finished, he disappeared quickly into the ranks of the soldiers amid the applause that followed.

The officers exchanged salutes, and the men began filing up the gangway to board the *Mintaka*. The soldiers waved at the people below who had come to see them off as they made their way onto the ship while a band played the "Stars and Stripes Forever" and the "Colonel Bogey March."

After supper, Wiley and I took a walk around the main deck. It was a warm evening, and we stood on the port side, resting our forearms on the rail, looking out to sea. The setting sun painted the sky, bringing the day to an end as we watched the blood-red ball sink below the black line of the horizon. We weren't much for talking right then, and we just stood together, lost in our own thoughts.

Chief Turk came by, a folder tucked under his arm, on his way to file a report or take care of some request from one of the officers. He saw us and stopped to talk. "You two okay? Saw you at mail call looking down in the mouth. Bad news?"

Wiley turned away from the view and looked at the chief. "Yeah. One of the boys we knew at home. Killed in Europe somewhere. Older than us, joined up right after Pearl Harbor."

"That's tough. I've lost some friends myself. First one hit me hard. Been some more since then, but you don't get used to it. Like a little piece of you taken away every time it happens."

"Hard to tell what to do, what to think, you know?"

"I know. At home, folks have a service, friends come around, help say goodbye. There's some comfort to that, even if they can't send the body home. Out here it's not the same. But you have to put it behind you, so you can move on." He paused, glanced out to sea, then looked at us again. "Listen, boys, I've got a suggestion. I'm on the way to turn in my report. If I can get past that idiot Weems, I'll talk to the captain. Go get cleaned up, put on your dress uniform, and meet me here in a half hour."

We weren't sure what the chief had in mind, but we did what he said. We needed to shed our dungarees and take a shower anyway. Half an hour later, we headed back to meet Turk. After a few minutes the chief came down the ladder from the bridge deck and made his way over to us, holding something in his hand.

"Look, I can't do anything about your friend, but I want my boys to be able to shoot straight when the time comes— can't do that when your minds are somewhere else." He handed each of us a slip of paper. "These are three-hour passes. Like I said, New Zealand is a good place. Go down to the Majestic Cabaret on Willis Street. Not more than a half-hour's walk from here. Ask anybody for directions. Be a lot of people there, nice music. Nice girls—not the other kind—might want to dance with you. Pubs close at six, but you might find a beer, listen to some music, put your friend to rest."

We thanked him, and he left us standing there. "What do you think, Wiley?"

"I don't know what to say. Chief's just being nice, I guess. Not what I expected. I suppose we could go see what he was talking about."

"It'd be nice to get off the ship for a while. It's only a few hours, anyway."

Even after dark, The Majestic was easy to find. We only had to ask for directions twice before we found ourselves looking up at the tall building with big pillars at either side of the entrance. Soldiers and sailors in groups of two or three stood on the sidewalk, smoking and talking. A few girls in small groups came down the walk, glanced at the men, and giggled to each other before heading inside. When the doors opened, "Moonlight Serenade" washed over us, reassuringly familiar, and we were swept inside as other folks crowded in behind us.

The band was lined up on a big stage, the musicians seated behind music stands with a fancy letter M on the front. A huge oval sign behind them had the New Zealand flag on the left and the Stars and Stripes on the right, a big eagle with raised wings between the two.   It was about the swankiest place I'd ever been, and it was packed with people having a good time.

Even with Glenn Miller's help, we weren't really "in the mood," and Wiley and I headed for an out-of-the way corner and found a table by ourselves. The song came to an end, and the band took a break. Dancing couples parted, some going off to sit with friends, others holding hands and moving off the dance floor together.

Two girls found us sitting together and decided to join Wiley and me, regarding us with bright eyes and friendly smiles. Wiley looked up at one of the girls, a perky redhead in a polka dot dress, then looked away, staring out across the room at the crowd.

"Why so glum, Yank? You look like you've just lost your best friend." She pulled out a chair and sat down. "My name's Violet, what's yours?"

Wiley looked up at her then, blushed a little, said, "Wiley."

The other girl, a dark-haired woman a little older than us, I thought, sat down at the table and introduced herself. "I'm Emma," she said, extending her hand to me.

"Justin," I said, holding her soft hand in mine for a moment. "We just came to listen to the music for a while. We're not looking for anything more. Got some bad news from home earlier today. Letters from our girlfriends said a friend of ours was killed in Europe."

"Sad news is hard to bear, I know. My brother was killed in North Africa last year," Emma said. "Most of our fellows were sent there to fight. Many were lost. A sad affair all around, this awful war."

Violet looked at Wiley and then at me. "I know what you need. I'll be right back," and she got up abruptly and left the table. We all watched as she made her way between the tables and disappeared in the crowd.

"Violet's a good girl, likes to come here for the music and the dancing. You Yanks have turned her head. I'd not be surprised to see her marry one someday, though I think her folks would pitch a fit, especially her father. He thinks the Yankee invasion is a threat to Kiwi manhood, says you boys show up looking like Clark Gable, charming the socks off

Kiwi girls with flowers and taxi rides, paying more attention to girls than they got from their own lads. 'Over-paid, over-sexed, and over *here*,' he says." She turned and pointed.

Violet returned with a small tray that held four glasses of beer. "Just what you need," she repeated, setting the tray down and passing a glass to each of us. "Cheers," she said, as she sat down and held up her glass. "To your friend. What was his name?"

Wiley ran his finger around the rim of the glass and looked at her. "Curt," he said. "Curt Spencer."

"To Curt, then," and we all raised our glasses and took a drink.

We sat quietly for a minute or two, drinking now and then as we watched the band return to their seats and listened as they tuned their instruments. In a minute or two the band leader raised his baton, and the band played "String of Pearls." I knew that song about a string of pearls from the five and dime, "every pearl a star above, wrapped in dreams, and filled with love." I wondered if Annie thought that way about the cowrie bracelet. I hoped so.

Violet jumped up, grabbed Wiley by the wrist, and pulled him to his feet. "Come on, sailor boy, dance with me!"

Wiley looked at me and blushed. Violet dragged him out onto the crowded floor, put her hand in his, placed his other hand at her back, and they began to sway to the music.

Emma looked at me and smiled, "Care to give me a whirl? I won't bite, you know."

"Sorry," I said. "I don't know how to dance. Annie and I never had a chance to learn. I like to watch, though."

"Annie's your girl back home?"

"Yeah. Funny—I don't think I ever said this to anyone but her, but she's all the world to me—the moon and the stars, the whole shebang."

"I can tell. Lucky girl, that one," she said, putting her

hand on mine for a moment before taking it away. "Looks like your friend Wiley didn't get dance lessons, either."

I looked up to see Wiley struggling to keep up with Violet and failing miserably. Finally, Violet just put her arms around Wiley and leaned against his shoulder. They stood still, holding each other, her red hair pressing against his cheek, moving together as the music played on.

"Two left feet, just like me. But Violet seems a lot like Wiley's girl Agnes back home, strong-minded, same fiery red hair."

When the dance was over, Wiley and Violet returned to the table and we finished our beers. Violet was game for another round, but we told them we had to get back before our leave expired. We thanked them for a good time, and exchanged hugs all around. I hoped Emma understood when I told her how much I enjoyed talking with her—her kind words, her soft presence, the warmth of her hand on mine did a lot to lift my spirits. I hoped she'd meet someone who'd "give her a whirl" and wrap the stars in dreams filled with love.

The air was cool outside the Majestic. The sky was clear, and I looked up to see the Southern Cross, its four bright stars the same ones represented on the New Zealand flag we'd seen inside next to the Stars and Stripes. We didn't have much to say to each other on the way back. I thought about Curt being gone and all, and I'm sure Wiley did, too. But we had laid him to rest in our minds. Violet was enough like Agnes to make Wiley miss her even more, and Emma's kindness reminded me of Annie.

I thought about those we had lost and the ones who waited at home. I thought about the war and the senseless heartbreak that had ripped our world apart. I walked along in the dark beside Wiley. Tears were streaming down my cheeks, and I didn't care. We would get through this together, kick this misery to the shadows, and find our way again.

16

When I woke up the next morning, the *Mintaka* was already underway. Wiley wasn't around. I took a shower, pulled on my dungarees, laced up my boots, and headed for the mess deck. Wiley wasn't there, either. It wasn't like him to miss breakfast. Me, either, for that matter, but I just grabbed some toast from the chow line and poured myself a cup of coffee. Opar and Dilly were eating and talking at one of the tables.

"Either of you seen Wiley this morning?" I asked.

"He was here earlier, I think," Opar said.

"Yeah," Dilly drawled. "Didn't say much, just grabbed a cup of coffee and left. Seemed off, somehow."

"He'll turn up sooner or later." Opar chuckled, "No place else to go."

I dipped a triangle of toast in my coffee and chewed for a while, wondering what was up with Wiley. After a bit, I grabbed the cup and headed outside. Our new passengers were scattered about in twos and threes, talking and smoking. I overheard them telling war stories or reliving their time in New Zealand. Some just stood along the rail, taking in the view.

I found Wiley sitting by himself in one of the gun tubs above the main deck. I climbed the ladder and sat beside him. "You okay?" I asked.

"Yeah, I guess. Just thinking about last night."

"Still thinking about Curt?"

"Not so much. Mostly thinking about those girls, about dancing with that girl Violet."

"What about her?"

"I dunno. Makes me feel guilty somehow."

"I can see how you might feel that way, but I don't think you need to."

"That Violet was a lot like Agnes, you know—perky and sassy as all get-out. Had red hair, too." There was a little catch in his voice before he continued. "When we were dancing, she put her arms around me and leaned her head against my shoulder. When I closed my eyes, I felt like it was Agnes in my arms."

"Yeah, I thought about that when I looked at the two of you out there on the dance floor.

"But it was just a dance. We were in a bad place, with Curt's death and all. You needed a hug, and that's all it was. It just reminded you of how much Agnes means to you.

"Emma was nice to me, too, talked to me a little like Annie would, made me feel okay. They just made us realize what we were missing, and that made us miss it all the more. I couldn't talk on the way back, kept thinking about Annie, how it felt just to sit with her and hold her hand. I thought about Momma and Waters, everybody at home—Curt , too, I guess. Tears were running down my face most of the way."

"Me, too, I think. Guess that don't make us tough guys, does it?"

"Probably not so much, but I bet those tough guys cry once in a while."

We sat there a while longer, not saying anything. When I heard Wiley's stomach grumble, I said, "Wanna see if they're still serving breakfast?"

Wiley came back from wherever his thoughts had taken him. He looked up at me with a sad smile. "Sure, why not?"

We steamed to New Caledonia and dropped off some of the GIs we'd picked up in New Zealand, embarked with some new troops aboard, Marines this time, and headed northeast toward an island called Espiritu Santo in New Hebrides. It was a quick turnaround, one of many to come in the next months, and there was no need for Cubby or me to worry about our friends getting into trouble in Sailors' Alley.

As we got closer to the equator, the muggy air pressed down on us, turning to rain showers that provided some relief from the heat, but didn't do much to lift our spirits. Wiley and I went around in tee shirts and dungarees like the rest of the crew, complaining about the weather as the *Mintaka* plodded toward its new destination.

One morning the alarm went off, general quarters was announced, and the order to man battle stations echoed throughout the *Mintaka*. Wiley grabbed a couple of helmets, tossed one to me, and we scrambled up the ladder to one of the anti-aircraft gun mounts. We were passing near an island where the enemy had been driven out by our guys. It was an atoll, shaped like a donut with a bite taken out of it and a lagoon inside the hole. One of their ships had been destroyed, and its hulk lay half-submerged in the lagoon. On the beach beyond the wreck, a burned-out jeep lay on its side just above the water's edge. Other equipment, reduced to twisted and blackened bits of debris, littered the sand around it. Trees above the beach had been torn to shreds. Their ragged stumps stood in the air, like hands with missing fingers, reaching up from the ground that was strewn with broken limbs. Tire tracks through the rubble trailed away out of sight. A few palm trees that rose behind the shipwreck had been spared from the shelling. Coconuts clustered below the fronds that hung down, stirring in the breeze that blew onshore.

It was an opportunity for a little target practice, and Wiley, for one, couldn't wait.

"Strap me in. Hurry up, strap me!"

Wiley leaned into the shoulder rests and I strapped him in. The straps kept the gunner from getting knocked off his feet from the vibrations set up by the rapid fire of the gun. Gino Manfredi and I loaded the sixty-round spiral magazines as we felt the ship reduce its speed. The Jap destroyer would give everyone a chance to fire at a distant target while the *Mintaka* was underway, though we were moving pretty slowly.

When the order was given, the crews fired in turn, taking aim at the derelict ship. It was exciting, fun even. Wiley certainly looked like he was enjoying himself. Sweat trickled down from inside his helmet as he concentrated on the target. His aim was high at first as the gun rode up, and palm fronds and coconuts went flying, but he brought it down, led the ship in the sights, and soon had our crew scoring hits. The spent shells tumbled into the cartridge bag as he swung the gun around to follow the target.

As we passed the wreck and began to leave it behind us, the five-inch gun mounted on the stern swung to and let off several rounds—smoky, deafening blasts that tore away sections of the destroyer's bridge. Everybody cheered and whistled as we sailed away.

"Most fun I've had so far," Wiley said. "Wish we'd been shooting at the Japs for real, though."

"Might not be so much fun when they shoot back."

"Yeah, I guess. We'll see what that's like when we get a chance. Sure knocked hell out of those coconuts, though."

The target practice had been exciting, but the lift it gave everyone faded when the guns went silent and our ship plodded on toward Espiritu Santo. The gyrenes did a lot of calisthenics, practiced landing drills, and maintained their equipment. They read books or magazines., wrote letters home, shot craps, or played poker. The sailors stood watch, prepared meals, chipped paint, greased ammunition, and kept the *Mintaka* afloat. Sometimes at night we got radio broadcasts, and once in a while we got to see movies.

The movies we saw were often screwball comedies, like *Keep 'Em Flying* with Abbott and Costello. In that one they joined the Army Air Corps and did a lot of goofy things that would never really happen, but were funny. Most of the Marines seemed to enjoy their crazy antics, but then there wasn't much choice.

The soldiers gathered on the main deck to watch movies on a makeshift screen, a sheet of canvas that hung down from the bridge deck. Sitting in a crowd of GIs that talked to the actors and whistled and made catcalls whenever a woman appeared on the screen wasn't my idea of fun.

Glory didn't have a movie theater, and I'd always wished it had. Kids who grew up in bigger towns had watched a lot of movies, and I had felt left out. I wondered what it would have been like to sit in the dark, holding hands with Annie, watching a real movie in a real theater with stage curtains and ushers in uniforms with bow ties who showed people to their seats and made folks in the theater behave so everyone could enjoy the show.

The crew watched movies on the mess deck. The crowd was smaller, but behaved just as badly. Sometimes we saw musicals, which some liked and others didn't. Deanna Durbin wasn't too popular, but when the guys got a look at Rita Hayworth in *You'll Never Get Rich*, they just about popped their corks.

One time we got to see *Stormy Weather*, with Lena Horne and Bill Robinson and a whole cast of Negro performers. I remembered hearing Ethel Waters sing that song on the radio when we were with the beach patrol, and I wanted to see the movie. I crowded into the mess deck with Wiley and Opar, Dilly Brown, and most of the other guys we knew. The room was really packed. Cubby and his friend Jenkins came out of the galley still wearing their white aprons tied around their waists and stood in back to watch the show.

That movie was really amazing. Cab Calloway performed a song called "Jumpin' Jive" and the Nicholas Brothers did a number that was hard to believe, dancing on tabletops and leaping over each other on a big staircase. There wasn't much of a story, but the musical numbers were swell. Most of the sailors really liked it, even clapping and cheering after some of the song and dance numbers.

When it was over, we all headed out to the main deck. It took a while for the room to clear out. As I stood there with Wiley, I heard two men a ways in front of us, talking about the show. "Them niggers really know how to sing and dance. Comes natural to 'em I guess."

I looked at Cubby and Jenkins, who were near the door. Jenkins bristled when he heard what the man said, squared his shoulders and opened his mouth to say something, but Cubby grabbed his forearm, looked up at the man as he passed them, rolled his eyes and said with a big grin, "It sho' do, Boss. Just like bowin' and scrapin' and cookin' fo' y'all. How you like yo' eggs?"

The other man looked at Cubby like he was crazy. He turned to his buddy and jerked his thumb over his shoulder, "What's the matter with him?" he said as they cleared the hatch to step out on deck.

"I think that asshole gonna get *his* eggs scrambled," Jenkins said.

"Another time," Cubby said, leading Jenkins back toward the galley.

I was standing watch from midnight to four two days before we reached Espiritu Santo. Nothing much happened at that hour, since most everyone was sleeping. I headed down to the tween deck where the troops were quartered. It was hot and smelly down there, lights were out, and it was pretty quiet, a few coughs and sputters, and some colossal snoring that must have made sleeping a challenge for those nearby. Canned sardines had more room between them than these guys had.

I heard the unmistakable clink of a Zippo lighter opening and headed toward the sound to tell the guy to put it out or go topside to smoke, but two or three guys yelled, "Hey, knock it off," and "Take it outside, pal," and saved me the trouble. Fire was the biggest danger aboard ship, and the rules were clear. Apparently most of the troops realized that.

The rest of the watch was uneventful, and I returned topside, reported in, and stood at the rail for a bit, looking at the moon sailing on its own cloudy seas. I was about to turn in when I saw Cubby coming along, headed to the galley for the early shift.

"Anything new, Cubby?" Cubby often served the officers' mess and sometimes overheard interesting tidbits of information the rest of us weren't privy to.

"Be in Santo pretty soon, big place with lots of troops. Want to keep the sea lanes open between Hawaii and Australia. Supposed to be the closest allied base to Guadalcanal, was real important in beating the Japs there. Captain said we were going to Luganville, got airfields nearby."

"Hear anything else?"

"Not too much—did hear a kind of interesting story, though."

"What was that?"

"Well, Ensign Weems, he like to gossip and I hear him ask Captain Briggs did he know anything about some pilot named Boyington, and the Captain told this long story about this guy they call Pappy who been a pilot with the Flying Tigers in China someplace, I think, before we got into the war. Shot down a bunch of Jap planes over there.

"Then the Captain said he got into the Marines after the war started, put together a squadron called the Black Sheep, and flew Corsairs out of Santo. Captain said he not too big on rules, this Boyington, but he got the job done, had twenty-five kills, some kind of hero, supposedly."

"That's quite a story" I said. "He still flying missions from here?"

"Story don't have a good ending, far as I can tell. Captain said he got shot down a couple months ago, first part of January. Captain said he got another kill on the way down. Ain't heard anything more about him since. Mighta got captured, but he probably dead, seem more likely."

"How come all the heroes seem to be dead?"

"Don't know, Justin. But I ain't anxious to be one of them. I aim to get back to the henhouse before my goose is cooked."

"Me, too, Cubby. Let's keep this boat right side up all the way home."

I caught up with Wiley about 1300 the next day. I'd had eight hours off after my watch ended and had spent most of them sleeping. I managed to grab a snack from the galley and found him chipping paint near the base of the cargo winches between the number four and number five holds.

Wiley looked up when he heard me coming, "Ship's hardly a year old. Don't seem like it should be rusty already."

"I remember somebody saying it only took a month to build. Probably in too big a hurry to get it launched. Maybe they didn't have time to put on a good coat of paint. Salt water's hard on ships anyway."

I grabbed a brush from the paint bucket beside him and started painting over the rusty spots. While we were working, I caught Wiley up on the news from Cubby. When I told him the story about that pilot Boyington, Wiley's ears perked up.

"How come some guys get to be heroes while the rest of us have to peel spuds and chip paint? Must be nice to be a big shot."

"I think everybody's a hero to somebody, even you and me. Folks at home look up to us, say we make them proud. Don't want to be a dead hero, though. Don't even want to be a big shot. Hell, somebody's got to sit on the curb and wave at 'em as they go by."

Wiley smiled. "That's us all right—waving as the world goes by."

17

Cubby was working with a different crew now, preparing supper menus. He was learning a lot, working with a chief cook named Branson. "Hard to get used to recipes, call for forty pounds of meat, but I'm gettin' a feel for it. Chief Branson a good guy, don't yell at you if you make a mistake—'less you make the same one twice. He *show* you how to do stuff, don't just point to a page in the book."

Cubby was a quick study. Once he saw how it was done, he got the hang of it right away. Lamb had been the main dish ever since we hauled those crates aboard in New Zealand. We were still working on it when we set out for New Hebrides. I didn't know there were so many ways to cook lamb, but Cubby showed me the cookbook. There were recipes for roast lamb and braised lamb, which we had at first. I never ate mountain goat, but Chief Turk's colorful description didn't seem too far off to me. There were recipes for lamb chops and steaks, too, but the officers got those.

The cooks didn't let anything go to waste, and when we got down to the leftovers and small pieces, we had a lamb biscuit roll, and an Irish lamb stew, which of course had potatoes mixed in. My favorite was a lamb pot pie, with a top and bottom crust that was tasty and soaked up some of the grease. When we got down to lamb croquettes, I figured we were just about done.

"Yeah," Cubby said. "We about done with the lamb. How you like those croquettes?"

They were bits of meat mashed together in a paste, then breaded and deep-fried. They were hard and greasy and not very tasty. "Not so great, since you asked. Make good ammunition, though. We run out of shells, you could toss 'em at the Japs."

Cubby chuckled, "Prob'ly they just toss 'em back."

"Yeah, they wouldn't want 'em either." I was glad the lamb was finally gone. I was pretty sure I'd had enough for a lifetime.

The *Mintaka* made its way between smaller islands and steamed into the harbor at Luganville on the southern tip of Espiritu Santo. It was only about four hundred miles from New Caledonia. Even at twelve knots, it hadn't taken long. The sun, sinking behind the mountain ridge on the western side of Santo, as Cubby called it, lit the clouds in shades of pink and lavender that began to fade as we entered the harbor.

Santo had been an important support base in the Guadalcanal campaign. The island was mostly mountains and forest, but the Allies had cleared a lot of land, built airfields, put in miles of roads, and built warehouses for maintaining and repairing equipment. They had put up hundreds of Quonset huts for use as hospitals and housing. I hadn't seen anything like it before.

As we pulled up to the dock, Cubby joined Wiley and me on deck. "Welcome to Luganville. Hospitals and whorehouses. Shoot 'em up, patch 'em up, give 'em the clap. Great way to run a war."

"You in a bad mood?" I asked.

"Not really—just makin' a joke. Mostly true, though— what this place be about. They come here to gear up for battle, later come back to the hospitals or the cemetery. The ones ain't in the hospital or the cemetery got nothin' to do with themselves when they off duty, so they usually gamblin' or drinkin', sometime get into fights over stupid stuff.

"You like baseball? They put up teams once in a while, play a game or two. Give the men something to root for, something to watch. Got outdoor movies, too. Might be okay if you don't mind the mosquitoes. Got malaria here, too."

"You're not much of a tour guide, Cubby," Wiley said.

"Ain't much to recommend this place," Cubby said. "I know guys who been here before." Then he looked at us and laughed. "They tell me the line start outside the whorehouse at ten in the morning. Imagine that."

The Marines disembarked early the next morning. A lieutenant showed up in a jeep with two sergeants in the back. The driver stayed in the jeep while the others got out. The lieutenant trotted up the gangway. Captain Briggs and Ensign Weems were waiting. The three exchanged salutes and Weems held out a clipboard. The lieutenant scanned the papers, took a pen from his breast pocket, and signed. Weems gave him a copy of one of the papers and the lieutenant saluted again and started his new charges down the gangway.

The Marines assembled on the dock, and the sergeants got them in formation, barking orders as the men lined up. The lieutenant followed the last of the soldiers down the gangway, got in the jeep, and signaled his driver, who started the jeep and drove him away.

The sergeants called the men to attention. One of the sergeants yelled, "Forward, March!" and the men moved out. The sergeants marched along beside the formation, one of them calling out, "your left, your le-eft, your left, right, left!" When they were all in step, the other sergeant called cadence with a song, calling out a line which the soldiers all repeated in a booming chorus:

"A-round her hair she wore a yellow ribbon." They all marched in step as they repeated the line. "She wore it for her true love, who was far, far away." Again they soldiers echoed the sergeant's line. "Far away" he sang. "Far away," they repeated. Then they all joined in on the last line: "She wore it for her true love, who was far, far away."

They marched along for a little while, moving away from the *Mintaka*. As they rounded a corner and began to move out of sight, I heard the sergeant begin another verse, singing, "Behind the door, her daddy kept a shotgun…"

Later in the morning, Chief Harper caught me and Wiley on deck after breakfast. "Either of you two know how to drive a truck?"

I looked at Wiley, and then back at Harper. "How big is the truck? I can't drive one of those deuce-and-a-halfs, but I'd be okay with a jeep or one of the smaller trucks, sure. What do you need, Chief?

"We got a load of medical supplies that 'sposed to go to one of the hospitals. They brought two trucks, but they're short on drivers. The two guys who came left in the same truck, said we'd need to find one of our own guys to haul those supplies."

"Sounds good to me."

"Take Travers with you. He can look at the map while you drive. Drop the stuff off first. You're going to hospital #3. Take this with you," he said, handing me a clipboard. "Make sure you get a doctor to sign these papers. You can take a look around afterwards. With the troops gone, most of the crew's gonna get some time off, anyway. Just remember where you live.

"Supplies are waiting on the dock – you'll have to load them yourself. I sent Opar down already to keep an eye on things. Get him to help you, then send him back up here. I got another job for him."

We headed down the gangway and found Opar sitting on a pallet loaded with supplies. He looked up when he heard us coming. "You the lucky stiffs got picked to deliver this stuff?"

"Yeah," I said. "Harper said you'd help us put it on the truck."

"I bet he did. Probably got some other job for me, too."

"As a matter of fact, he does. Said you should report back to him when we're done."

"Yeah, most guys gettin' time off now the troops are gone. You'll be drivin' around the island while I'm stuck on some detail with Harper's gang."

"I think your turn's coming—just help us load up."

Wiley dropped the tailgate and tied back the flaps on the canvas that covered the bed of the truck while Opar and I pulled the cargo net off the pallet. We all pitched in and stowed everything in the back of the truck. We said goodbye to Opar and hopped in the cab.

"You sure you know how to drive this thing?" Wiley asked.

"Probably as well as you can read that map. First time for everything, don't you know? This one's pretty easy, I think. Just a good-sized pickup. Not too different from the Model A. Those deuce-and-a-halfs are a different story, got a dual-range transfer case. I wouldn't know how to shift gears in one of those." I got the truck started, stirred the gearshift lever around to get the feel of things, and shifted into gear. "Hang on to your hat. Here we go."

I let out the clutch, gave it a little gas, and we pulled away from the dock. When I got it up to speed, I tried to shift, but missed, and there was a terrible grinding noise till I put in the clutch and tried it again. Wiley looked at me and groaned, but after a few tries, I got the hang of it and we putted along smoothly.

Wiley oriented the map as he held it on his lap and gave me directions as we rolled along. The road was rough and muddy in spots, carved in a mostly straight line between the palm trees that were everywhere around us. As we left the harbor, we passed warehouses with big trucks outside and airfields with rows of planes lined up beside long landing strips. We stopped at one to watch a Corsair touch down, bouncing once before it rolled to a stop. We drove past big steel storage tanks on a little hill above the road and a crew of men putting up some Quonset huts, bolting together the steel frames and standing them up on their foundations.

After a while we left all that activity behind as we drove along the tree-lined road. I was beginning to think we were getting lost when Wiley looked up from his map.

"Should be comin' up soon," he said. "On the right side—look for a sign."

Apparently Wiley was a good navigator. A few hundred yards further along, I saw a big white sign with black letters that said "Hospital Number 3" with an arrow below pointing to the right. We turned into a cleared area off the road, where rows of Quonset huts were lined up side by side. I stopped in front of one with a signboard hanging over the doorway that said "Entrance." Wiley jumped out with the clipboard and went up to the door. He came back in a few minutes and climbed back into the cab.

"Building number 5, last one in the row. They said a doctor would meet us there."

When we got to the end, two men in scrubs and a fellow in uniform were waiting for us. Lieutenant's bars glinted in the sun as the officer stepped forward. "I'm Lieutenant Andrews. Glad to see you men. We've been running short. Hopefully you've got what we need."

"Don't really know what all we've got, sir," I said. "Our ship just docked last night. We were told to get this over to you right away. Hope it's what you want." I handed him the clipboard, and he looked over the papers. He frowned a little, signed the form, and handed the clipboard back. The guys in scrubs began unloading the truck.

"It's not everything we need, but every bit helps. Thank you, men. Drive carefully." He smiled, "Don't end up in my hospital."

When everything was off the truck, we saluted the lieutenant and headed back to the truck.

As I drove out to the main road, Wiley said, "Let's look around a little before we go back, like Harper said we could."

"Okay with me. I'm not in a hurry to get back on the ship. Where you wanta go?"

"Keep going the way we were headed. See what's up ahead a ways."

I drove along the road for another half mile or so, but didn't see much to look at, just more palm trees with the road sliced between them. Up ahead it curved to the right around a hill. When we rounded the curve, we saw two men walking along together at the edge of the road. As we pulled up closer, I recognized Cubby and his friend Jenkins. I pulled up behind them and stopped.

I got down from the cab as they turned to see who we were. Wiley got out and came around to the front of the truck, too.

"Hey, Cubby, where you headed?"

"Just up the road a bit. What you boys doin' out this way?"

"Harper had us deliver a shipment to the hospital back there. Short on drivers or something. Said we could look around a bit when we were done. You want a lift?"

"Guess so. Turned out to be a longer walk than we thought."

"All right, then. You get in front with me and tell me where to go. Wiley can ride in the back with Jenkins."

Wiley paled when I said it, but then he looked at Jenkins,

smiled a little, and walked around the back. I went to see them get settled while Cubby climbed up in the cab.

Jenkins dropped the tailgate and hopped up in the bed of the truck. "Come on, Whitey, climb aboard."

"It's Wiley," he said, looking a little worried.

"I know, kid—just havin' a little fun with you." He reached his hand out to Wiley, "Come on up, now. The view ain't so bad from the back of the bus."

Wiley took Jenkins' hand and levered himself up into the truck bed. I latched the tailgate and climbed back into the cab. I fired up the engine.

"Where you want to go, Cubby?"

A truck was coming up the road behind us, and I waited for it to pass. It was a carryall, what some folks call a panel truck, enclosed, with two big doors on the back that met in the middle. Across the doors the word "cemetery" was painted in big white letters.

"Just a little further down the road, I think," Cubby said. "Just follow that truck."

I wondered what was going on, but I figured Cubby would tell me in his own time. I drove along behind the carryall, waiting to see where it would lead us.

After another quarter mile or so, he spoke up. "You know Jenkins' name is Caleb? Prob'ly never got around to introducin' him, did I? Anyway, folks call 'im 'Leb, though I wouldn't try it just yet if I was you. 'Leb got a friend out here someplace. Somebody he knew since they was kids. They kep' up with each other even after they got into the war. He lookin' to find him.

"Friend's name is Thomas, but 'Leb call him Toots, say he called him that all his life. 'Leb heard Toots' Momma tell him his daddy was a big ol' windbag, but he was just a little toot. I guess the name just stuck after that.

"Anyway, Toots was with one of the colored outfits, 24th

Infantry, I think. They s'posed to establish a perimeter on some Jap-held island. 'Leb don't know all the details, say Toots tried to save some of his guys pinned down by a Jap machine gun. He got close enough to toss in a grenade, blew the Japs all to hell. But Toots got shot up pretty bad . They sent him here to recover. Then he come down with malaria. Been a long time getting back to himself, but 'Leb got a letter from Toots sayin' he okay now. We were on our way to see 'im when you came along."

The truck ahead of us slowed, then turned off on a little road to the right. When we turned in, there was a big white sign that said, "Espiritu Santo Military Cemetery." I drove along the lane behind the truck. It bumped along a little further, then pulled off and stopped in the shade of a banyan tree that had wrapped itself around some palms.

"Stop right here. Let me go get 'Leb out the truck." Cubby got down from the cab and walked toward the back of the truck. I got out and joined him.

I put down the tailgate, and Wiley and Jenkins clambered out, looking around. Ahead of us just to the right of the lane, a man with a corporal's stripes on his sleeve stood at a table that was made of two wooden crates stacked one on top of another. A cigarette dangled from his lips as he laid a white-painted cross on the table. We watched as he put a cardboard stencil on the crossbar. He picked up a short, stubby brush, dipped it in a jar, daubed it around on a board by the jar a few times, then tapped it gently over the stencil. When he was done, he peeled away the cardboard, and a name appeared on the cross. He examined his work, then stood the cross on end in a long rack beside him, with other crosses lined up behind it, their crossbars resting on the edges of the rack.

Further along, opposite the parked carryall, there was a cleared area where two men with their shirts off were digging graves, one beside the other. As they dug and tossed the dirt with their shovels, they kept cadence with a song. First one of the men would call out a line and then the other would answer, repeating the line. "Ain't no use in goin home," the first man sang in a deep voice that made his words seem big and round. Then the second man repeated the line, starting a little higher and bringing it down as he sang. "Jody's got yo' gal and gone," the first man sang in his big voice and the second fellow repeated it. Then they both sang: "Wo-oh-oh-oh, Wo-oh-oh."

Two men stepped out of the carryall and threw open the back doors. A simple wooden coffin lay inside, and the two men each took an end and carried it out, setting it on the ground. The gravediggers kept on with their work, singing:

> "Ain't no use in goin' back,
> Jody's got yo' Cadillac.
> Wo-oh-oh-oh, Wo-oh-oh.
> Wo-oh-oh-oh, Wo-oh-oh."

The two men with the coffin unfolded an American flag and draped it over the coffin as it laid on the ground. As I watched them work and listened to the singing, it suddenly dawned on me that all the cemetery workers were Negroes.

Jenkins stood watching for a minute, then stepped away from the truck and walked out to where the men were digging. I heard him call out Toots' name and watched as his friend set the shovel beside the hole and took Jenkins' hand as he climbed out of the grave.

Toots was a big man like Jenkins, muscles rippling under dark skin that glistened with sweat. Raised scars stood out on his right shoulder, twisted like the legs of a spider squashed underfoot. The shoulder sagged just a little. The two men hugged, then stood back, looking at each other.

Cubby stood next to me, watching Jenkins and his friend.

After a minute, he said, "You guys can go on back, do your look-see, whatever, take the truck back."

"What about you? How are you going to get back? Won't you need a ride?"

"We be all right out here. Give friends time to catch up. Maybe hitch a ride in that cemetery truck. Don't need to worry about us."

Wiley and I headed back in the truck. Wiley seemed a little confused about what we'd seen at the cemetery. As we bounced along, I filled him in on what Cubby told me, about 'Leb and Toots and all he'd been through.

"Jesus, Justin, the man's a war hero. What the hell's he doing out there digging graves?"

"Lot of war heroes these days. Probably a lot of them under the dirt out there if we knew their stories. People like Jenkins and his friend—war heroes or not—don't always get what they deserve. I think maybe you figured that out by now."

"Yeah, I guess so. Really stinks, don't it?"

18

Santo was a big base, spread out all over the area around Luganville. Thousands of troops were stationed here, others like us, passing through on our way to somewhere else. As we drove back to the docks to return the truck, we passed all sorts of vehicles, carryalls like the one at the cemetery, adapted for different purposes: an ambulance with a white cross painted on the side, one with ladders strapped to a rack on the roof. Trucks of every description rumbled along: dump trucks, a deuce-and-a-half pulling a trailer with a giant spool of electrical cable, smaller trucks like the one I was driving, their cargo hidden under the canvas covering the bed. Dozens of jeeps scurried along the road, too, darting in and out among the bigger vehicles.

When we pulled up to the dock, we parked beside the *Mintaka*. Wiley grabbed the clipboard, and we headed up the gangway. Chief Harper was waiting on deck. Wiley handed him the clipboard.

"Have any trouble finding the place?"

"Not really," I said. "We just followed the map."

Harper looked at the papers the doctor signed. "What'd the doc say? Everything okay by him?"

"Lieutenant Andrews said they were running short of supplies. He kinda frowned when he read over the list, said it wasn't everything they needed, but then he brightened up a bit, said 'every bit helps' and told us to be careful driving so we didn't end up in his hospital."

Chief Harper smiled, showing us his gold tooth. "Probably tells everybody that. Good advice, though. Lotta men don't keep their mind on their work—get in accidents of one kind or another. It's why I gotta keep an eye on my guys all the time.

"Anyway, thanks for filling in. Go get cleaned up. Be chow time pretty soon."

By the time we hit the showers and put on clean clothes, supper was being served on the mess deck. I followed Wiley in the chow line, pushing the metal tray along the edge of the counter. I looked into the galley, but didn't see Cubby or Jenkins anywhere. I thought they'd have made it back by now.

Wiley held out his tray, and the server slid a slice of meatloaf off his spatula onto the center. Wiley pushed his tray along, and the next guy plopped some mashed potatoes into one of the depressions. He put gravy over the top, pushing the ladle into the potatoes to make a little well. Another server scooped up some canned peas with a slotted spoon and filled in another spot.

"Meatloaf. Hope it ain't lamb."

"Relax—Cubby told me the lamb's all gone. Mystery meat, maybe, but not lamb. "

We each grabbed a biscuit and a little dish of tapioca pudding and headed over to find a place to sit in the crowded room. We squeezed in across from each other at the end of one of the tables.

We hadn't eaten anything all afternoon. Wiley split his biscuit, dipped one half in the gravy, and started eating right away. He was making up for lost time. I was hungry, too, but my mind wasn't on food.

"You seen Cubby or Jenkins since we got back?"

"Wasn't really thinking about them," Wiley said, chewing. He swallowed. "Now that you mention it, I don't remember seeing them anywhere since we came aboard."

"Makes me wonder. They should be back by now."

"Don't worry about them, Justin. They'll be all right.

That Jenkins scared the shit out of me, callin' me Whitey, then givin' me a hand up into the truck."

"He was just playing with you. Gave you an idea of what it feels like when folks call him names. That hand up was a peace offering."

"Maybe so—still scared me, though."

"People are afraid of things they don't know. Jenkins is used to white folks treating him a certain way. He sees guys like us, thinks he knows who we are 'cause we're white. Probably take some time for him to come around. Both of you are making some progress, I think."

When we were done eating, we scraped our trays into the garbage bin. I headed toward the hatch that led outside, then stopped.

"Go on out," I said. "I'll meet you on deck in a minute. I want to talk to Chief Branson."

Wiley stepped through the hatch, and I turned back and walked over to the galley. Chief Branson was the one training Cubby. I wanted to see if he knew what was going on with him.

I found Branson in the back, supervising the clean-up detail. He saw me coming, gave me a *You don't belong here* look, and walked toward me.

"Sorry to interrupt," I said. "I know you're busy, but I was wondering if you'd seen Cubby or Jenkins?"

"Sure as hell haven't. You know where they are?"

"No. I saw them this afternoon when Chief Harper sent us on an errand, but I haven't seen them since we got back. I'm a little worried."

"I ain't worried so much as I'm pissed off. They didn't show for dinner, left me short-handed. Would've been hell to pay if we'd had the troops aboard."

Then the chief's attitude softened a little. "Look," he said.

"I like Cubby. He's a good worker, learns fast. I don't have to tell him twice like some of the others. He cares about what he's doing. He'll make a good cook.

"But Jenkins is a different story. He's trouble standing on two legs. Gotta chip on his shoulder so big it's pulling him down. If they aren't back by morning, I'm going to have to report them to the captain."

"Okay, I understand. Sorry to interrupt your work. They'll probably show up soon."

I found Wiley on deck watching Sticks Bentley and Andy Feltzer playing cribbage. They had been trying to teach Wiley and me how to play. I remembered Tommy Rainwater and Red Morgan from the beach patrol spending a lot of evenings with the crib board between them. It looked like fun, and we were slowly getting to know the game.

We watched them play for a while, then decided to call it a night. We were taking on a load of cargo tomorrow before shipping out again, and I expected we would get called on to help. We were supposed to get some time off before we left. Since our trip to the hospital had been a work detail, I hoped we would get another chance to go ashore.

Wiley seemed to fall asleep when his head hit the pillow, but I kept wondering what had happened to Cubby and Jenkins. I must have dozed off, but woke up with a start in the middle of the night. I got up, threw on some pants, and went to check on Cubby.

I passed a sailor on fire watch—Rawlins, according to his name tag. I'd seen him before, but I didn't know him. He worked in the engine room, a boiler tech or something like that.

"Little late to be up. Everybody asleep, 'cept the ones keeping us afloat."

"Couldn't sleep," I said.

"Wanna trade places? I wouldn't mind hitting the rack

for a few hours. This keepin' watch is for the birds."

"I was looking for my friend Cubby. He's a cook. You know him?"

"He that nigger cook, the one on Branson's crew?"

I cringed when he said that, but held my tongue. "Yeah, have you seen him?"

"Not since supper last night. Why ?"

"Doesn't matter. Thanks, anyway."

I went out onto the main deck. It was cooler outside. A little breeze stirred the air. The sky was mostly clear, with a few clouds drifting across the moon and a handful of stars. It was quiet enough to hear the water lapping at the pier, even with the generators humming below deck. A truck rumbled along a road in the distance, shifting gears as it climbed a hill.

I walked over to the rail and looked down at the dock below. It would be a different story in the morning when the sun was up and the trucks arrived with brakes squealing, smoke pouring from their exhausts. It was a routine that had become familiar: men shouting orders as they dropped off tons of supplies, the cranes swinging out over the dock, raising one load after another and lowering it into the holds. It would be a crazy morning.

I'd been wandering the main deck for about half an hour when I heard something that caught my attention. Not the night noises surrounding me, but voices in the distance, a ways off, but getting closer. When I looked over the rail, I saw three men heading toward the *Mintaka*. I watched them walking along close together, weaving a little from side to side. When they came closer, I saw it was Jenkins in the middle with Toots and Cubby kind of propping him up and moving him slowly along. I couldn't hear what they were saying, but Jenkins was grumbling and complaining and Cubby and Toots seemed to be trying to keep him quiet as they shuffled along together.

When they got close, I heard Jenkins tell his friends, "I'm awright, just leave me be!" Toots let go of Jenkins then, said something to Cubby, and rested his hand on Jenkins' shoulder for a moment before he turned and started back down the street.

Cubby kept his arm around Jenkins and steered him toward the gangway. Jenkins pulled away from Cubby and started slowly up the stairs by himself. Cubby trailed along behind him, looking like he expected to have to catch him any second.

I thought they'd probably all been out drinking somewhere and Jenkins had overdone it, but when they neared the top of the stairs, I could see things weren't exactly what I expected. I could smell liquor, but 'Leb's right eye was swollen nearly shut and his lower lip was split and crusted with blood.

I was rushing over to see if I could help when Cubby looked over, saw me coming, and held up his hand, waving me off. Jenkins didn't look my way as Cubby hustled him through the hatch and headed for the galley. Cubby had as much as told me he had things in hand. Probably gone to the galley to get some ice, I thought. I left them to sort things out and went back to bed.

We were up early in the morning, with most all the crew assigned to getting our supplies squared away and the cargo loaded. The ones in charge told us if we worked hard, they'd do their best to cut us some slack, give us some time off. I'd heard that lie before, especially on some grunt detail like galley duty. A shift would change, a new crew would come in, and we'd hear the same story again. That only had to happen once to make me skeptical, but I hoped they meant it this time. Some of the crew hadn't had a chance to go ashore.

That included Wiley and me, too, unless Harper's hospital run got counted as a pleasure trip. We'd just have to wait and see.

The parade of trucks along the dock seemed endless. The ship's stores were replenished with fresh meats, fruits and vegetables, eggs, flour, sugar, salt, coffee, and supplies that were dried, condensed, powdered, and tinned for when we ran out of fresh food. Field rations for the troops were hauled aboard, too, mostly tinned and dried items, including crates of K-rations.

The holds were carefully packed with all kinds of equipment, lots of machinery and machine parts, some clothing, boots, helmets, weapons. A small convoy of reconditioned jeeps from one of the island shops appeared on the dock and were lifted aboard along with a few trailer-mounted guns. Heavy metal ammo cases and medical supplies were brought aboard, too.

"Bullets and bandages—how about that?" one of the men said. "Go together like soup and crackers, don't they?

19

When the loading was complete, Chief Harper kept his word. The *Mintaka* would depart at 0800 tomorrow. We had the rest of the day off. Those who hadn't had shore leave up to now, including Wiley and me, were free to explore the island.

Wiley headed for the showers, but on the way I spotted Cubby leaning on the rail outside the mess deck, smoking and looking out to sea. I wandered over to talk, not really knowing what to say. I was worried about what I had seen last night, but I knew it was really none of my business.

"Hey, Cubby." I stood beside him, leaning my forearms on the railing. "Everything okay?"

Cubby kept looking out to sea. After a minute or so, he turned, squinted at me through the cigarette smoke. "Suppose you want to know 'bout last night."

"Only if you don't mind talking about it. It's not really my business. I tried to find you guys last night, but you didn't come back. I got worried something had happened. That's why I was sitting out there when you finally showed up."

Cubby chuckled, "Makes you the first white boy ever worried was I okay." He looked at me and smiled. "First time for everything, I guess."

"What'd Chief Branson say?"

"Branson's pissed. Cussed us up one side and down the other. Threatened to report us. Restricted us to the ship.

"Kinda feel bad about lettin' him down. He been good to me, say I do good work, even complain to me sometimes about other guys have to be tol' two or three times how to do somethin'. He mostly mad at 'Leb, though. Ain't really fair—we both late gettin' back. But 'Leb don't warm up to others much, always expectin' the short end of the stick. I think the chief decided he never gonna change. Might even be afraid of 'Leb. I don't know."

"I saw him with Wiley today. Kidding around, called him 'Whitey'—thought he had warmed up a little."

Cubby smiled, "Yeah—think he scared Wiley, though. But you right—maybe 'Leb has to take it one man at a time."

Eventually, Cubby filled me in on what happened. The three of them had gone with two guys from the cemetery crew across the channel to a place called Aore Island. The Fleet Recreation Center was there, a big place with all kinds of things for the sailors and soldiers. "Got ball fields over there, guys playin' football, baseball—even got some basketball courts. We been tossin' the ball around on the court for a while when some Aussie guys came over from another court, asked did we want to play against them.

"'Leb didn't think much of that idea, but the rest of us didn't mind, so we said we'd play. Didn't much happen for a while—just the usual back and forth. Aussies were pretty good, played in school, I guess. Hard pressed to stay even with those boys, but we were holding our own. One of their guys, a big red-headed fella with a nose looked like it had been busted a few times cussed at 'Leb when he hit 'em a little too hard tryin' to block his shot and take the ball away. 'Leb didn't mean nothin', but there were red streaks and a handprint that showed clear as day on that boy's white skin when he walked away.

"When 'Leb heard him say something about 'that damn bloody nigger', he took out after the guy, and the rest of us had to pull them apart. The two of them had words and wouldn't settle down. Aussies dragged their guy off, and we tried to get 'Leb to settle down. They walked off a ways, looked like they were leaving, but one of the other fellas came back by himself and talked to us. He said, 'We didn't mean to stir up trouble. It was just a game, everyone enjoying himself. But our Ralph's a hothead—always has been. How about letting the two of them settle what's between them in the ring? Me and my mates will put up fifty dollars against it if you're willing to back your man.'

"So that was it. We headed over to the boxing ring they got there. 'Leb and the other guy put on the gloves and climbed into the ring. That fella Ralph was a big guy, tall, with a lot of muscle, but he don't know much about boxing. Be the kind they call a brawler. He just put up his mitts and wade in—count on his size and strength to take a few punches before he get lucky and knock somebody out.

"'Leb got a few moves, but he forget everything when he lose his temper. I been tryin' to make him see what my daddy taught me. You get mad, you can't think straight. Gotta keep your mind in the fight. Let the other fella make you mad, you bound to lose.

"Big Ralph, he just smart enough to figure that out. Called 'Leb a lot of names, made 'im mad enough to let his guard down, throw some wild punches. Ralph charged in, got 'Leb hard in the face, closed that eye right up, had blood runnin' down his cheek. That punch seemed to bring 'Leb to his senses. I was hollerin' at him, tellin' him what to do, but I don't think he heard me, with everybody shoutin' like they were. Anyway, after that 'Leb stepped back and went to work. I could see him take that Aussie's measure. He waited for an opening, then stepped in and delivered a punch that staggered that big lug. Couldn't even bring his gloves up to defend himself. After that, 'Leb moved in and never let up till the big guy was down.

"We collected our winnings and took the boat back to Santo to have a few drinks and celebrate. Wasn't much of a celebration, but that's what we called it. You and Wiley should go over to the island. You probably have a better time than we did."

When I told Wiley what happened, he didn't seem too surprised. "Kind of wish I'd been there to see it. Can't imagine what that Aussie was thinking—picking a fight with a scary-looking guy like Jenkins. Thought those guys were smarter than that."

"There are guys like that everywhere, I guess. They think being big makes them tough. 'Leb rattled his brain pretty good, but I don't think he'll change his ways. Some folks never change."

Wiley and I caught the shuttle to Aore Island in the afternoon. The boat was packed with sailors and GIs. Some were from the *Mintaka*, but a lot of folks we didn't know had scrambled aboard at the last minute. When the boat pulled up to the dock, we stepped off, following the others toward a big white sign at the end of the dock. It was mounted on tall posts and stretched all the way across the dock so you had to walk under the sign to go ashore. It said "Welcome to Fleet Recreation Center" in black letters across the top and underneath in smaller letters was a list of all the sports they had there: baseball, horseshoes, boxing, football, volleyball, soccer. We walked along together, stopping here and there to watch men playing football and shooting baskets on courts with wooden backboards painted white. A little crowd had gathered to watch some GIs pitching horseshoes. One of the GIs held a fistful of dollar bills, showing they had money in the game. Loud cheers went up when the metal shoes clanked loudly against the post, and some groaned when they fell short.

We watched a baseball game for a while. It looked like something I'd like to try. We'd never had enough kids in

Glory to make sports important. Our recreation came from hunting and fishing, and hiking around in the woods. Workouts came from farm life, taking care of cattle and horses, making hay and splitting fence posts and firewood. We were strong, but nobody would say we were athletic. Boot camp had toughened us some, and we'd put in a lot of miles on the beach with Jig and Doc. Still, we weren't ballplayers.

Wiley and I took in the sights as we walked along. We came to a sandy beach and walked along the shore. Some guys were wading in the gentle surf, little waves lapping at their feet as they stood looking out to sea where heads bobbed as others paddled around further out. When we came to the end of the little beach, there was a building with a wide deck on three sides. The roof extended over the deck and the sides facing the sea were open. A bar was set up on the back wall, and tables and chairs set out so you could sit and take in the view while you had something to eat or drink.

We headed to the bar and ordered a couple of beers. Bill, the bartender, introduced himself, and set our drinks in front of us. "First time on the island?" he asked.

"Yeah," I said. "Didn't know all this was here till a friend told us about it. Shipping out tomorrow—wish we had a little more time to spend here."

"Aore's a nice place. Government did a nice job. Lot of guys passin' through Santo stop in here. Get some famous people sometimes, too."

Wiley looked skeptical. "Really? Probably big shot officers—generals and such?"

"Well, you'd be surprised. Back in November, Mrs. Roosevelt dropped by. She visited the hospitals in Santo, pinned some purple hearts on the wounded fellas there, took a boat out here and looked the place over."

"She a big hit with the troops?" I couldn't imagine the guys lining the streets of Santo to watch Eleanor Roosevelt drive by. Rita Hayworth, maybe, but not Mrs. Roosevelt. She wasn't exactly a movie star.

"Not so much," Bill said. "But she had a lot of reporters with her, took a lot of pictures. It'll make the newsreels. Folks at home will see her visiting with the boys in the hospital, watching the troops at play. Raise their spirits, you know. Lot better than the ones that show the bodies drifting in and out with the tide.

"Rumor has it that Bob Hope might do a show out here. They don't tell us a lot of details, but the word is maybe sometime in July. That would be something to see."

"I'd wanta see that, for sure," Wiley said. "He always brings all those movie stars. Imagine seein' folks like that up close."

"We're leaving tomorrow," I said. "Looks like we'll miss our chance."

"Probably get a better look at them when they're on the screen, anyway," the bartender said, wiping the bar with a rag. "Good luck, fellas."

Wiley and I bought two more beers, thanked Bill, and took them out to a table on the deck. We sat looking out at the sea. It was a warm afternoon with a little breeze stirring the palm trees. The roof provided some shade and the cold beer hit the spot.

"This is nice, just sittin' here," Wiley said. "Guess we ain't done much to earn it. Other guys done a lot more before they come here."

"Our time will come. I'm not in a hurry to catch up with trouble. "

"Maybe so. Hope we're up to it. Some of these guys we seen look pretty beat up. Don't understand some of the things they do, gettin' drunk and fightin' with each other."

"They're just blowing off steam most of the time, looking to have a good time, forget what they been through. I just hope to keep my head above water no matter what. Those guys that get drunk all the time make me think of those toughs that hung out at the Snug back in Glory. They never did any good for anybody. I saw enough of that to put me off hard liquor.

"The applejack Waters made won him some friends, but didn't make drunks out of anybody."

"True enough," Wiley said. "Guess we'll just have to see how we act when the time comes."

We sat for a while, not saying anything. Seabirds wheeled in the warm air. Their cries blended with the shushing sound of the surf rolling in and out. Once in a while, a plane would pass above us, heading for one of the airfields on Santo.

"How far you think it is from here to Glory?" Wiley asked.

"Too far to swim, that's for sure."

"Used to like swimming in the creek. Water was colder, though. Couldn't stay in very long, remember?"

I remembered. We used to dare one another to jump in first. Sometimes Wiley pushed me in when I wasn't looking. Most of the time we just counted to three, held our noses, and took the plunge. Annie and Agnes changed all that.

"I remember when you tried to push Agnes in. She came up sputtering and beat you with that stick."

"Yeah, I learned my lesson that time. Can't play with girls that way. Agnes can be tough as nails sometimes, but she's soft, too. Expects to be treated right. Wish she was here."

"I miss Annie, too."

We always had fun when we went swimming with the girls. They brought a picnic lunch, and we hiked to a spot we found where there was a good-sized pool with a sandy shore. The girls would strip down to the swimsuits they had on under their clothes and wade a little, complaining about how cold the water was.

Wiley and I peeled off the clothes we wore over our swim trunks. We climbed up on the big rock beside the pool and jumped in, splashing water as far as we could. The girls ducked and turned their backs toward us, hoping to stay dry. We paddled around for a while till our teeth started chattering and we had to get out.

Annie and Agnes waded in together, groaning when the cold reached the tender spots, and finally ducking in up to their necks, trying not to get their hair wet. They paddled a little and got out when they couldn't stand it anymore. Wiley and I enjoyed the view when they stepped out, their wet suits clinging tightly. It took my breath away the first time I saw Annie like that. We tossed their towels to them and pretended we hadn't seen anything. When everybody'd warmed up, the girls spread out a blanket, and we had our picnic lunch, just sitting together in the sun and talking.

Later, when Agnes and Wiley finally discovered each other and Annie's kisses had won me over, things changed. After lunch, Wiley and Agnes usually made some excuse, said they were going for a walk, and left me and Annie alone. We laid out on the blanket and looked up at the trees shifting in the breeze. Annie put her arm across my chest, resting her hand over my heart. She drew her fingers along my cheek, leaned in, and kissed me. I put my arm around her and we kissed some more, her body pressed against mine. Her suit was still damp, and the softness of her breasts against my bare chest gave me goosebumps. We laid like that for a long time, pressed against each other, our hands exploring gently.

After a while, Agnes would call out, "You guys okay?" or something just as meaningless, letting us know they were coming back. We had a pretty good idea what they'd been doing while they were "gone for a walk," but we never admitted anything. I'm sure the girls knew. They had probably planned it that way.

Wiley and I had been sitting awhile contemplating the long swim from here to Glory. I heard boots scraping across the floor as someone came up behind us. I turned and looked up to see a big red-haired man standing behind Wiley. He had a worn look about him, like other GIs we'd seen before, the ones whose faces showed they'd been to hell and back. He clapped a rough hand on Wiley's shoulder.

"How's my sister?" he said.

20

Jesse'd always had that sly *I'm-gonna-get-you* look when Wiley and I saw him at school in Glory. He and Curt were the oldest kids, nineteen or twenty probably—too old to sit cramped behind the little tables in Mr. Phillips' classroom. Agnes had warned Wiley about her brother, how he didn't like it when he was made to look bad in front of the younger ones. He and Curt had come too late to the classroom. They were old enough to shave, broad shoulders filled out by years of farm work with their folks. I used to think they were just big and dumb, trying to make up for their lack of smarts by swaggering around the schoolyard, giving us all the stinkeye. But I wasn't so sure anymore. Maybe you didn't have to win the spelling bee or know how to do long division to be smart.

The man standing above us, his hand resting on Wiley's shoulder, had lost that playground sneer. He'd given up his place as the biggest rooster in the yard. Life had put lines in his face that weren't there when we knew him in Glory. Crow's feet pinched the corners of Jesse's eyes. His cheeks were hollowed. He seemed to be made of lean and leather, someone who had lived up to his own notion of who he was and didn't need to prove anything to anyone else.

"Jesus!" Wiley nearly jumped out of his skin when he looked up and saw Jesse standing over him. "You scared the shit out of me, Jesse. What the hell are you doing here?"

"Came in to get a beer, watch the sun go down. Saw you and Justin sitting there–took me a while to realize who I was looking at. You ain't little kids no more. Everything's changed for all of us, I guess."

"Where you been all this time?" Wiley asked. "Agnes and your folks don't know what happened to you, they've been worried sick."

Jesse walked around to the other side of the table, pulled out a chair, and settled into it.

"Curt and me got shipped over to Europe together, but we didn't stay together long. After a few months, we got reassigned—sent to different infantry units. I ended up in North Africa, Libya to be exact. I got hit by a mine on patrol. It blew the guy in front of me all to hell. Hit me in the leg, tore it up pretty good. Sent me to a hospital run by a New Zealand unit. I was laid up for a while, but I'm okay. "

"What're you doing out here in the Pacific?" I asked.

"Not much, seems like. Got me doin' admin duties. When my leg healed up, I was itchin' to go back and fight, kinda got used to it, you know—the smoke, the noise, shit rainin' down, bouncin' off that steel pot on my head. Kind of liked being in the thick of it all. I think there's a big push comin' over there. I wanted to be part of it.

"They wanted to send me home when I got hurt, but I still got all my parts and they work just fine. Doctors think I'm not fit for combat—won't send me back 'cause they think my head ain't on straight exactly. Guess you're not supposed to ask for more when they think you've had enough. Anyway, the war's not over yet, and I didn't want to go home till the job was done, so I got myself reassigned—do something more before I settle down and go home."

I couldn't help myself. I had to ask, "Did you hear about Curt?"

He looked at me sharply, like I had slapped him, then dropped his gaze to stare at the beer in his hand. A pained look came over his face. "Yeah—buddy of ours found me in the hospital. Told me what happened. Not much to it, really. Curt just stuck his head out of the hole to see what was going on, got his hair parted with a Mauser. End of the story—end of Curt."

"The girls sent us letters, told us he'd been killed. They didn't know the details. I wasn't sure whether you knew," I said. "Didn't mean to cause any more pain."

"It's okay. I've had plenty of time to put Curt to rest."

Wiley looked at Jesse. "Felt bad ourselves when we heard the news. Kind of brought the war home to Glory. I know you were good friends."

"Yeah, we were. Used to give you kids a tough time, didn't we? Seems so long ago—another time. It ain't comin' back, either—just like Curt. Sorry we gave you guys a hard time."

It's okay," I said. "Like you said—another time."

Wiley told Jesse about our time on the beach patrol, but left out the part where he almost drowned. We told him about the shuttle runs with troops and cargo aboard the *Mintaka*, how we were shoving off in the morning.

We all sat there for a while, watching the sun go down behind the mountains of Espiritu Santo, painting bloody streaks across the sky. It was peaceful where we were, more so than we deserved, I thought. A quiet evening of memories shared by the three of us. The war had brought many changes already—many more were to come, I was sure.

After a while, Jesse asked, "So how's Agnes?"

Wiley brought Jesse up to date, telling him about Agnes joining the Marines, working as an airplane mechanic, wishing she could fly the planes herself.

"Can't slow Agnes down when she got her mind set on something. I always knew that about her. Might be a good thing—used to drive me nuts trying to look after her like my folks expected." The ghost of a smile appeared as he gave Wiley a knowing look. "She still got that lasso 'round your heart?"

Wiley blushed, looked away for a second. "I sure hope so.

I'm hanging onto the end as tight as I can."

"Don't see any need to worry. Folks wanted me to look after her when she was little, protect her from boys like you." Jesse gave us another glimpse of that near smile. "Did a hell of a job, didn't I? Like I said, Agnes makes up her own mind. Had her cap set for you before you even saw her coming."

Jesse pushed back his chair and stood up to leave. "You can write to Agnes, tell her I'm okay—just tryin' to work things out in my head. Got a plan I'm workin' on. I got a notion things will work out. "

Wiley stood up. "Don't you want to tell her yourself?"

"Might do that—just need some time. You guys try to keep your heads above water. I'll see you again when we get back to Glory."

Wiley reached out, and the two of them shook hands. "Maybe we'll be family then. Take care of yourself, Jesse."

"Don't worry about me. I'm good at sharpening pencils and takin' out the trash. I'll be okay."

We sat there for a while, letting it all sink in. Finally, Wiley said, "Jesse sure don't seem like the same guy we knew back home. Still scared me when I felt that big paw on my shoulder and I looked up and saw who it was."

"I think Jesse might be smarter than we used to think he was."

"Yeah. He's just as big as he always was, but you're right. He's not the same guy we used to know. War's changed him for sure. Hard to imagine what he's seen, how that stays with you afterward."

"Think we're gonna change like that?"

"Hard to say. Depends on what happens along the way."

Wiley put on a worried look, a line forming between his eyebrows. "I don't know what's gonna happen, but I wanta go back to bein' myself when it's over."

"I think we might all be changed in some way when it's over. Take some time to get back to being ourselves. I'll let you know if I see you heading sideways."

21

We made our way back and caught the shuttle across the channel to Santo. After a quick trip through the chow line, we headed to our quarters to write letters home, letting the folks know we had found Jesse and that he was all right, at least for now.

"What do think Jesse meant when he said he had a plan?" Wiley asked.

"Hard to say. Maybe he's just hoping to get his head on straight, like he said. Give himself some time to sort things out before he goes home."

"I don't know. He seemed okay to me. Lot calmer than he used to be, but he didn't seem crazy or anything like that. Says he 'got a notion things will work out.' That could mean anything."

"Maybe he just didn't want to tell us what he's got going on. Just finish your letter so we can get 'em sent before we shove off."

At 0800 the *Mintaka* got underway, with troops and cargo aboard. Lines were cast off, the gangway swung alongside, and we were on our way. We steamed northwest from Santo, headed to Guadalcanal, some five hundred miles away.

The trip was uneventful, the usual drills and maintenance tasks occupying us during the days, taking turns on fire watch and galley duty. Off duty, the men played cards, wrote letters home, and did what they could to entertain themselves.

Rex and Frank Oparowski recreated the quartet from the crossing ceremony with Sam Benson and Bobby Carco. One night they treated everyone to a medley of Opar's novelty songs. In addition to songs we'd heard every time Frank was in the shower, Opar had added new ones. We were treated to their rendition of "The Hut Sut Song" and "The Monkeys Have No Tails in Zamboanga." Frank had been saving that last one, he said, "till we were in the neighborhood."

We were a long ways yet from the Philippines, but I guess he thought we were close enough.

The first verse went like this:

Oh, the monkeys have no tails in Zamboanga,
Oh, the monkeys have no tails in Zamboanga,
Oh, the monkeys have no tails,
They were bitten off by whales,
Oh, the monkeys have no tails in Zamboanga.

There were lots of verses, most of them funny, with not so flattering remarks about the plants and animals and people. Of course, some of them were a little dirty, too. I remember one that said:

Oh, the ladies wear no teddies in Manila,
Oh, the ladies wear no teddies in Manila,
Oh, the ladies wear no teddies,
They're a bunch of ever-readies,
Oh, the ladies wear no teddies in Manila.

The GIs that gathered round Opar and the boys cheered and whistled when it was over. They seemed to enjoy the show as much as Frank and his crew liked putting it on.

We arrived at Guadalcanal on April 9. They had a big map on the wall in the mess deck, and we'd all got a chance to study it. Guadalcanal was a big island with high mountain peaks sticking up out of the jungle. The south side was steep and we steamed around Cape Esperance on the northwest tip of the island, headed east toward the grassy plain on the north coast of Guadalcanal.

As usual, we had caught the late bus again and missed the big battle that finally ended here last year. Wiley always seemed to be disappointed, afraid that we were missing out, somehow, but there was plenty of devastation to be seen. The GIs crowded together on deck to get a look. There were three Japanese transports beached near Cape Esperance, and we spotted another as we passed a little bump on the coast called Tassafaronga Point. Aircraft from Henderson Field had attacked the ships and blown up their supplies and ammunition, but a lot of Japanese troops had made it ashore. It was pretty much scorched earth on this side of the island, but palm trees still waved in the distance, and the mountain peaks kept watch above.

The battle for Guadalcanal had been a costly one. We had lost thousands of lives here. It was hard to imagine what those guys had gone through. I thought Wiley and I would do what we had to if the time came, but I wasn't in a hurry to be cast up on some foreign shore like driftwood caught in the tide.

The next few months were spent on shuttle runs from the Admiralties to Fiji, carrying supplies and transporting thousands of troops to and from staging areas. We were kept busy all the time, with little relief, but letters from home caught up with us from time to time. It was May, apple blossom time in Glory, and I thought of the song that says, "I'll be with you in apple blossom time." But the Andrews Sisters weren't singing for Annie and me, and the news from home wasn't all sunshine and flowers.

22

It took a while for the mail to find us as the *Mintaka* shuttled troops back and forth between the islands. The first letters to reach Wiley and me were filled with good news, hopeful thoughts that kept our spirits afloat. Folks at home were doing their part, planting victory gardens, complaining about rationing, but making do in spite of it, knowing that they were doing what they could to help the war effort.

Everyone was relieved and happy when our letters arrived with the news that Jesse was safe. But Agnes was mad that Wiley didn't get an address so they could write to him and find out more about what was going on with him.

"Damn, Justin," Wiley complained. "She really baked my beans over the whole thing, said sometimes she thinks I don't have the brains God gave a goose."

"Sounds mad, all right," I said. I could only imagine that red-haired fury unleashed. It was comforting to know she was six thousand miles away.

"Thing is, he still scares the shit out of me. When I looked up and saw him with his hand on my shoulder, I felt like I'd seen a ghost."

"Maybe you did, kinda. He's not the Jesse we used to know."

"Maybe not, but when you're heart's leapin' outta your chest, you're not gonna go huntin' for a pencil to take down somebody's address."

"It'll be okay. Underneath it all, she has to be happy to know he's safe."

"I suppose so. Don't make her happy with me, though."

Other letters followed, sometimes two or three at a time,

with hints that even though the community rallied for the war effort, not everything turned out as expected. Mr. Babcock at the Rexall had been visited by people from the Red Cross. They were stopping in small towns like Glory, organizing a blood drive. They asked him if he thought folks in Glory would be interested in taking part. He was soon sold on the idea, and took the posters they had left with him to all the stores to put in their windows. One of them was a color poster that showed an army medic on the battlefield holding up a plasma bottle over a wounded soldier. The writing under the picture called on folks to donate blood. The other poster was simpler. It had a big Red Cross symbol on the top and announced that Red Cross volunteers would come by to collect blood from volunteers on a certain date. The date line was blank, but Mr. Babcock's visitors had filled it in, giving Glory time to get the word out.

Annie's parents had put the posters up in their windows, too, but they had some ideas of their own. Folks that could afford it had been buying War Bonds. Eighteen dollars and seventy-five cents bought a twenty-five dollar bond. At least it would be worth twenty-five if you waited ten years to cash it in. Folks did what they could. Annie's parents thought that the blood drive was great, but decided there might be a way to raise money to donate to the Red Cross, too.

Mr. Sadler put a cardboard standup on the counter in the market. It had seventy-five slots that held a quarter in each. When it was full, it would have the eighteen seventy-five needed to buy a twenty-five dollar War Bond. He asked folks to donate their quarters and gave them a ticket for each quarter they donated. The tickets were for a raffle held during the blood drive, and the winner would get the bond. The Sadlers would donate twenty-five dollars of their own to the Red Cross.

Other folks were inspired by their example, and pretty

soon it was a community affair. The blood drive was going to be held at the school, with a bake sale and home-made goods to be sold and the money donated to the cause.

It took the two of us a while to piece together the whole story. Letters from Wiley's folks told us part of the story, and I got letters from Momma and Waters. All of them hinted that the blood drive had taken some unexpected turns, but the details were sketchy. Eventually, it was Annie who told us the whole story.

Momma had used most of the sugar ration allowed for canning to put up jars of applesauce, apple butter, and cinnamon apples for pies. Annie's mom had cut out circles of red-checked cloth with pinking shears, and they tied them over the tops of the jars with ribbons to make them look pretty. Annie and her mom baked cookies, dipping into their own allotment. Wiley's mom turned out pies with the cherries she'd put up from the tree in their yard and donated loaves of nut bread and pumpkin bread as well.

Other folks crocheted doilies and potholders, embroidered pillow cases, all donated to the cause. A group of ladies in a quilting circle hurriedly finished a victory quilt they'd been working on together and sold tickets to raffle it off to some lucky person.

On the day of the blood drive, the Red Cross people drove up in a white panel truck with "American Red Cross Blood Donor Service" on the sides under the familiar symbol and began setting up their equipment on the stage at the end of the room while the people who came to give blood looked at the items being sold to raise money.

The raffles were set up on two tables in front of the stage. The Sadlers were waiting to pick the winner of the twenty-five dollar bond, and the quilters were selling tickets for the quilt, which they had draped over Mr. Phillips rolling blackboard so everyone could get a good look at it. Other tables had been set in rows out in the center of the room. Momma had laid her jars out on her table. The other ladies set out their offerings on their own tables. They sat on folding chairs and chatted up the folks who strolled along looking at the items for sale.

According to Annie, it wasn't all sweetness and light. Waters was outside with Sully and Uncle Hal, waiting for the Red Cross folks to set up. Momma sat at her table with Rebecca beside her, happily drawing in a coloring book. Folks milled about, stopping here and there to talk with neighbors and admire the homemade goods, but they gave Momma dirty looks when they saw her with Rebecca.

"I swear," Annie wrote, "those snooty people acted like she was the poison apple witch.

They looked at your Momma and Rebecca and tsk-ed and humphed, and walked right past, muttering shameful things as they went. I felt so bad for her—it went on for such a long time."

There was apparently a little stirring among the crowd when Mrs. Spencer, Curt's mother, came in. Ladies went to her, hugged her tight, asked her how she was doing. She walked along the row of tables, looking at the donated items for sale, the seated women offering their condolences.

"When she got to your momma's table," Annie wrote, "she looked at Molly and then at Rebecca, who was concentrating on staying inside the lines in her coloring book. Your momma had done her curly hair up in side switches tied with pink ribbons. 'Such a precious child,' she said." Annie said Curt's mother kept looking at Rebecca, and her lips trembled as she spoke.

"Your Momma stood up, took Mrs. Spencer's hand, and told her, 'All the children are precious—the ones we hold in our arms and the ones we hold in our hearts.' The two of them just stood there, and I could see tears running down as they spoke. It made me want to cry, too. Those two mothers, one wanting her son to come home and the other knowing hers never will."

After they talked for a while, Curt's mother left a donation and stepped away with a jar of apple butter. Other folks who had seen Mrs. Spencer with Momma apparently softened up and bought some things as well, but others still stared and walked past.

When the Red Cross workers were finally set up, people started lining up outside in the vestibule, and stood at the bottom of the steps going up to the stage. One of the volunteers sat at a card table with papers for the blood donors to sign. When they were finished registering, the donors moved up onto the stage, where cots were laid out and the blood was drawn.

Annie wrote that her brother Bobby, who now insisted on being called Bob, was out of sorts because he wasn't old enough to enlist. He was worried that the war would end before he got a chance to serve. He'd caused a fuss when he tried to give blood and found out he wasn't old enough for that, either.

I remembered the pesty ten year-old Bobby that followed us around when I first visited Annie and her folks. He was the little kid that spied on us from the upstairs landing, hoping to catch us kissing at the bottom of the stairs before I left and headed home to the ranch. He was growing up, I knew. Waters told me once when I did something foolish that it was natural for me to want to put my toe in to test the water. He warned me that sometimes the water was deep and that trouble was never far away. I hoped the war ended before Bobby could find out just how deep the water was.

Momma and Waters eventually got around to telling me about the blood drive in their letters, and Annie filled in the gaps on the rest of the story.

Waters and Uncle Hal were near the end of the line, talking with Sully and Pearl while they waited for their turn to donate, but it took twenty minutes or more for a person to answer the questions the Red Cross volunteers put to them and to get their blood drawn. A couple of folks fainted, and the people in line had to wait while they were revived and led off to be propped up with juice and cookies. Some were rejected for various reasons and put up a fuss like Bobby had when he was turned away. Sheriff Max was there to keep things moving along, but things went along pretty slowly.

When Waters stepped up to register, the woman at the table told him the Red Cross didn't accept blood donations from Negroes. Waters knew that wasn't exactly the whole truth. He read his newspapers, kept up with the news in the world. Momma remembered the article he'd cut out that said "American Red Cross Bans Negro Blood!" He'd pasted it on the wall of the cabin with other articles that came after, about the protests when Negroes were turned away at donation centers. He also knew that the policy had been changed a year later to allow Negroes to donate, but the blood was only to be used on other Negroes.

When the sheriff saw Waters being turned away, he called over the doctor that was supervising the blood drive.

"Is there a problem, sheriff?" the doctor asked.

"This man wants to donate blood," Sheriff Max said. "Your nurse says you don't take donations from Negroes."

The doctor pursed his lips and pushed his glasses up on his nose. He acted like he'd just choked on something. He hesitated for a moment longer, and then he looked at the sheriff. "It's not exactly like that. Negroes who wanted to donate were turned away at first, but after the protests, they changed the policy. Negro donations are accepted, but they have to be kept separate and used only with Negro service personnel. Some of our volunteers don't go along with the new policy."

"Seems to me everyone's blood is the same color. Maybe your volunteer lady should look at those posters you put up. Think that soldier fellow's worried about where the blood came from?"

Waters got to take his turn for the war effort after that, but there were more than a few stares from others who didn't think folks like Momma and Waters measured up to their notion of patriotism. Annie wrote, "I don't understand how people can be so mean." I didn't understand it, either.

In one of the letters, Waters said he pretty much knew how it would go at the blood drive, but he and Momma wanted to take part anyway. He told me about another article he'd read that told how the American Medical Association had come out and said that segregating blood was not only unscientific but "an insult to America's largest minority." Waters summed it up with his usual patience, "This war going to change a lot of things, Justin, but Jim Crow still trumps scientific fact, at least for now."

Rebecca was just learning to color within the lines, but everyone else already seemed to know how.

23

The *Mintaka* spent the next few months shuttling troops between Guadalcanal and the Green Islands, a spot that hardly made it onto the map. It was east of Rabaul and northwest of Bouganville. The biggest of the islands was Green Island, an atoll with a lagoon in the center that was about two miles wide and four or five miles long. There was a lot more lagoon than island as far as I could see, and it was full of ships and small boats of every kind, but there was room for two airstrips on the southeast side, one for fighters and a longer one for bombers.

Cubby still spent some time in Officer Country, serving meals to the captain and the visiting officers who came aboard, and he kept his ear to the deck for news. He had the lowdown on the gossip from up above, and he found out some interesting things about Green Island.

"Lotta Japs here, built one of them airstrips before the Marines and the Kiwi troops cleared them out. Seabees built a longer one for the bombers.

"One of the visitin' officers, Captain Staples, told a funny story. Said the Navy sent two officers out to take charge when the fuss was over, had duplicate orders. One of them, a lieutenant named Nixon, had two months seniority over the other guy, so he got to be the base commander."

"I thought you said it was a funny story," I said. "Just sounds like the usual Navy snafu to me."

"That wasn't the funny part. Nixon and the other guy got tired of sharin' their misfortune—getting' bug-bit, fightin' off infections and jungle rot. Said the las' straw was when their tent blew away in a storm. Got the Seabees to build them a regular cabin—got a hardwood floor, private water tanks, and an ocean view."

"Sounds like business as usual, Cubby. Big shots livin' high while other guys do the dirty work."

"You goin' sour on me, Justin. He might got himself the cushiest billet on the island, but folks say he all right. That Staples fellow called the place Nick's Snack Shack, say he give out burgers and snacks to the flyboys and Navy guys."

"Don't imagine *we'll* be stopping by for a beer, do you?"

"Don't hardly seem likely. He don't serve liquor anyway. He a Quaker, Staples say. Give out ice-cold pineapple juice instead. Wouldn't mind havin' a real burger, though."

"Me, too," I said. "Sounds like some folks manage to do better, no matter where they go."

"Yeah, seems like. Another guy called that Nixon fella the 'Green Island Gambler,' say he have other officers over to his place, have big-money poker games. Say he win a lot, send his money home."

I had to laugh at that. "Makes those burgers pretty expensive. Now I know we're not gonna be droppin' by."

"Welcome to the club, Justin—welcome to the club."

A motor torpedo boat squadron was based on the island, and a dozen or more of the PT boats were nosed up to the beach, with t-shaped steel pontoon docks between them that stretched out into the water. The boats had two torpedo tubes on each side and were bristling with gun mounts. A lookout tower stood near the trees at the end of the row. Below the railing at the top of the tower a big sign said, "Motor Torpedo Boat Squadron" with a hand-painted picture of a PT boat cresting a wave and "Green Islands" below the picture.

"How'd you like to be part of the gun crew on one of those?" Wiley asked. He was impressed, I could tell from the excitement in his voice.

"A dinky plywood boat in the middle of the ocean? Not

my idea of fun."

"Come on, Justin. Wooden ships and iron men. What about all that?"

"Yeah—*ships*, not wooden dinghies with torpedoes. Wouldn't take much to turn them into kindling."

"Jesus, Justin—where's your sense of adventure?"

"Got more adventure than I signed up for already. I'm not so sure about that iron men business, either. I think I'll stick with the *Mintaka*—lot harder to sink an iron ship."

Bigger ships were anchored in the lagoon, with Higgins boats and other smaller craft shuttling between them, taking on or dropping off men and supplies. Nearer the shoreline, a couple of PBY Catalinas rode their sea anchors, bobbing in the water. The twin-engine seaplanes with the waist gunner bubbles on the sides were used in combat missions and rescued air crews downed over water. They also brought cargo and mail.

The *Mintaka* had dropped anchor near the other ships, its heavy chain rattling as it was pulled from the chain locker. Wiley and I were working on maintenance, stacking shells and greasing mounts, the routine tasks that kept the ship ready for battle. We were so familiar with our jobs by now that we could have done everything in our sleep. As we worked, we kept an eye out, watching the shifting scene that surrounded us.

Chief Harper was on deck nearby, bossing his crew as they pulled cargo from the hold and lowered it over the side to one of the flat, barge-like Higgins boats that had tied up to the *Mintaka*. Suddenly, a siren in the lookout tower went off, and we all looked around to see what was going on. One of Harper's men pointed out toward the inlet to the lagoon. About half a mile out, a PT boat was making its way toward us. Black smoke was streaming from its Packard V-12 engines as it struggled along. We could tell it was in trouble. When it got closer, we saw the bow was ripped open, and the radar mast was blown away, leaning off the port side, which was stitched with bullet holes. It was a wonder the thing was still afloat.

Smaller boats raced to meet the laboring PT boat. Lines were tossed and the boat was taken in tow. The clattering engines died, and the black smoke drifted away on the wind. When they got to the dock area, the PT boat was tied up. Men on board lifted two aluminum stretchers and carefully lowered them to men waiting on the dock. The bodies on the stretchers were completely covered and tied to the frames. When the dead were lowered, the remaining crew dropped down onto the dock, joining a small crowd that had gathered.

We watched the PT boat settle in the shallow water as an ambulance and a small truck pulled up on the shore. Four men from the PT crew hoisted the stretchers and carried them along the pontoon dock, followed by the other crewmen. The stretchers were laid on the ground. Two Navy corpsmen knelt beside them, pulled aside the body coverings, and checked the dog tags of the dead sailors. The PT crewmen held open the rear doors while the bodies were loaded inside. The remaining crew climbed aboard the waiting truck. With the ambulance in the lead, both vehicles drove along the shore. We watched until they drove out of sight into the palm trees that lined the shore. The knot of onlookers that had gathered drifted away.

I felt my own dog tags hanging from my neck. I looked at the St. Christopher medal, the one Momma had sent me, attached with the tags. I hoped he was still on the job and gave the medal a little squeeze. Wiley was looking a little grim. His sense of adventure had lost some of its luster.

Chief Harper pulled off his cap and wiped his forehead with his sleeve. "Poor bastards," he said. "Trading one plywood coffin for another, looks like." He set his cap back on his head and turned back to his crew. "Show's over, fellas—back to work."

We were heading into the dry season, but we left Green Island under gray skies that promised warm afternoon showers. We refueled at sea, pulling alongside an oiler for what the Navy called an underway replenishment. Both ships traveled at a steady twelve or thirteen knots, pushing into the sea to avoid the side-to-side motion that would cause them to collide. It was a tricky maneuver that required real seamanship on the part of the helmsmen on both ships. The crew fired a shot line from the oiler to the *Mintaka* to bear the heavy hose that carried the fuel oil. The two ships traveled alongside each other until the transfer was complete and the ships parted.

We kept to a busy schedule for the next few months, shuttling between Manus Island in the Admiralties and Fiji, carrying thousands of troops to staging areas. In late May, the *Mintaka* carried 1500 troops between the Green Islands and Guadalcanal. In September, we left Guadalcanal and returned to Manus, our new operating base.

Letters from home kept our spirits afloat as we steamed from one island to the next. Agnes and Wiley had patched things up, but she was still worried about Jesse and wished he would let her or her folks know what was going on. I could just see her building her own plane and flying out to Santo to snatch him by the ear and drag him home herself.

Uncle Hal had a new batch of calves to keep him busy. He was looking forward to turning last year's pair into steaks and chops, especially the one that head-butted him in the pasture. He had chained it to a stake to keep it from wandering into Waters' orchard, and when he went to move the stake, the "damned fool thing" as he described it, drove into him and nearly knocked him out. He couldn't wait to turn that one into mincemeat.

Momma and Waters had gotten over their disappointment with the blood drive. The apple crop looked to be a good one this year. Waters was pleased to tell me the different kinds of apples we had grafted to the crabapple tree he called the All-American were all producing fruit. Apparently apples of different colors could all get along on the same tree. It was a shame people weren't as smart as apples.

Rebecca was old enough to start school this year, and Waters and Momma were worried about how that would turn out. Annie thought she might have some ideas but didn't say what they were. I only hoped they could all work together to find a way. The home front battles weren't being fought with bombs or bullets, but some of the weapons folks used were just as ugly. I wished I could be there to fight that battle with them.

24

Manus Island was just north of the eastern end of New Guinea. It was the biggest of the Admiralties, about sixty miles long, with a tall mountain in the middle, rising up out of heavy jungle. Two and a half months of fighting between the end of February and the middle of May had rid the island of more than three thousand enemy troops. The First Cavalry Division attacked nearby Los Negros, a smaller island separated from Manus by a narrow channel. They secured a place called Momote and the airstrip the Japs had built there. Allied forces then got control of Manus and Seeadler Harbor, a fifteen-mile-long stretch between Los Negros and Manus.

The Seabees improved the airstrip at Momote, which was only long enough for Kittyhawks and Spitfires. They repaved it and doubled its length, making it suitable for the B-24s we heard roaring overhead from time to time.

By the time the *Mintaka* arrived at Manus, the base was well-established. There were two Liberty ship wharves, an evacuation hospital, bulk fuel storage areas, warehouses, and administration buildings in Quonset huts that sprang up everywhere like mushrooms in the pasture after a rainstorm. It was hard to believe how much they had accomplished in only four months' time. Every time we returned to Manus from one of our shuttle runs there was something new—a base for repairing seaplanes or landing craft, a water treatment plant—always something we hadn't seen before. They were building like the war would never end.

Letters from home caught up with us as we shuttled troops and cargo between islands. The latest letter from Momma was full of news about getting Rebecca ready for school. She talked about how ready she was, how she knew her letters and numbers, how she already knew how to write her name and count a little. She had bought her new clothes to wear and a new winter coat. Momma only seemed worried about how she was going to get her to school. The gas ration wasn't enough for daily trips to town and back. The tires on the Model A were thin and new ones nearly impossible to come by. The car was old now and a rod knock had developed in the tired motor. When Hal drove to town, that rod started pounding every time he went up a hill. Hal had learned to retard the spark and shift to a lower gear till he eased over the top of the hill and started down the other side. He knew it wouldn't last much longer and only used it when necessary.

The Sadlers came up with an idea that Momma thought had some promise, but I had my doubts. Across the street from their store, Mr. Babcock had rooms above his Rexall drugstore that he rented out. I remembered the narrow door beside his store window and the little sign with the arrow pointing up that said "Rooms to let." There were only two rooms up there, but one of them was vacant. Carol Sadler had convinced Mr. Babcock to let Momma and Rebecca stay in the vacant room during the week in exchange for helping out in the drugstore. Waters would take care of the apple crop and keep an eye on Hal if he needed help.

Billie, the waitress at the Bon Ton, lived in the other apartment. I didn't know what side of the fence she was camped on, but I didn't expect her to be too keen on sharing the bath at the end of the hall with Momma and Rebecca. She was always nice to me and Annie when we stopped in at the Bon Ton, but I wondered how much her attitude had been changed by all the ugly things she heard people say about Momma and Rebecca.

The Rexall was on the same side of the street as the Snug,

with just a little cross street separating them. The locals that hung out there weren't exactly known for their generous dispositions, and I could see them causing trouble sooner or later.

Waters and Momma had made some friends in Glory. Annie's folks had kind of taken me in because of Annie, but soon warmed up to Hal and Waters and helped us out when Momma was gone and Hal was down with his broken leg. Sheriff Max stepped in to haul away Hal's attackers and visited him when he was laid up. He stood up for Waters at the blood drive, too.

There were other good folks in Glory. Sully, who brought us our mail, had kept Momma's letters to Waters hidden in his newspapers and never told anyone where she was. When the time came, he had brought Momma and Rebecca home. Pearl the postmistress knew everybody's business but kept it to herself when it was important.

McManus at the feed store lent Hal his truck for the scrap metal drive and applauded when Momma and Waters rode into town standing on the running boards. Mr. Babcock had rushed out to take pictures while folks stood on the sidewalks and cheered.

Other folks lived in Glory, too—people with hardened hearts and minds that wouldn't be changed overnight. Waters said the war was going to change everything, but I knew some things would never change. There was bound to be trouble.

I tried to talk all this over with Wiley, but he didn't really seem to understand why I was so worked up about Rebecca and school.

"Don't worry so much," he said. "It's too bad about the car, but things will work out. Mr. Phillips will take care of her at school. They can spend weekends at the ranch, maybe find a new car, I dunno."

Wiley was making progress, I knew. He didn't know what to do when he first met Waters, but he was coming along. Sometimes it seemed he only opened his mouth to change feet, but Cubby had been patient with him even when he said stupid things. It had taken a while for Wiley to realize Jenkins was teasing him when he called him Whitey, but the depths of his understanding could still be plumbed with a pretty short stick.

By now Cubby pretty much knew everything that went on in Glory. He was a good listener and knew about the kind of trouble that worried me. I told him about the folks in Glory, the good ones that helped each other out in hard times, the ones who backed us up when it mattered. I told him about the others, the ones who snubbed Momma and Rebecca wherever they went, ones we didn't even know who made snide remarks when they thought we couldn't hear.

"Your Momma a good person, sounds like. She makin' friends as she go along. Tryin' to build her house in heaven one brick at a time. Take a while for that to happen, prob'ly."

"Let's hope she doesn't run out of bricks," I said.

Cubby chuckled, "Might need to save some to throw at those other folks."

It was Annie, of course, who told me what really happened on the first day of school. She met Momma and Rebecca at their door to walk to school with them. Even in the morning, there were a couple of toughs leaning against the wall of the Snug. One of them whistled and called out to Momma, "Hey Sweetie, wanta invite me up for some fun?" The other one laughed and punched his pal in the shoulder. "Don't waste your time, Floyd. That one only likes dark meat."

Momma ignored the men and took Rebecca's hand, leading her down the street. A few men coming out of the

Bon Ton across the way stopped to stare at them as they passed. Al leaned against one of his gas pumps, scowling and slowly shaking his head.

"Your momma's got a lot of grit," Annie wrote. "I hope you know. I was plenty scared, just walking beside her. But she just held her head up and carried on like nothing was happening. It made me proud to be with her. She made me promise not to tell Waters. She's worried about what he might do. You can't ever tell him, either.

"When we turned the corner and headed down the street to the school," Annie said, "we saw Sheriff Max outside his office. He was leaning against his patrol car, watching as we walked up to the school with the other children and their mothers. It made me feel a little safer seeing him there. Some of the children, mostly the older ones, stared at Rebecca. The littler ones didn't seem to care. The other mothers chatted with each other, turning their backs on your momma and me."

I thought long and hard about what Annie said. What would Waters think if he knew what went on? What would he *do*? What *could* he do? He knew trouble was to be expected. But he knew Momma was determined to get Rebecca started in school. He would wait and see for now, wait to see if the hurtful words turned into sticks and stones.

Annie walked to school with Momma and Rebecca every day. One morning later in that first week Annie met Mr. Babcock outside the door that led to the upstairs rooms. He had a can of turpentine in one hand and a rag in the other. He was busily scrubbing away at something on the door next to the arrow pointing up. When he moved aside to let her in, she saw what he was doing. Someone had scrawled the words *nigger lover* on the door in red paint. Mr. Babcock had gotten a lot of it off, but enough was left to tell what it said.

"He apologized, said he didn't see who did it, but nodded

his head toward the Snug and said, 'I don't think we have to go far to look for suspects.'"

I could only imagine what Momma felt like when mean folks treated her like that. I remember telling Al off when I stopped to buy gas and he took me aside to talk about Momma and how she should have left Rebecca at the mission. Sometimes the war at home seemed closer to me than the one we were fighting in the Pacific. I knew who the enemy was. I wasn't a kid anymore. I wanted to punch somebody.

There were other things going on at home. Waters sent me a letter telling me a story about "a bit of trouble they had" with one of Uncle Hal's cows. The cow had taken a liking to apples and had gotten out of the pasture and made its way up the hill into the orchard. It had gorged itself and foundered on the apples it ate before anyone noticed what was happening. All those apples were fermenting in its stomach and the expanding gas was puffing up inside. The pressure was building up faster than the cow could belch out the gas. Waters knew the cow was in trouble and ran down the hill to get Hal.

When Hal got to the orchard, hobbling along with his cane, he threw a halter over the cow's head and tried to keep her walking, even as she belched and wheezed and bawled in distress. "If she lays down, the pressure on her insides will kill her," he said.

Waters was worried that his apples were going to kill the cow, so he took off down the hill and hopped in the Model A to go get Doc Abernathy, our only vet. But the doc's place was close to town, and by the time Waters got there, babying the Model A, and returned with Doc, they were both surprised to find the cow still alive, calmly walking about in the pasture with Hal holding the lead on the halter.

Hal knew his way around animals. He knew the cow

would die before the vet could get there. He had taken out his pocketknife and saved her himself. He made a small cut on her left flank about a hand's width behind the last rib to get through the tough skin and then stabbed her in the same place, twisting the knife to let the gas out. " 'Smelled like somebody tipped over the outhouse on a hot day,' Hal said, but it did the trick. Scared the mess out of me, though. The doc just stitched up the hole and told Hal what a fine job he done."

I had never known Waters to be at a loss for what to do, and I was impressed with Hal's quick thinking. I could just see Hal stabbing that cow. I could hear that smelly gas spewing out of the cow in a kind of sideways fart. I was sorry to have missed it.

25

In early November, we sailed in convoy for shuttle duty in the Palaus. With troops and cargo aboard, we sailed from Kossol Passage south to Peleliu, arriving on Thanksgiving Day, the twenty-third. Stories had filtered down to us about the bloody battle raging on the island. D-day on Peleliu had been September fifteenth. The First Marine Division had expected a three- or four-day battle would be enough to retake the island, but it had taken more than two months to beat the ten thousand Japs on Peleliu. The island was riddled with hundreds of caves, and the Japs had dug miles of tunnels connecting them. They had hunkered down behind pillboxes and gun emplacements reinforced with concrete. They had created an overlapping field of fire that made our amphibious assault on the island a deadly one.

The island wasn't yet ours when we arrived. The beaches were secure and most of the Japs had been wiped out, but the battle continued on a hill called Bloody Nose Ridge, where enemy holdouts were dug in, refusing to surrender.

The devastation was worse than anything we'd seen so far. The island had been covered with jungle, but there were hardly any trees standing now. Blackened palm and mangrove stumps stuck up here and there from the scorched earth. Smoke curled from smoldering brush. Flamethrowers had tossed napalm into caves and pillboxes, sucking the air from the enemy inside, forcing them out to be cut down by rifle fire. Gaping holes in the hillsides stared at us like empty eye sockets. Charred bodies still littered the blackened earth.

The convoy lined up off Purple Beach on the southeast side of the island, the best logistical location for offloading troops and cargo. The assault beaches, named White 1,

White 2, Orange 1, Orange 2, and Orange 3 were out of sight around the southern tip of the island on the southwest side. The troops aboard lined the rail, trying to get a look at what was ahead for them.

The gun crews were manning their stations, helmets on and battle gear at the ready. Wiley and I looked out at the scene from our post at the anti-aircraft gun.

"Don't look like a friendly place," Wiley said. "Looks bombed out and burned to hell."

"Yeah," I said. "Bombers pounded the island before the troops went in. Even so, the chief said, it wasn't enough. Lot of the first wave got cut down before they made any headway at all. Went in ahead of the troops with LVTAs, those big armored tractors with the 75 millimeter howitzers, supposed to take out anything left after the fighter planes strafed and bombed the beaches. But the Japs were hard to get to in their holes, had the beaches covered up and down."

"Makes me dizzy just thinking about it," Wiley said. "Imagine those Marines in the first wave, those LVTs making their way ashore, pushing past our gunboats shelling the trees above the beach. Our cruisers and battleships behind them sending bombs overhead while the Japs hurl mortars at them from their hideouts in the jungle.

"Guys just like us, crammed into those landing craft, wading into that smoky hell. Lot of 'em never got off the beach, I bet."

We could hear gunfire from the mountain that rose up in the center of the island, but it was off in the distance, far away from where we were. The smoking thunder and chaos of that first assault was something to think about. A lot of those Marines were probably the same age as Wiley and me, but it took more guts than we had to go through the hell they had seen.

Landing craft, mostly LCVPs, pulled alongside our ship,

and the troops shouldered their gear. They clambered down the cargo nets and dropped to the deck of the boats. As each boat was filled, the mooring lines were cast off, and the little Higgins boats chugged away toward the beach.

Other boats arrived to take on cargo, and the deck cranes pulled one load after another from the holds, swinging around to lower them over the side. Chief Harper barked at his men, directing the operation as Wiley and I kept watch, perched above the main deck at our post by the gun mount.

We'd arrived in the morning, and most of the offloading was complete by lunchtime. Wiley and I joined the deck crew in the galley for the noon meal. We ate quickly, thinking to replace the others who were still keeping watch on the main deck.

When we headed topside again, Harper and the chief gunner's mate were having some kind of confab, looking down over the rail. When they saw us, the chief called us over. We glanced over the rail and saw another of the boats had pulled up alongside. The deck was covered with cargo, wrapped in nets. Mostly ammunition and rations, it looked like. Apparently the crewmen who hadn't gotten to break for lunch had been busy while we were in the galley.

Our chief gunner's mate, Turk, pointed down to the Higgins boat bobbing in the water below us. "Look, boys. I don't know exactly what's going on, but there's only one guy driving the boat—says they're short of men. Sent him out by himself. Only takes one man to drive that thing, but there's no one to man the guns, protect that cargo. Chief Harper wants to send a couple of our guys back with him. I volunteered you two."

Chief Harper smiled, giving us a look at that gold tooth of his. "Piece of cake, fellas. Just go along for the ride. Stand by the machine guns, maybe help unload when you get there.

Get your steel pots and rifles in case you need them when you go ashore."

It seemed like an easy job—just a little boat ride, like Harper said. I could tell Wiley was champing at the bit. So we gathered our helmets and rifles, made our way over the side, and dropped down onto the deck of the waiting boat.

The sailor piloting the little barge was named Paulsen, a short bosun's mate second class. He had a dead cigar stub parked in the corner of his mouth. A greasy dixie cup hat that had seen better days perched on top of his head. An old scar above his left eye gave him a permanent squint that unnerved me.

"Just call me Popeye," he said when he saw us staring. "Everybody does—I'm used to it." He smiled then, and we relaxed a little. "Look, boys. This whole thing is one big screwup. Lot of folks got shot to hell when this place went up. Not enough left in some units to get everything done like it's s'posed to be. I appreciate you comin' along to help out. You just stand by the guns while I get this tub underway."

Wiley and I cast off the lines and took up our places at the machine guns on each side near the stern. "Popeye" stood between us at the control panel and fired off the engine. The propeller dug in, and we pulled away from the *Mintaka*, headed for the shore.

As we approached the island, Popeye veered south, headed away from Purple Beach, where the other LCVPs had taken the troops. I asked him where we were going.

"Our dropoff point is a little further south," Popeye said, "kind of a detour, you might say."

Wiley looked me, a little puzzled. "Hope he knows where he's going."

We passed the southern tip and turned northwest. The waves rolling in toward the shore tossed the boat from side to side, making me a little queasy. I hadn't been seasick for ages, but even with its cargo holding it down, the little boat lurched up and over the rolling swells. I hoped our pilot found somewhere to park this boat soon.

Finally Popeye turned toward shore, headed toward a tiny spit of sand bordered by trees that had survived the shelling. The boat tossed from bow to stern as we slid onto the beach. The engine roared as the propeller churned hard, pushing us up onto the sand. Popeye showed us how to lower the ramp at the bow. We stepped ashore, looking around.

After a few minutes, a Negro Marine corporal stepped out of the brush, rifle slung loosely over one shoulder. His clothes were torn and dirty, his boots caked with dried mud and white saltwater stains above the ankles. He looked us over, looked at the supplies stacked on the deck of our boat. "Been waitin' here a while—glad to see you got here."

Popeye looked at the soldier. "Sorry it took so long. We're short-handed. Had to get these fellows to come along with me. You by yourself?"

"Naw—my buddy off in the woods somewhere. He saw you comin', went to see could he get a truck to carry that stuff. You can just drop it off anywhere you like."

"We can wait a while," Popeye said. "Some of that shit's heavy. No sense liftin' it more than you have to. Folks call me Popeye. This here's Justin and Wiley."

"Name's Jones. Eldon Jones. Folks call me EJ." We shook hands all around.

"You look like you been here a while," Popeye said. "Don't see many Negro Marines."

Popeye didn't sound like he meant anything by that remark, but it made me nervous, knowing where most people would be steering the conversation with a comment like that. But EJ didn't act offended, kind of acted like people do when asked where they're from and they say "Texas" or

"Tennessee."

"Got two Negro units here," EJ said. "Sixteenth Field Depot sent in with the First Marine Division to support the assault troops. I was with the Seventh Marine Depot Company. Others with the Eleventh. We supposed to bring supplies and ammo to back up the First Marines when they landed. But the Japs was fierce, tore up our boys from the First. We couldn't get in until the beach was secure.

"Got desperate watchin' the beatin' the Japs gave us. But we all Marines first, trained to shoot and fight. Went ashore on the third day—went in on the barges, rifles blazing. Lost a lot of good men, but we turnin' it around. Won't be long now."

Popeye looked at EJ and smiled. "Yeah, the Marines done good. Make anyone proud to be part of that."

While EJ and Popeye chatted, I looked around for Wiley. I'd been listening to EJ's story and hadn't been paying any attention to what Wiley was doing. He'd been standing beside me, his rifle slung over his shoulder, his right hand clutching the strap. Now he was gone.

I looked at EJ and Popeye. "Either of you seen Wiley?"

EJ said, "Your buddy walked into those trees," pointing behind me. "Probably went to take a leak."

"Thanks," I said. "I'll just go see where he went."

I took off in the direction EJ indicated. The sounds of distant gunfire on the ridge above us made me jumpy. Wiley wasn't in sight, and I didn't want to call out since I didn't know who else might be around, but I didn't think he could have gone very far. As I plowed through the underbrush, I began to think Agnes was right. Sometimes Wiley really didn't have the brains God gave a goose.

After a few minutes, I came over a little rise, stepping out into a clearing. The soil was thin, and the coral crunched beneath my boots. The hillside ahead was steep. Heavy shelling had knocked down trees that lay in a tangle like pickup sticks cast from a giant hand. Rocks had tumbled down onto the scorched earth. It was tough going, and I stopped to rest, looking around for Wiley.

I spotted him further up the hill, standing beside a big iron door set into concrete. The door was hanging open, not quite off its hinges, but sagging into the earth. The area around the door was scorched from the earlier shelling and the ground littered with rubble. I was more than a little steamed when I finally caught up with him.

"What the hell are you doing?" I asked. He looked at me like he didn't understand what my problem was.

"Hey, Justin. C'mere—look what I found."

"I don't care what you found. You can't just go runnin' off by yourself. There are still Japs on the island. You could get us killed."

"Aw, come on. Ain't nobody around here. This must be one of those caves everybody's been talking about. Let's go have a look."

"You come on. We need to go back now. Forget about what's in there."

As I started back down the hill, I heard Wiley say, "I'm goin' in." I looked over my shoulder and he was gone. I cussed him under my breath and went back after him.

I unslung my rifle and stepped inside the door, peering into the dark interior of the cave. Light from the open door showed a narrow hallway carved into the rock. Twenty or thirty feet in, the tunnel opened into a larger natural cave, a room that was maybe fifteen by twenty feet. On the other side, the tunnel continued, stretching away into darkness beyond.

"Where are you?" I said, trying to keep my voice down. Some light spilled inside from the open door, but it was hard to see any details.

"Over here, Justin."

My eyes were getting used to the dark, but I still couldn't see much. I almost jumped out of my skin when I heard a click and a light came on at the far side of the room. Wiley had pulled the flashlight from his utility belt and was shining it around to see what was in the room. "Hang on a second," he said.

There were some scraping sounds after that, and then I saw Wiley rummaging through some boxes at his feet. The flashlight had a right-angle head and Wiley had the light pointed down, looking at something that had caught his eye. Not too long after that I heard popping sounds, distant gunfire coming from that dark tunnel on the other side.

"You hear that? Dammit, Wiley, the Japs are shooting out the other end of this tunnel. We gotta get outta here!"

"Sounds pretty far off to me. Let's see what we can find in here."

Wiley toured the room, tipping the flashlight up to see what was there. It looked like a storeroom of some kind. Boxes were piled around, some of them torn open, like someone had been in a hurry to find something. Empty sake bottles and other trash were piled in a corner. There was a small table and a chair against one of the walls. On the table amid a bunch of papers was a small framed picture of a smiling girl in a kimono.

Wiley was peeking into the boxes, trying to see what was inside. He pulled out a pair of sniper shoes, looked them over, then tucked them under his belt. He was still poking around in the boxes when there was a scurrying commotion in the tunnel. The beam from Wiley's flashlight bouncing off the walls had caught someone's attention, and they were headed our way. Wiley heard it, too. He took his rifle off his shoulder, clicked off the light and stood beside the dark tunnel.

I was on the opposite side of the room. I had my own

rifle at the ready, waiting. The sounds got closer, then slowed as someone neared the opening from the tunnel. I could be seen in the light from the outer door, but I had nowhere to go. I raised my weapon, not sure what was about to happen.

A voice from the tunnel called out in Japanese, and an outstretched arm appeared, gun in hand. The soldier stepped into the room. He saw me standing across from him and raised his hand, aiming the gun at me. Before he could fire, Wiley swung his rifle and bashed him in the head. It was Babe Ruth swinging for the bleachers, and the man went down without a sound, except for the sickening thud of the rifle butt smacking his skull. His gun skittered harmlessly across the floor.

I was stunned. I couldn't believe what I'd just seen. I braced myself for other faces appearing from the tunnel, but no one came. When the shock wore off, I looked at Wiley and then at the soldier on the floor. The side of his head was a bloody mess, but his chest was rising and falling with ragged breaths, and I knew he was still alive.

"What are we gonna do, Wiley? He's still alive."

"Shoot him, strangle him? I dunno."

Neither of those ideas had much appeal. We couldn't leave him behind. If his friends came looking for him, they would certainly come after us. We ended up finding some cord and tying his hands and feet. Wiley searched him, removed the knife from his belt and tucked it into his own. When he was trussed up like that, we each took one of his arms and dragged him outside the cave into the light.

We made our way back to the beach, dragging and carrying our unconscious captive with us. When we got to the boat, EJ's friend had arrived with the truck, and he and his men were loading the supplies into the back. Popeye saw us coming. He looked at EJ with his usual squint, "Is that a helluva souvenir, or what?"

The Marines took charge of the Jap soldier while we helped load the supplies onto the truck. They tied him to a stump and pulled off his shoes, split-toed sniper shoes like the ones Wiley found in the box inside the cave. "Not so likely to go dancing away on the coral if he got no shoes," EJ explained.

The soldier was coming around just as we finished loading the truck. He probably had a hell of a headache, but he had a fierce look in his eyes, staring back at Wiley and me from the truck until it disappeared into the trees.

Wiley didn't say much as we bobbed along in the Higgins boat, manning the machine gun stations. I hoped he thought about how stupid he'd been going off on his own. I wondered what he would say to Agnes.

As Popeye steered us toward the *Mintaka*, I remembered that it was Thanksgiving. There was a lot to be thankful for—even without the turkey and dressing. Maybe next year we would be thankful for that, too.

26

Chief Turk was standing at the rail when Wiley and I climbed aboard the *Mintaka*. "Everything go okay? You guys were gone a long time. I was about ready to send out a search party," he said, smiling.

Wiley jumped in before I had a chance to say anything. "Everything's okay, Chief," he said. "We just had to wait for some guys to show up with a truck. Took a while to unload everything and pack it on the truck." Wiley didn't want to give up any more details.

"They were down the coast quite a ways," I added. "Took some time to get down to the dropoff point and back."

"All right, then. You guys go get cleaned up. See if you can get some chow before they close down."

Wiley and I sat on the boat deck watching the stars come out and listening to the occasional gunfire from the mountain ridge that rose above Purple Beach. Since we'd come back, he'd worn a hangdog look, like he'd stepped in cowflop and couldn't figure out how to get it off his shoe. Neither of us had much to say.

I didn't know what Wiley was thinking now, but I was still shaken up. His recklessness had come close to getting us killed. He hadn't been thinking at all when he decided to poke his nose inside that cave. Waters' warning that trouble was never very far away rang in my ears when I stepped inside. Wiley seemed to forget what it was that killed the cat.

Wiley had saved my life when he whacked that soldier over the head, but I was too mad to feel grateful. Wiley tended to jump in with both feet before he knew how deep the water was. That might not be such a bad thing sometimes, but he wouldn't have had to save me if he had thought about what he might find inside that cave. Wasn't much thinking involved when he clubbed that soldier, either. It was just a reflex. He didn't have time to think about what he was doing. My heart sank when I thought how close we'd come. I was glad he kept us alive.

After we had sat there a while digesting the events of the afternoon along with our supper, Cubby and Jenkins stepped out from the galley, heading our way. Their shift was over, and they were taking a breather. Cubby came over to us, leaned against the rail, and lit a cigarette. 'Leb was working over a toothpick he'd parked in the corner of his mouth.

"Hey, Justin," Cubby said.

"Hey. You guys done for the night?"

"Yeah. How'd you like your supper? Not exactly Thanksgiving at home, was it?"

"No, but you did pretty good with what you had on hand. That chicken pot pie was real good."

"Came out okay, considering." He smiled, squinting against the smoke from his cigarette, " How you think they get those chickens in them tins, anyhow?"

"Sweet talk 'em, I suppose. Either that or just chop off their heads and push 'em in before they have time to think about it."

Cubby and Jenkins chuckled over that one.

"Best thing was that sweet potato pie," 'Leb said. Didn't think those dee-hydrated potatoes be much good, but they come out awright."

Cubby smiled at the compliment, raising his hands in front of his chest. "Be magic in the master's hands, don't ya know?"

Jenkins looked at Cubby and rolled his eyes. "I know you fulla shit, sometimes. But that pie was good. Have to give you that."

Wiley hadn't said anything since Cubby and 'Leb showed up. He had been sitting by himself, just looking out at the island, still sifting his thoughts.

'Leb looked over at Wiley sitting alone. "What's up with Whitey? He usually got plenty to say. Cat got his tongue or somethin'?"

"He's got a lot on his mind," I said. "We went ashore with some supplies this afternoon. Got into a little trouble."

"Hey, Whitey," 'Leb called out. "Come join the party."

Wiley turned and looked over at the three of us. He stood up and walked over. "Hey," he said.

Cubby took in Wiley's droopy expression. "You look like the guy in line ahead of you just took the last slice of pie. What's goin' on, kid?"

"I was just thinkin' about what happened this afternoon," Wiley said. "Chief Turk sent us ashore to guard some cargo on one of those Higgins boats."

When he didn't continue, I said "Wiley wandered off by himself while we were waiting for some guys to come back with a truck. When I went to look for him, he was poking his head into one of those caves the Japs got."

"I just wanted to look around, you know? See what I could while we were waiting for the truck."

I was still pissed at him for nearly getting us killed. "Saw a little more than you expected, didn't you?"

"I didn't really think about what might happen. I was just curious to see what was there."

The story of our afternoon adventure trickled out little by little. Wiley was pretty embarrassed about the whole thing and swore Cubby and 'Leb not to tell anyone what happened.

"You guys captured that Jap by yourselves. Didn't even fire a shot," 'Leb said. That's something to show what you made of, Whitey."

Wiley looked at 'Leb. "I suppose so. I'm not sure what I think. Justin's right, though. We shouldn't have been there in the first place." After a moment, Wiley's expression brightened. "You should have seen the expression on that guy's face when they put him on the truck. Blood runnin' down the side of his face, and he was mad as hell."

"Japs got a thing 'bout honor," Cubby said, "'bout dyin' for the Empire. Some shit like that. You boys took that away from him when you tied him up like a hog. No wonder he be mad."

"Might be you ain't a hero yet," 'Leb said, smiling. "But you findin' out what you made of. That be somethin' worth knowin'. We'll hold off on sharin' the news with the other guys till you ready."

Cubby and Jenkins were nice about the whole thing. There was a little more starch in Wiley's shoulders after he got the story out. I know it helped him feel better about getting us in over our heads, and I knew I wouldn't stay mad at him forever.

In December, the *Mintaka* returned to Guadalcanal and resumed shuttle runs in the Solomons and what the map called the Bismarck Archipelago, a string of islands that included New Britain and Rabaul—battlegrounds every one. The Allies had secured them all before we arrived. We brought supplies and replacement troops, once again falling into that familiar routine.

With Christmas approaching, Wiley and I turned our thoughts toward home, so many thousands of miles away. We got to pick out V-mail Christmas cards There were different designs, and we pored over them, trying to find something we liked. I found one that said, "To My Sweetheart" under Christmas bells with "Merry Christmas" on one side and "Happy New Year" on the other. It had a little poem that I hoped would let Annie know how I felt. It said:

> Thinking of the happy hours
> I have known because of you—
> Sharing in your dearest wishes-
> Hoping every one comes true-
> Knowing that, when this is over,
> We will never be apart--
> Working for that happy day, dear--
> Loving you with all my heart!

It was kind of corny, but I knew I couldn't do any better myself. I wrote "With all my love, Justin" next to the crossed flags at the bottom.

I had a harder time finding something for Momma, Waters, and Rebecca. There were cards for "Mother" and "Mom and Dad", but none of them seemed right. I ended up with a card that showed a tall sailor standing on a tiny island with palm trees and little mountains sticking up around his feet. Across the way was a curved horizon line and a city skyline with the word "Home" above it. The sailor had his hands cupped in front of his mouth as if he were shouting, and the words "Merry Christmas" stretched across the empty space between him and the little town so far away. I added a line at the bottom: "To everyone at home. You're all the world to me. Love, Justin."

When we could get them, we still saw movies aboard ship. Just before Christmas, we saw the movie *Casablanca*. It was a war movie with a great love story, but it didn't turn out so well at the end. Rick, the hero, puts Ilsa on the plane so she can help Victor Laszlo carry on his work, the thing that keeps him going. Rick tells her that if she doesn't go, she'll always regret it. When she says, "What about us?" he tells her, "We'll always have Paris." It made me sad to hear that.

Then Rick says he's no good at being noble, even though he just gave up the love of his life for a noble cause. What he said next made me even sadder. He said, "It doesn't take much to see that the problems of three little people don't amount to a hill of beans in this crazy world," and tells her someday she'll understand.

I thought of Momma and Waters and Rebecca—three little people in a crazy world that didn't think they were worth a hill of beans. Like the song in the movie said, "It's still the same old story." The war in the movie was a fight for love and glory, the soldiers fighting for the countries and the people they loved.

But there was another fight going on in Glory. "Moonlight and love songs" might never go out of date, but "jealousy and hate" were everywhere, too. I knew the world didn't always welcome lovers. But I hoped it had room for a few more.

At the end, Rick puts his hand under Ilsa's chin and raises it so their eyes meet. Then he says, "Here's looking at you, kid." Wiley loved that line. Every morning at breakfast, he'd raise his coffee cup and look at me, repeating that line. After a week, it got pretty old.

We were best friends, but we didn't always see the world in the same way. I couldn't talk with him the way I talked with Annie. Everything was on the surface with Wiley. We slapped backs and twisted wrists and kidded each other around, but I mostly kept how I felt inside. Wiley was as loyal to me as Doc had been to him when we were on the beach patrol. He was faithful to Agnes, too, but I thought her love bewildered him. The movie was different for him, I was pretty sure, but it didn't hurt him to think about love and sacrifice once in a while. Maybe it would keep him out of trouble.

I tried to talk to Cubby about my worries, about what was going on at home. He was a good listener and was pretty good about sharing his thoughts with me. I was surprised by what he had to say.

"Look, we all on the same boat now—won't be the same when this war over. We be friends here if you want. But things go back to the way they was when the war over. You prob'ly know that if you think about it."

"I kinda hoped things would change for the better. Waters says the war will change everything."

"Waters understand how the world is. This war change a lot of things, for sure, but it won't make folks give up the hate in their hearts. They come together to beat the Japs, maybe, but they go back to themselves when it's over."

The more I listened to Cubby, the more I thought he was probably right. But it made me feel empty inside.

"You just go back to that girl waitin' for you. Maybe her and you make Glory a better place, even if you have to do it one person at a time."

27

Christmas found the *Mintaka* at sea, steaming between Guadalcanal and New Britain. Our mail had caught up with us before we left port. Folks at home were urged to get Christmas packages in the mail before the end of October in order to reach the servicemen on time. By the look of the heavy sacks filled with letters and packages, everybody had gotten the word.

Wiley's mom had sent the inevitable fruitcake, her specialty. Guys made fun of the fruitcakes, sent by mothers everywhere, it seemed—called them doorstops and other unflattering things. But Wiley was right. His mom's fruitcake was delicious. I remembered sitting at the oilcloth-covered table in her kitchen on Wednesdays during school when Wiley invited me to lunch at his house. His mom always had something fresh-baked to serve us.

Wiley's gift from Agnes was something special. It was "a promise ring," she said in her letter. She had made the ring herself in the shop where she worked on the planes. Made it from a piece of stainless steel tubing, shaped it on a lathe, and polished it till it shined like silver. She had it engraved, too. On one side it said "Come home to me," and when you turned the band, it said "Keep your head down" on the other.

I hadn't seen Wiley with a tear in his eye since he said goodbye to Doc when we left the beach patrol, but his eyes were shining when he saw that ring.

"Guess she really loves me after all," he said, turning it on his finger.

I knew it all along, but if Wiley'd had any doubts, Agnes had just pulled that lasso around his heart a little tighter.

My package from home was a group effort, with

something from everybody. Annie sent me a little bottlebrush Christmas tree. It had frosted tips on the branches and stood on a red wooden base. Her father had gotten a camera from Mr. Babcock at the Rexall, and Annie sent me two pictures. One showed Annie standing outside the market. She was wearing a new dress her mother had made for her. She said it was light blue, though the black-and-white picture made it look gray. She had on a cute white hat with a dark band, and I could just make out the little spritz of freckles on her nose and cheeks. Her eyes sparkled as she smiled at the camera. It made me think of the picture I'd seen in the cave, the one with the girl in the kimono. It was a sad thought, and I put it out of mind.

Annie had used her father's camera to take a picture of Momma and Waters and Rebecca. They were standing together in front of the All-American apple tree. The tree still had apples on it when the picture was taken. Momma and Waters stood together, with Momma resting her head against his shoulder. Rebecca stood in front, looking up at them with laughing eyes and a pretty smile. I imagined her giggling at something Annie said when she took the picture. Rebecca had ribbons in her hair that looked like they matched the little dress she was wearing. It was a great picture. It made me a little sad, too, but in a good way.

Uncle Hal sent along some venison jerky he had made. He had built himself a little smokehouse out behind the barn and had been dying to try it out. I have to say the jerky turned out great. It was sweet, a little bit spicy, and just soft enough to chew easily. Wiley liked it, too, but I had to keep an eye on him. His mom's cake was good, but fruitcake for Hal's jerky didn't make an even trade.

Waters put in some dried apple slices he was experimenting with. They were thicker than potato chips and dusted with cinnamon. They weren't bad exactly, but probably what some would call an acquired taste. I didn't think they would be a big seller. Wiley was free to help himself to those.

Annie's mom sent some homemade fudge and divinity. She had wrapped it in waxed paper and tinfoil and put it in a tin to keep it fresh, but it had lost a little during its long journey. The edges of the candy had hardened some, but I didn't mind, and neither did Wiley. It was a taste of home that melted in your mouth.

I was surprised to find a Christmas card from Mr. Phillips, our teacher. He had come into the store one afternoon, given it to Annie, and asked her to send it in her Christmas package. It was a card he had made himself. Mr. Phillips could draw pretty well, as we had discovered in his class. Sometimes when the class read a story, he would draw a picture while the students read the story out loud. It was usually a quick sketch, a line drawing with enough detail to show everyone what the story was about. He didn't do it often, but it was always a treat to watch him when he did.

On the outside of the card was a drawing of a boy sitting on a little hill, looking up at the night sky. There was a little peppering of stars, but the boy was looking at a single bright star in the distance. Inside Mr. Phillips had written a short note, saying that he had enclosed a poem he was planning to read in church on Christmas Eve. It was a poem called "Kid Stuff," by Frank Horne. He hoped we would find it meaningful.

Mr. Phillips had printed the poem inside the card, filling up both sides.

At the bottom, Mr. Phillips wrote, "Hope you are well and safe wherever you are. Wishing you peace in the New Year. Merry Christmas."

The wise guys
tell me
Christmas
is Kid Stuff . . .
Maybe they've got
Something there —
Two Thousand years ago
three wise guys
chased a star
across a continent
to bring
frankincense and myrrh
to a kid
born in a manger
with an idea in his head

And as the bombs crash
all over the world
today
the real wise guys
know
that we've all
got to go chasing stars
again
in the hope
that we can get back
some of that
Kid Stuff
born two thousand years ago—

It was a nice poem, hopeful for sure, but the bombs were still crashing all over the world. We were chasing the Japs all over the Pacific. Maybe we would find those stars somewhere along the way.

Opar and his boys put together some entertainment for Christmas Eve. Chief Braddock, the Royal Baby of the line crossing ceremony, dressed up as Santa Claus, sitting in King Neptune's big chair. Andy Feltzer, the little guy who couldn't say no to a soldier earlier, sat on Santa's lap and sang about dreaming of a white Christmas in that sweet, pure voice of his. Opar and his boys gathered around, providing a soft harmony. Rex Lambert, Sam Benson, and Bobby Carco joined Opar to sing some carols. When they sang, "O Holy Night," Opar's booming voice rose above the others, filling the room. It was better than being in church.

Everyone was invited to sing along with the boys when

they sang "Silent Night" and the new Bing Crosby song, "I'll Be Home for Christmas." Some people just hummed along with the others who knew the words, but everybody seemed to know the part that said, "I'll be home for Christmas, if only in my dreams." That last part seemed to pee on the fire a little as the men thought about what they were missing, and an awkward silence settled over the room.

After a minute or two, Santa rubbed at his eye, stood up, and looked around the room. "Merry Christmas, you guys. Now, let's beat the Japs and go home. The next Christmas is at your house."

Christmas Day was pretty much like any other at sea. Thin clouds hung over the empty gray sea that surrounded us. It was eighty degrees, and an afternoon thunderstorm was likely, but that, too, was ordinary fare. As long as the skies weren't hiding any enemy planes, we could relax a little. The Japs had begun their kamikaze attacks at the end of October, suicide raids where pilots crashed their bomb-laden planes into our ships. The attacks were mainly aimed at carriers, but trouble falling out of the sky began to seem more likely as the Allies tightened their grip on Tojo's neck. Sailing in convoy seemed safer, but some said that just made us a better target. When we sailed alone, as we often did, I always worried about being caught out. The droning sound of planes flying above the clouds overhead made everyone tense. I hoped the ones running the show knew what they were doing.

Our evening meal was the highlight of the day. Chief Branson had managed to load up all he needed for a real Christmas feast before we sailed. We had turkey with stuffing and gravy, raised dinner rolls, fresh vegetables, and several kinds of pies for dessert. It wasn't Christmas at home, but it was the next best thing. How the folks who supplied all the ships at sea and the troops ashore managed to do their jobs as well as they did dazzled me. I thought about the guys in combat who were probably happy when they saw the waxy chocolate bar in their K-rations and read the label on the tinned treats inside. Sometimes being on the *Mintaka* didn't seem too bad.

28

Important announcements on board the *Mintaka* were usually made through speakers located throughout the ship. The intercom was affectionately known as the "bitch box," and all hands stopped what they were doing to listen when they heard it come to life one morning in April: "Attention all personnel. This is the Captain... It is my sad duty to inform you that Franklin Roosevelt, our President, died yesterday of a cerebral hemorrhage. Vice-president Truman has taken the oath of office in his place. Mrs. Roosevelt has informed their four sons who, as you may know, also serve in the military... It saddens me to think that the President, like so many, did not survive the war... We will have to win it without him. That is all for now."

I was with Cubby when we heard the announcement. "I think it means he had a stroke," I said.

"Used to be Abe Lincoln we looked up to," Cubby said, "but FDR did a lot of good for our folks, turned a lot of us who could vote into Democrats. Still a long way to go, but made some headway, for sure."

I wondered what Waters would have to say about that. He kept up with things better than me, but I was brought low by the news. Roosevelt was the President as far back as I could remember. Mr. Phillips had taught us about the Revolution and George Washington and some of the "founding fathers," as he called them, but he had a picture of Franklin Roosevelt on the wall by the flag. Every morning in school FDR looked back at us when we stood and recited the *Pledge of Allegiance*. He was the man who ran the country, the one, Waters said, who lifted us up when the Depression had us down. He *was* the government.

I had listened to the news on the radio and talked with Waters about what he read in the paper, but the world was smaller then, and I hadn't spent much time looking beyond the front porch. Waters said FDR tried to keep us out of the war, but he thought the President knew we would be drawn into it sooner or later. Pearl Harbor had made up everybody's mind and changed everything forever.

Near the end of April the *Mintaka* left Guadalcanal with 968 Seabees, bound for Okinawa. We were steaming in convoy, heading north nineteen hundred miles from Guadalcanal to our first stop at Eniwetok, another tiny dot on the map. It was an atoll made up of thirty-some islands that ringed a lagoon about ten miles wide. Eniwetok Island was the biggest, two and a half miles long, but only fifteen hundred feet wide. Our guys had taken the island at the end of February, and by the time we arrived, they had already cleared a bomber strip 6800 feet long and four hundred feet wide and set up Quonset huts for aviation personnel. Bombers were already flying missions from the island.

On Parry Island about three miles further north, the construction battalion had taken over a ramp built by the Japanese and were developing a seaplane base to support the patrol bombers. The place was buzzing with activity everywhere we looked.

The *Mintaka* didn't linger long at Eniwetok. She refueled, offloaded some cargo, and took on provisions before heading out to sea again, steaming west fifteen hundred miles further, to Ulithi, our next stop on the way to Okinawa.

There were seventeen other ships in the convoy, with destroyer escorts protecting the troops and cargo we carried. We steamed along together, a necklace of gray shapes floating on the sea. Drawing nearer to the action, we manned our stations around the clock, ready for what might fall from the skies or rise from the depths to attack. When nightfall came, the lights on our sister ships winked out one by one, leaving us in the dark. Blacked out to keep from being seen, we couldn't see each other. But it was comforting to know we weren't alone.

The captain had met with the chiefs, and Chief Turk passed on what he knew about Ulithi to the gun crews. "You won't see this place in the newsreels," he said. "It's a big deal, but pretty much on the QT. Japs had a weather station here, parked a few ships now and then, but abandoned it last year.

"Japs really dropped the ball on this one. Last September the Army and the Seabees moved in, started settin' up shop. Within a month, they had a base up and runnin'. It's another atoll, runs north and south about twenty miles and about ten miles across. Somethin' like forty little islands surroundin' a lagoon that can hold more ships than Pearl.

"By now it's a big deal, a floatin' service station, got floatin' drydocks and repair stations, shops that can build most anything. Fleet oilers can meet warships at sea to refuel closer to the action. They got a rec center, too, on an island called Mogmog—can handle eight thousand men a day. Got a theater with 1200 seats and a chapel with 500." Turk looked around at our group and smiled. "More calls for popcorn than prayer, I guess."

Turk looked us over again and got more serious. His eyebrows narrowed, and his voice took on a more serious tone. "We ain't really advertisin', but the Japs know we're here. Back in November one of their *kaiten* manned torpedoes sunk the *Mississinewa*, one of our oilers, killed 63 crewmen. In January the *Mazama*, an ammo ship, was damaged by another *kaiten* torpedo. One of our carriers, the *Randolph*, was hit by a kamikaze attack in March—crashed into the stern starboard quarter, killed 27 crewmen, more than a hundred wounded. Poor bastards were watchin' a movie on the hangar deck.

"Point is—it's a big place where we're goin'. Hundreds of ships, thousands of men, makes it look safer than it is. Japs may be losin' the war, but they still got some fire in their bellies. Keep your eyes and ears open. Even when we get to Ulithi. This ain't a cakewalk—nobody's safe till it's over."

Westerly winds pushed a few clouds across the sky above the lagoon when we arrived at Ulithi. The rainy season was coming to an end, and the days were warm, usually in the eighties.

Chief Turk said there were forty or so islands surrounding the lagoon, but most of them were tiny, barely rising maybe ten feet out of the water. They reminded me of the Christmas card I'd sent with the sailor standing on the tiny island. Without the palms and other trees sticking up like flags, they would have been impossible to see at any distance.

There were some bigger islands, of course. Turk had mentioned Mogmog, where the rec center was supposed to be, and we would learn the names of others—Asor and Sorlen and Falalop. But as the convoy steamed into the lagoon, what everyone noticed first were the hundreds of ships that were already at anchor there—cargo ships, transports, tankers, barges, oilers, repair ships—ships that looked like they'd been towed in and set up as floating warehouses. We passed battleships of every kind: the "small boys"—destroyers and destroyer escorts—cruisers, and a row of Essex-class carriers with Hellcat fighters lined up on the flight decks, their wings folded back like ducks on a pond. A white-painted hospital ship with a big red cross amidships steamed past us, headed out to sea as we entered the anchorage.

The gunner's mates were on duty all the time now. Keeping watch, maintaining guns and ammunition—Chief

Turk's warnings were taken seriously. "We're in the shit now," Wiley said. I couldn't disagree. Most watches were four hours on, four hours off, giving us time to sleep, but off-time was limited and often spent on maintenance tasks. Two teams traded off throughout the day, with the dogwatch between 1600 and 2000 hours split into two-hour shifts, allowing each team time for their evening meal.

A lot of the guys stationed at Ulithi got shore leave, swam in the surf on the white sand beaches, got four-hour passes to drink three-two beer and play volleyball on Mogmog island, but we were passing through on our way to Okinawa, where a big battle had begun on April 1, and we were kept busy all the time, now.

Team 1, which included Wiley and me, along with Gino Manfredi, a skinny kid named Terry Sykes and a couple others, had just completed the first of the two dogwatches. We were heading for the mess deck to get our dinner when the mail clerk caught us outside. He reached into a tray he carried, and pulled out a handful of letters. We stuffed our letters in our pockets and got in the chow line.

Falalop, the biggest of the four larger islands, was just wide enough for the 3500-foot airstrip that could handle the R4Ds and R5C Commandos that flew in from Guam with passengers and cargo—and mail. It never failed to amaze me how the mail found us wherever we went. We had been at Ulithi for less than a week. Folks at home had only the vaguest idea where we were and, frankly we didn't really know, either, but when they put that FPO address on an envelope, it always seemed to find its way to us.

We hurried through the chow line with the others, heading for a table by ourselves, where we could eat and read the news from home. We plowed through the food, not giving much thought to what we were eating. Wiley pushed his tray aside, pulling the letter from his pocket, looking it over carefully. "Might be the last letters we get," he said. "For a while, anyway."

"Could be. Especially now that we're 'in the shit', as you put it." I didn't think we were *in it* yet, but it certainly looked like we were heading that way. Okinawa was still thirteen hundred miles northwest of us. The battle there was still raging.

My letters were full of happy thoughts. The spring rains had let up, the creek was behaving itself, and Momma and Rebecca had managed to melt the frosty reception folks in town greeted them with at first—if only a little. But it was something I hoped would grow like the new shoots on Waters' All-American and one day bear fruit. Momma had shown Rebecca my shellback certificate that I had mailed home. She was quite taken with the drawings of mermaids on the borders. She wanted to know if I had seen any mermaids yet. It made me smile when I read that, but I was more worried about other things rising out of the sea to meet us.

Annie was happy, too, full of news about folks in town. Everyone was optimistic that the war in Europe would end soon, and all the boys could come home. She hoped our war in the Pacific would be over, too, so we could be together again. I hoped so, too.

Wiley's letter must have been filled with good news, too. He had a dreamy look in his eye when he folded the letter and put it back in the envelope. He didn't say anything. He just sat there, holding the letter with one hand, resting his chin on his hand, the letter pressed against his lips.

"Everything okay?" I asked.

"Yeah—Agnes is making plans for when we get back. Says she can't wait till we're together." Wiley set the letter down on the table. He twisted the promise ring on his finger, the dreamy look back on his face. "Got a surprise for me, she says."

Agnes never failed to surprise. She was as unpredictable

as the weather. She had Wiley hooked, for sure—always had. I just hoped she meant to keep that promise in her heart.

Team 1 had the middle watch from zero hundred to 0400 hours the night before the convoy pulled out and headed for Okinawa. Ulithi was a beehive during the day. Small boats rushed to and from larger ones, delivering mail, picking up messages. Distilling ships replenished fresh water supplies to patrol vessels and escort ships. Cargo ships offloaded freight, taking on new shipments bound for other destinations. Submarine patrols flew overhead, looking for enemy vessels.

At night, the entire fleet was blacked out. Hatches were dogged to keep light from escaping and compartments watertight in case of attack. Communications were silenced, though some TBS "talk between ships" communication was possible on the marine VHF radio band. All was quiet. A thin cloud layer hung over the lagoon, the quarter moon little more than a dim glow above us, but enough to cast shadows on the deck. My eyes were accustomed to the dark, and I could see Wiley sitting on the floor of the gun tub, leaning back against the low wall surrounding us. I thought he might be asleep.

My mind wandered as I stood there in the dark. I remembered what Jack's daughter Lucy told me about the water when we were on the beach patrol—how the sea can be unfriendly if the water doesn't know you. Jack told her the water watches you, takes your measure, decides what to think about you. We had been at sea a long time now. The water'd had enough time to take our measure. A warm breeze drifted in from the west. Little waves lapped against the ship, and I remembered part of a poem Mr. Phillips taught us, something about "the little waves, with their soft white hands..." The familiar rhythm of those gentle sea hands was somehow comforting as I stood there in the dark.

I thought at first I was imagining it, but I heard a different noise, one that didn't belong to the usual night sounds. Off in the distance, beyond the north end of the lagoon, I heard a faint, but steady drone. "You hear that?"

Wiley raised his head, twisted right and left, working out the kinks. "Hear what?"

"The other end of the lagoon," I said, pointing. "Listen. Something's up there."

The sound got louder as the plane passed over our heads, circling around. Sirens went off then. Alarms rang, and crews went to general quarters everywhere. Wiley scrambled to his feet and swung the gun in the direction of the noise. A little wind pushed the clouds aside. The plane circled once and began a howling dive that made me want to head for cover even though the plane was more than a mile away from us. As we watched, tracer rounds from the nearer ships stitched bright holes in the dark sky, searching for the screaming bandit headed their way. Cannon fire erupted from the bigger guns. We saw an orange flash in the sky, followed by the sound of the Zero exploding. We watched as it came apart and fell into the sea.

It hadn't lasted more than a minute or two. My ears were still ringing when the all clear was given. The wind stirred, pulling the thin blanket of clouds across the moon, and the night sounds returned. The lapping waves patted the *Mintaka*'s hull: *Go back to sleep. It was just a dream.*

29

Red skies greeted us as the convoy made its way out to sea the next morning. They were a bloody reminder of the fireball in the sky the night before, when the Jap bomber exploded and fell into the lagoon. But the sun soon rose above the gathering clouds, and a freshening westerly breeze greeted us as we headed northwest, steaming toward Okinawa.

Captain Briggs usually met with the chiefs and had them pass along his orders to the crew, so it was a surprise when the bitch box crackled one afternoon and the captain's voice echoed throughout the ship. All hands stopped what they were doing to listen.

"Attention all personnel. I have just received news of importance to everyone aboard the *Mintaka*. As of this date, the war in Europe is over. The Nazis have surrendered." The voice paused as cheers were heard from every quarter. After a few moments, the speakers crackled with static, and the captain continued. "The lights are on again in England, but not all over the world, as you well know. And unlike what the song says, rain is not the only thing that may fall from the skies above us. As long as the kamikazes swarm over our heads, the Japs still pose a deadly threat. Celebrate this victory in your hearts, but keep your eyes and ears open as we head to Okinawa. Our time to celebrate will come."

It was good news for sure, but like the captain said, the war wasn't over for us. I remembered that song he talked about, and the part that said something about going back to kisses that won't just mean "good-bye" and how "we'll have time for things like wedding rings when the lights go on again all over the world." We steamed into the unknown with our sister ships beside us, gray shapes huddled together on a dark sea, our lights out at night, hiding in the dark. I hoped someone in Glory was leaving a light on for us.

Wiley's eyes lit up when he heard the news. He was over the moon like the cow in Mr. Phillips' *Mother Goose* book, the one he read to the little ones in school.

"Don't pack your sea bag just yet," I said. "The captain's right. It might be over 'over there', but we still got a ways to go."

"I know. But it means something. It has to. First Italy, now Germany—two down and one to go, right?"

"Yeah—I want it to be over, too, but there's more to do. Hard to tell what's ahead."

"Eyes and ears open, like the captain said?"

"Yeah—just like that."

I was as excited as Wiley, but I was trying to keep a lid on it. I wanted to go home as much as anybody. I went home to Glory in my mind, felt the welcoming arms of Momma and Waters and the long-awaited "hello, sailor" kiss from Annie. But the sea road was long, and Glory was still far away. So I held it all in, trying to celebrate in my heart, like the captain said, hoping our war would end soon, too.

The battle for Okinawa had been going on since the beginning of April, and it was still raging when the *Mintaka* steamed into Nakagusuku Bay on the eastern side of the island. Okinawa was about seventy miles long and seven miles wide. The bay was nearer the southern tip of the island than Chimu Bay, a little further to the north. We were only about four hundred miles from Japan, a notion that was difficult to imagine.

"Naka-what?" Wiley said. "We came six thousand miles

to end up in a place with a name we can't pronounce. Oughta be something simple, like Glory."

"We're a long ways from Glory. Don't worry about the names," I told him. We'll just give 'em new ones. Name them after some general or something. Like the reporting names they use for the Jap planes. Gave the bombers women's names—Betty and Sally and Val. Fighters got men's names like Oscar and Zeke—for the Zeros. Lot easier to say when you're in a hurry."

The bay was about twelve miles long and nine miles wide, filled with hundreds of ships of every description. We began debarking the troops and unloading cargo as soon as we arrived. A line of LCVP's drew alongside, scramble nets were tossed over, and the Seabees made their way down to the rolling deck below. Groups gathered at the rail waiting their turns. When one of the little Higgins boats departed, another pulled up to take its place. The men, loaded down with their gear, climbed over the rail and scrabbled down the nets, some of them dropping the last few feet as arms reached out to catch them.

When the last of the landing craft were away, other boats appeared alongside the *Mintaka* to take on the cargo we carried. Chief Harper barked orders as the deck apes scrambled to shift ammunition and other supplies brought up from belowdecks to the waiting boats. Winch motors whined as cables tightened and the big cranes swung loads over the side. The ground war had been stalled by steady rains and mud that bogged down heavy equipment and made mounting an attack difficult. Offloading our cargo would take several days.

On the 22nd of May, our second day at anchor, five twin-engine Jap bombers called "Sallys" swept down from the north and attacked airfields on the island.   At 2200 hours the sky lit up when the antiaircraft batteries came to life, and we watched as the bombers were blown out of the sky. We didn't have ringside seats exactly, since they were several miles away, but it was close enough to prove Captain Briggs was right. So was Wiley. We were "in it" now.

During the day, we continued offloading supplies as aircraft patrolled overhead and a ring of radar picket stations surrounding the island covered possible approaches by the enemy. Blacked out and buttoned up tight, the nights were long as we lay under the smoke screen pumped out by generators aboard destroyers anchored nearby. Night watches were the worst.

Wiley and I drew the middle watch, from midnight to 0400 on the morning of the 24th. The *Mintaka* had tied up beside another liberty ship, the *William B. Allison*, which was loaded with construction materials for the Seabees who'd traveled with us earlier—lumber, structural steel, spools of cable, and other things. The weather had cleared, and even though we were bundled up in the smokescreen, the full moon could be seen through the thin layer of clouds overhead. From time to time we heard the sound of a plane droning above us.

The first few hours of the watch were uneventful. Wiley and I whispered back and forth, passing the time, but not saying much. About 0300, a little breeze came up and parted the clouds. Five minutes later, a Jap bomber fell out of the sky on the far side of our sister ship. It dropped a torpedo that struck the *Allison* amidships. The plane vanished into the sky before we could even bring our guns to bear on it. The explosion rocked the *Mintaka*. Sirens went off on both ships as the call to general quarters was announced.

The torpedo had scored a direct hit on the *Allison's*

engine room, killing three men and severely wounding four others. It ripped a hole thirty feet wide in the side of the ship. Flooding in the engine room caused the ship to settle in the water, but compartments on either side were sealed, preventing the ship from sinking.

Rescue boats arrived, carrying the dead and wounded to the hospital ship *Mercy*, anchored further offshore, away from the hostilities. Afterward, concern shifted to saving the *Allison*'s cargo in case she sank. Without power the *Allison* was dead in the water beside us, the crew scrambling about in the dark. Steam lines were sent across from the *Mintaka* to power her generators. Other boats pulled alongside to receive the cargo as the power came on and the crew hurried to pull material from the holds of the damaged ship.

We kept watch until we were relieved, climbing down from the gun mounts and heading to the galley. Cubby and Jenkins saw us come in, walked over to us as we got coffee and made our way to the nearest table.

"You guys okay?" Cubby asked, as he and 'Leb sat down with us.

"Yeah," I said. "Can't say the same for the guys on the *Allison*. They got hit real hard. That torpedo blew a hell of a hole in her side. Bad as it is, it could have been a lot worse."

It wasn't cold, but Wiley held the thick mug in both hands, like he was trying to ward off a chill. He twirled the spoon in the mug, watching the coffee swirl near the rim.

'How 'bout you, Whitey? You lookin' a little paler than usual."

Wiley looked up. "I'm okay, 'Leb. Everything just happened so fast is all. There wasn't time to even fire back. By the time we saw the plane, it had already dropped that torpedo and was zooming into the clouds."

"That's the thing now," Cubby said. "Hit and run. Crash and burn—hope to blow up a ship by diving into it."

"I know, but I missed my chance—maybe could have saved those boys next door."

"Their guys didn't see it comin' either," Jenkins said. He put his hand on Wiley's shoulder. "Japs ain't run out of bombers yet. Maybe you get another chance to take one down."

When we left the mess deck after breakfast, the crews were still busy salvaging cargo on the *Allison*. We watched the offloading for a while. Chief Turk came over to talk to us. He said it would take some time before the work was complete. He said the ship would be towed to Kerama Retto, an island nearby, for repairs. "Engine room's a total loss, but they'll patch the hole, tow it somewhere, turn it into a floating warehouse." Chief Turk warned us to keep a sharp eye on things. He didn't blame us for not getting that Sally, but like Wiley, he wished we had.

I was suddenly tired. I told myself I wanted to rest up before Team One's next watch at 0400 the next morning, but it was more than that. I told Wiley I was going to hit the rack and left him leaning on the rail, watching the crews transfer the cargo from the damaged ship.

Chief Turk sometimes changed the gun crews around a little. Today he had posted Wiley and me on the Oerlikon 20mm cannons on opposite sides of the foredeck. Gino Manfredi was with Wiley on the port side. I shared the starboard gun tub with Terry Sykes. Terry chewed tobacco and sometimes spit into the wind when he got rattled. Ducking the blowback made working with him a challenge, but kept me alert. He was a scrawny kid, but strong enough to hoist the heavy ammo canisters into place.

Work on the *Allison*'s cargo had been completed while we slept, and the ship had been taken under tow to Kerama Retto. Word was received and passed along that other ships had been damaged in similar attacks. Another swarm of kamikazes had been intercepted north of Okinawa and been destroyed. The Japs were throwing everything at us, it seemed.

Heading across the bay to take on cargo from another ship, we scanned the skies as the sun rose above the horizon, painting the clouds with color. The clearing weather and the full moon at night had opened up doors we'd been trying to keep closed. Everyone was on edge, expecting trouble to appear at any moment.

We didn't have to wait long. About three hours into the watch, a sharp-eyed spotter noticed a few dark specks against the red-orange of the sky and sounded the alarm that brought everyone to their battle stations. The dark specks grew into a flock of Zeros with the red Japanese "meatball" painted on the wings. The planes closed in on the ships in the harbor, breaking away from each other as they chose their targets.

One of the Zekes peeled away and headed toward us. It dropped down from the sky at high speed, swinging around so that it came at us out of the sun, making it harder to see. The ship was turning to face the attacker as it came in low over the bow. The 3-inch forward gun fired, but missed as the Zero screamed overhead. Wiley and I got off a few rounds, but the plane roared on, stitching holes in the deck as it passed. I saw Jenkins and a few other men caught on deck dive for cover about sixty feet away, near the opening to the number 2 hold, as the pilot banked above, dropping down for another run along the port side from stern to bow. The *Mintaka*'s guns blazed as the attacker dove toward us. The five-inch gun on the stern barked repeatedly, belching flames and smoke, but its rounds missed their mark. The 20mm cannons struck home, shattering the cockpit as the plane dropped downward toward us. When it got lower, it would be out of my line of fire behind the bridge.

I looked over toward Wiley's gun mount. Gino's body hung lifeless over the edge of the gun tub. Wiley was giving it hell, hammering away as the plane approached the ship. As I watched, a dark shape topped the ladder to the gun mount and pushed Gino's body aside. It was Jenkins. He reached up to replace one of the ammo canisters. Where the hell had he come from? Wiley and the other gunners continued to pound their target, trying to keep the plane from exploding on the deck.

As the Zero headed in for the kill, spraying rounds from its machine guns, men in the direct path of the falling plane dove for cover, diving into the hold or jumping overboard in panic. My eye followed the tracer rounds from Wiley's gun as they finally ripped a wing off and the plane began to rotate away from us. The wing fell onto the deck, carving a path as it slid forward, cutting cables and taking out anything in its way.

An explosion rocked the plane as it neared the main deck, and part of the fuselage took out a section of the port side railing before falling into the sea. The explosion sent a shitstorm of shrapnel that flew everywhere. Airplane parts rained down on the deck, bouncing and slamming into things. A propeller blade clipped the wall below the bridge deck, bounced off, and went spinning though the gap in the railing. Terry and I dove down in the gun tub, ducked behind the wall, faces down on the deck. I shut my eyes and pulled my helmet tight with both hands as pieces of metal beat against it and peppered the back of my vest.

When the sky stopped falling around us and the only noises were the shouts of men and the siren that continued to wail, I looked over at Wiley's gun mount. Wiley was sitting in the gun tub, leaning back against the low wall. Jenkins sat beside Wiley, his arm around him, his hand holding something against Wiley's shoulder where a dark stain was beginning to spread. I rushed over to the starboard mount, fearing the worst.

When I reached the top of the ladder, Jenkins was holding on to Wiley for dear life, talking to him softly. Wiley seemed to be listening, but his head was down, and his eyes were closed. There was a bloody smear on the wall behind him. Jenkins had been hit in the leg. It was stretched out before him as he sat, holding Wiley. He had used his web belt to fashion a tourniquet, but there was a lot of blood on the deck. Gino lay on the far side of the tub, a hole through the helmet that was still strapped under his chin, blood pooling beneath it.

"I'm okay, kid," 'Leb said. "It's Wiley who needs help. Caught a round, maybe shrapnel, in his shoulder. I'm keeping pressure on it. Go get a corpsman, someone who can help him."

30

The whole crew hustled to deal with the aftermath of the attack. Some men had tossed a scramble net over the side, and two men made their way down it with a boat hook to reel in the fellow who jumped overboard to escape the Zero's machine gun fire. Smoke lingered in the air, drifting up from the sea where the burning wreck had splashed down. Deck apes pushed aside debris, clearing a path to get to several men who sat, dazed and confused, some slightly wounded. I made my way past them, hoping to find someone who could help. "Doc" Kelly, one of our small number of corpsmen came rushing toward me.

I told him Wiley and 'Leb were down near the bow, but he was already on the way. Spike Harper had been coming up the ladder from the number 2 hold when the attack began. He saw Gino fall and Jenkins take his place. The chief knew Wiley and 'Leb had been hit.

"Blew his whistle to get my attention," the medic hollered back at me as I trotted along behind him. "Said somebody was hanging from the gun tub. Other guys wounded, too." The red cross on the flap of his shoulder bag swung back and forth as we dodged the debris and the holes in the deck.

"My friends are hurt bad. Stuck with it when the plane attacked until they tore the wing off," I yelled back. A chunk of the Zero's wing had snagged on some cables, blocking our way. We clambered over it, trying to steer clear of the gap where the plane had taken out a long section of the port railing.

When we got back to the gun mount, Cubby was halfway up the ladder, calling out to 'Leb. I couldn't tell what he was saying, but I could see the worry on his face. I followed Doc up the ladder. He was already taking charge when I got to the top. He checked Gino first, then shook his head and turned to Wiley who was still cradled in 'Leb's strong arms.

Doc cut away Wiley's vest to get a better look at the wound in his shoulder. There was a ragged hole and a lot of blood. He reached into his bag and took out some iodine swabs. He did what he could to clean the wound, applied some pressure dressings and wrapped them tightly with gauze bandages that he pinned securely with safety pins. When he was finished, his hands were red with Wiley's blood.

"Looks like a shrapnel wound," Doc said. "Tore a helluva hole, but I think it passed clear through. Probably find it on the deck behind him somewhere. Lost a lot of blood, though. Passed out from that. Get him down to the main deck. We'll hook him up to a plasma bag. Looks like he'll make it."

Cubby and I worked together to get Wiley up and lower him down to the main deck. Doc was talking to 'Leb as he cut away his pants leg to look at his wound.

"Good job keeping pressure on your buddy's wound. Probably saved his life. Might have bled to death if you hadn't been there to take care of him." He examined 'Leb's wound carefully. "Looks like a through-and-through. Didn't hit the main artery, but you won't be dancing for a while." He swabbed the wound and replaced 'Leb's web belt with a tourniquet from the medical bag. He covered the wound with another bandage from his kit. "Gonna keep an eye on this, might have to work at it to stop the bleeding." He closed the flap on his bag, and slung it over his shoulder. "You'll be okay."

Cubby and I got Wiley down the ladder to the deck. It took both of us to do it, hooking our web belts together in a makeshift sling, and lowering him down to Terry and another guy who hurried over to help. Terry went to get a litter as I sat with Wiley and watched Doc help 'Leb negotiate the ladder.

Cubby and I lifted Wiley onto the litter and carried him over to join the other wounded men. 'Leb and Doc came along behind us. Doc walked with Jenkins' arm around his shoulder, his own arm around 'Leb's waist, helping him as he limped along.

When they were settled, another corpsman arrived, and Cubby and I watched as both of our friends were hooked up to plasma bags. The medic took out two tubes of morphine, pulled off the ends, and injected Wiley and 'Leb. "For the pain," he said. "Gonna hurt like hell when the shock wears off." He pinned the empty tubes to their collars. "Lets the doctors know what kind of dose they got before leaving the ship."

"They gonna be all right?" Cubby asked.

"Should be. Worst thing is infection. Doc put sulfa powder on those wounds before the bandages went on. Should get by till they arrive at the hospital ship and get a proper cleanup."

He looked at Wiley and then spoke to 'Leb. "Looks like your buddy got the worst of it. Take a long time to heal a wound like that. Be a bitch when it starts hurtin', like I said. But the infection shouldn't be a problem."

He glanced toward Cubby and me. "GIs get wounded in the jungle got more to worry about, got malaria, bugs, bad water, jungle rot—you name it. Not so big a problem aboard ship if we get you guys treated right away."

He turned back, looking at 'Leb again. "That leg will give you fits for a while, but you'll be okay, too."

'Leb cracked a little smile and looked up at the medic who'd dressed his wound. "Never was much for dancing, Doc. But it be nice to get off this damned boat." He looked at Wiley, still unconscious, propped up against the railing. "I

just worried 'bout Wiley, here. Got a gal back home, hopin'
to see him again. Wouldn't want to see her disappointed."

"She's gonna have to wait a little, but he'll make it home.
Probably get there before some of us do."

Cubby and I sat with Wiley and 'Leb, waiting for the
rescue boat to arrive and take them to the *Mercy*, one of the
hospital ships we'd seen earlier. Wiley stirred, groaning. His
eyes opened, and he looked around at us.

"How you feeling, Whitey?" 'Leb said.

Wiley turned toward 'Leb. "Like I been kicked by a mule.
You okay?"

"Yeah, guess so. Don't seem much worse than some of
the fights I been in, but the doc says it'll hurt some when the
morphine start to wear off."

"Morphine make you dizzy? I feel like my head's
swimming."

"It's okay, Wiley," I said. "Just take it easy."

It took a while for the rescue boat to arrive. Cubby and I
sat with 'Leb and Wiley, saying our good-byes, thinking our
private thoughts. I didn't expect to see Wiley again until we
met up in Glory. The war was over for him, but the battle
wasn't yet over for the rest of us. I hoped we'd all meet again,
like the song said, when "the blue skies drive the dark clouds
away," but there were still a lot of dark clouds on the horizon.

When the rescue boat arrived and people began to stir,
Wiley looked up at me. "This is it, then. I guess we won't be
seeing much of each other for a while. Gonna miss me?"

I smiled when he said that. I told him, "I'm kinda tired of
seeing you every day. Go home to Glory. You'll probably get
there ahead of me, 'less the war ends sooner than we think.
Give Agnes a kiss. Hug Annie for me and tell Momma and
Waters I'll be home one day soon." Some men came along

then, picked up the stretcher, and started carrying Wiley away.

"And when you get a chance," I said, walking beside him, "thank 'Leb for saving your life."

"'Leb's a good man…" Wiley nodded. He was starting to drift back to sleep.

"You were just scared of what you didn't know," I told him, but I don't think he heard me. Maybe 'Leb had been scared, too.

When the stretcher was lowered over the side, Wiley stirred and gave me a thumbs up. He said something, but it was too noisy to hear for sure.

The deck apes were all over the main deck, gathering up debris, repairing torn cables, putting up a barrier across the gap in the port railing. I wandered over to where the Zero's wing lay tangled up in some rigging. I watched as one of the men cut away some lines that had gotten fouled when the wing slid across the deck. He had some big shears in his hand and was working at untangling the mess. When he looked up at me, he set the shears down, and swiped his arm across his forehead, wiping away the sweat. "Hell of a mess. Gonna take a while to sort it all out."

"Guess we got lucky, though. Mind if I borrow those shears for a minute?"

He had a puzzled look on his face, but he handed over the shears. I looked at the wing, riddled with bullet holes, torn sections peeled away. I stuck the shears into the wing where a corner of one of the sections was split open. I carved out a square piece that had a bullet hole through the green paint and a sliver of the red "meatball" from the center of the wing. I weighed it my hand, looking at it for a moment before handing the shears back.

I went below then, headed for the quarters I shared

with Wiley. I tossed the metal from the wing onto Wiley's bunk and sat down on my own, looking at that little piece of destruction that had cost Gino his life and wounded Wiley and 'Leb.

Wiley had gotten his chance to be a hero, but I didn't think he'd given it any more thought than when he stumbled into that cave on Peleliu. He just did what he was supposed to do when the opportunity came along. I don't think Jenkins gave it much thought, either. He just did what needed to be done. Maybe he did it for Wiley, but I couldn't say one way or the other. He probably would have stepped up no matter who was stranded on the gun mount. He was that kind of guy. They both were.

I thought of Gino lying on the deck with a helmet full of blood. He'd been in the thick of it, too. Everybody was somebody's hero.

After a while, I noticed the drawstring from Wiley's sea bag poking out from under his bunk. He hadn't been able to take it with him when the rescue boat carried him away with Jenkins and the others. I wondered what to do with it. I pulled it out and laid it on his bunk. I dumped it out, looking at the contents. There was the usual stuff: uniforms, socks, underwear, shoes and leggings. He didn't need any of those things. He would be issued new stuff wherever he landed. I was looking for other things, the things he couldn't replace.

Rolled up in a pair of dungarees I found the knife Wiley had taken from the Japanese soldier in the cave. I set it aside and kept looking through Wiley's stuff. There was a picture of Wiley and me on the beach patrol, with Doc and Jig at our feet, their tongues hanging out, ears perked up. There were two pictures of Agnes, one from before the war, with Agnes in the polka-dot swimsuit she wore when we all went swimming together. The newest picture showed her in the aircraft plant, wearing overalls, with her hair tied up in a scarf, holding some kind of tool in her hands as she worked. She looked good in both pictures. I hoped Wiley would look as good to her when he got home.

There were two bundles of letters tied up with string. They made me think of the letters in my own bag. One bundle was from his parents. The other, thicker bundle contained all the letters he'd received from Agnes. I set them aside. I found another larger envelope. The end was held shut by two round discs that had a string laced around them. I squeezed the envelope between my fingers, wondering what was inside

When my curiosity got the best of me, I unlaced the string around the discs and opened the flap. There were two letters inside, one addressed to Wiley's parents and one addressed to Agnes. After some thought, I realized these were Wiley's "just in case" letters, with the things that Wiley would want his parents and Agnes to know if he didn't come home. Maybe Curt's death had prompted them, but they were a surprise to me. I had no idea. Wiley's thoughts went deeper than I gave him credit for. Love and sacrifice were on his mind, too. I looked at the letters for a long time before putting them back in the envelope and re-tying the string. I wrapped Wiley's things in a towel to protect them and stowed them in my own bag for safekeeping.

The Jap fighter that tore up our ship had ripped our friends away from us as well. Wiley and I were fast friends, always together through thick and thin. When it counted, he was the one who'd saved the day. I hadn't really done anything. I wondered what it would be like without him by my side every day

Cubby missed 'Leb, too. It wasn't hard to tell. Cubby wasn't one to mope, but I'd catch him outside the galley in the morning, usually smoking a cigarette and looking out across the bay. I stood with him at the rail and wondered, as he probably did, what the new day would bring. Just standing there together was a comfort. We didn't say much. But as one day followed another, talk came more easily. We still talked about the weather and the war, but more and more we talked about the end, about going home. I asked Cubby what he wanted to do when the war was over.

"Probably head back to Butterspring, little town where I'm from, see if anybody I know still there. Had me a girl there named Gussie, a big-eyed girl with a heart of gold. I told her I'd come by when the war over, but that was a long time ago now. You know I ain't much for reading, even with your help. Writing ain't exactly my strong suit, either, but Gussie know that. I sent her cards from different places we been. Just wanted to keep my name in the hat, you know?

"Anyway, I plan to drop by and see if she still know my name or if she give up on me and plucked another out of the hat. Wouldn't surprise me if she had. Be sad to see that. But that be the starting point. If she still in the mood, maybe we settle down, start a restaurant or something. My cooking ain't that bad.

"If she give up on me, maybe I just stay on the ship. Colored folks moved up a little during this war. Might not be such a bad thing— 'specially if people stop shooting at us."

Despite continuing *kamikaze* attacks that rocked the bay as more planes fell from the sky, the *Mintaka* continued offloading supplies and performing other duties during the next week. There were many ships in the bay to provide targets for the enemy. The *Mintaka* escaped further harm. A dozen more ships suffered casualties before we steamed out of the bay, headed for Ulithi. We hoped for a quick end to the battle we left behind.

31

The *Mintaka* steamed toward Ulithi, thirteen hundred miles away from Okinawa. While the battle behind us raged on, I was glad to escape the "hostilities," as Captain Briggs described them. What a strange word that was. I thought of the sailors blown up on the *Allison*. I thought of Gino lying in a pool of blood, of 'Leb risking his own neck to save Wiley, hugging him to keep his life from slipping away. Betty and Sally were still dropping bombs, and Zekes still fell on ships below. Soldiers fought through the mud and blood to take an island in the middle of nowhere that stood between us and Japan. "Hostilities" was a big word, but not big enough to describe those things.

The *Mintaka* was a mess, and we spent most of our time underway trying to put her to rights. Debris from the plane was gathered up and tossed overboard. Weapons were broken down, cleaned, and repaired when necessary. Ammunition was greased and loaded into fresh canisters for the 20 mm cannons. We scoured the decks, chipped paint, scraped at rust, and scrubbed and cleaned everything. It was catch-up maintenance, routine stuff that kept us busy. I didn't mind doing it.

Washing away the blood from the gun mount was the only thing that gave me pause. Chief Turk told Terry and me to grab scrub buckets and mops and clean things up. Terry started to climb the ladder to the gun tub, but I told him I wanted to do this myself. He looked at me like I had a screw loose, said "Suit yourself," and headed over to the starboard gun, pausing at the rail to launch a wad of tobacco juice over the side.

I lugged the bucket and mop and a scrub brush up the ladder. When I got to the top, I looked at the pool of dried blood on the floor of the tub and the red smears where Wiley had rested against the wall. The bloody stains were all that was left from Gino's sacrifice and a silent testimony to what Wiley and 'Leb had done there together.

I dipped the mop in the bucket and swabbed the deck. I scrubbed the smears from the wall, rinsing the mop and the brush in the bucket. I felt their presence as the water turned pink. I could wash away their blood, but what they had done here would stay with me always. I swirled my hands in the water for a moment before I dumped it overboard.

The *Mintaka* was still seaworthy when we arrived at Ulithi five days later, but necessary repairs had to be made before she could return to shuttle duty. The time it would take to get the ship back to fighting trim meant that there was time for the crew to go ashore for recreation. The off-duty time rotated among the crew, usually from 1300 to 1800 hours. This allowed them about four hours on Mogmog, the island where the rec center was located, with the extra time taken up by travel on the LCIs that carried the men ashore.

Mogmog was sixty acres in size, shaped like an old-fashioned three-corner hat, with a palm grove surrounding a swamp in the middle. The tallest part was only thirty feet above the water. The landing area was at the base of the triangle. The eastern corner was a big sandy beach with a swimming area. Further up the eastern side were ball fields and finally, the "beer gardens" that overlooked some coral dunes.

The western end of the island was Officer Country, and so labeled on the map that greeted arriving visitors to Mogmog. Clearly visible from the landing area was Crowley's Tavern, a thatch-roofed hut where officers could hoist a few. Closer to the landing was the Flag Bar, where junior officers could find refuge from sweaty underlings while still keeping their distance from the commanders above them. Off-duty Navy nurses were allowed to circulate between the officers' clubs, but were expected to avoid social encounters with enlisted men.

I wasn't much interested in going ashore without Wiley to keep me company, and guys like Opar and his gang weren't really the kind to pal around with. I asked Cubby if he was interested in going when our time came up in the rotation. I knew he missed 'Leb and thought maybe he wouldn't mind going with me.

Cubby was leaning against the rail on the boat deck when I caught up with him. When I asked if he wanted to go to Mogmog, he said, "Might be something to do." He looked in the direction of the island. "What I hear, that place mostly about the four b's."

I didn't know what Cubby was talking about. "What's the four b's," I asked.

"Bathing, baseball, boxing, and beer—the four b's."

"They got a movie theater and a chapel, too."

"Might be nice to stand on real ground again—almos' forgot what that feel like. We got movies on the ship. Don't need to be in church to send up a prayer. But the beer be the best part. Maybe we could take a look around, have a couple of beers." After a while, he looked at me and smiled a little, "'Leb woulda liked the boxing stuff, though."

When our turn came, we got ration chits for two beers each and lined up at the railing with a dozen or so others. The LCI arrived, already nearly filled with men from nearby ships. We made our way aboard, and the boat took off for the island. It was a warm afternoon, and the water was calm.

It would be nice to escape from duty, if only for a few hours.

When we arrived at the landing, we were greeted by two giant signs at the end of the dock. One was a map of the island, with all the areas clearly marked. Another, nearer sign had just four lines: "Enlisted Men's Area, Beer Garden, Baseball fields, and Bathing Beach"—each line ending with an arrow that pointed to the right.

"Hard to get lost with those directions," Cubby said.

I glanced over at the sign with the map of the island. "Officer Country" was clearly marked, but all the arrows on our sign pointed the other way. "Guess we know where we belong, don't we?"

"Always do," Cubby chuckled.

We made our way along the beach. Hundreds of men in various stages of undress swam and splashed in the water. Some of them weren't wearing anything, but most had shoes on to keep from cutting their feet on the coral.

"No wonder those Navy nurses kep' away from this bunch," Cubby said. "Might be one or two get talked into skinny dipping with an officer after a few drinks, but it be a lot more civilized over there in Officer Country."

"Probably so. Some of these guys look pretty rough."

We rounded the tip of the island and continued up the beach toward the ball fields and the beer garden. A turtle that had crawled up onto the beach was headed back into the surf, and two men were looking at it. One of them was poking it with a stick.

There were a couple of pickup games underway on the baseball fields. We watched for a while, stopping every now and then as we passed by, but we had no stake in the game, and continued on toward the beer garden.

It wasn't much of a garden, just a shady area under tall palm trees midway between the coral dunes and the swamp. It might have been nice if it weren't for the crowded mass of men that outnumbered the trees. They were crouching, sitting, and standing cheek-by-jowl—smoking, swilling beer, blowing off steam in a dozen ways. One guy with a gold earring and an eagle tattoo was reliving his last shore leave in the kind of salty language that would blister tender ears. Several men gathered around a group playing acey-deucey. One of the players swore as the dealer raked in his bet. Another bunch was telling jokes, their laughter erupting behind us as we passed by on our way to the refreshment stand.

The stand itself had a plywood front with signs stating various rules. "CHITS ARE NOT REDEEMABLE FOR CASH" and "THIS ISLAND SECURES AT 1800." Two men stood at a counter behind the plywood, below a rolled-up canvas flap that could be lowered when the stand was closed. Men ahead of us lined up to get beer. A couple guys bought cigars to go with the beer. Two guys who bought soft drinks were immediately cornered by a sailor already several sheets to the wind who traded a wad of cash for their beer rations and disappeared into the trees.

Cubby and I turned in our chits, got our beers, and made our way through the crowd. A couple of mean-looking types gave us the eye, their heads turning to follow us as we passed by.

"Be mixed company, you and me," Cubby said. "Things a little different with 'Leb around. He scared off a lotta trouble. You don't scare nobody. Some folks take offense just seein' us together."

"My daddy told me how some people got mad just seeing him and Waters together. I never did understand that. People are crazy sometimes."

"Them people crazy *all* the time. Yet and still, it don't make sense to hang around till trouble find us. Let's take a walk, see can we find us a place to breathe."

We walked along, rounded the swampy area, and found a spot on the other side, overlooking the camp area for the rec center personnel. We sat under some palm trees, looking out on the bay in the distance, the officers' clubs in full view near the shore below us.

Thin, streaky clouds drifted across the blue sky above us. Hundreds of ships, some on the move, others at anchor, dotted the calm waters of the bay. Music drifted up from Crowley's Tavern on the beach below us. Officers in khaki uniforms with saucer hats and garrison caps crowded together on a few tables set up beneath palm trees outside the thatched hut.

We took in the scene below as we sipped our warm beer.

"Story's the same wherever we go," I said.

"Which story is that?" Cubby asked.

"The one where the little people sit in the dirt and drink warm beer and watch the world go by."

"Can't do much to change all that. Most people born to be who they are. Little people do the world's work, but the big shots hog the credit." Cubby looked at me, hoisting his beer bottle. "Warm beer ain't so bad, Justin. Just a little hard to get used to, maybe."

"You sound like Waters. Always seems to find ways to be happy no matter how bad things get. 'Look for the joy and the misery keep to the shadows,' he says."

"Waters got the right idea. But sometime the joy spread a little thin, be harder to find. I know you worried about Wiley. 'Leb too, I expect, knowing you. They on my mind, too."

Halfway through the second beer, I remembered the earlier night at Ulithi when we watched the Jap bomber get blown out of the sky and the thoughts that crossed my mind just before the attack. I told Cubby about Jack Moon and his tales of how the sea watches you, takes your measure, decides what to think about you.

"Sound like bullshit to me, but a lotta people believe stuff like that." He took a drink, looked out toward the ships in the bay. "Had me a neighbor once, lived down the road a ways. Put in a garden every spring. Dug it all by hand with a shovel, raked it just so, planted his seeds, onion sets, and such. When he was all done, he chopped the head off one of his chickens, caught the blood in an old Mason jar. Took that blood and sprinkled it all around the garden. S'posed to bring a good crop." Cubby took out a rumpled pack of Luckies, shook out a cigarette, and set fire to it.

"All that heebie-jeebie stuff don't make sense to me," he said, snapping the lighter shut. "Never put much faith in that kind of thing." Cubby paused, looked up at me through the smoke and smiled. "Man always had a nice garden, though."

We made our way back to the landing under skies painted red by the setting sun. As we lined up to board the boat that would take us back, I wondered if there was any truth in what old sailors said about red skies at night.

Near the end of June, repairs to the *Mintaka* were completed. Word reached us that the battle for Okinawa was over. We took on fuel, loaded stores, and, finally, got mail. Annie's letter said Wiley's parents had been notified by telegram that he had been wounded, and they were stricken with worry. Eight days after the telegram arrived, his parents received a postcard from a hospital clerk on Guam, saying that Wiley had been taken there by the hospital ship. His wounds were serious, but he was recovering. Recuperation would be slow. Additional information would be provided as long as he remained seriously ill.

Wiley's folks were encouraged by the second notice, but didn't know how badly he was hurt. "Agnes is fit to be tied, too," Annie wrote. "You know how she is. She can't stand sitting around, waiting. Even though there's nothing she can do, she keeps trying to find something. She wrote me a letter when she got the news, said she had told Wiley to keep his head down—even though she knew he wouldn't, said she'd given that boy her heart and he'd damn well better bring it back. She just rambled on and on. That's how upset she is."

Not long after the attack, I had written letters to Annie and Momma. I wanted to let them know I was okay, no matter what they might hear about Wiley. I wanted to tell them what I knew, though I could never be sure what the censors would do with my letter. I had kept my word and never spilled the beans about how Wiley nearly drowned when we were on the beach patrol. I had kept quiet about his embarrassing escapade in the cave at Peleliu, too, though he would have some explaining to do when Agnes saw the Jap soldier's knife.

I was in shock from the recent events, and in spite of the corpsman's reassuring words at the time, I wasn't sure Wiley was going to make it. I wanted them to know that Wiley had done a good thing in knocking down that Zero at the end. They could decide what name to put to it.

There was no word on how 'Leb was or where he'd been taken. I hoped Wiley had been able to thank him for what he'd done.

32

When repairs were completed, the *Mintaka* resumed its duties shuttling troops and cargo between islands. As the weeks passed, the crew fell into the routine that had become so familiar. We steamed to Iwo Jima and Okinawa and Ulithi again, trading battle-worn troops with haggard faces for fresh replacements eager to "see action." Supplies were replenished and offloaded wherever they were needed. We were out of danger, it seemed, though we continued to stand watch and kept our eyes peeled, looking for trouble from above or below.

Letters from home gave me other things to think about as I waited to hear from Wiley. School was out for the summer in Glory, and Momma had left her room over the Rexall. She and Rebecca were back at the ranch with Waters and Hal.

People in Glory were getting used to seeing Momma and Rebecca. Carol and Mike, Annie's parents, had done what they could to make her feel welcome. "Mr. B at the Rexall says your mother's a good worker," Annie wrote. "He stood up for her a couple of times when some snooty ladies made snide remarks. I don't think she'll be invited to join their quilting circle anytime soon, but she's making some progress." So were the townsfolk, I hoped, but I was pretty sure that wasn't what they would call it.

Uncle Hal was waiting on his cows, expecting another round of newborn calves any minute. Waters was tending to his apple trees, looking forward to a better crop than ever. He and Momma and Rebecca had been taking picnic lunches down to the creek. Waters was trying to teach Rebecca how to fish, but she was more interested in throwing sticks in the water and watching them sail downstream. He said he would be glad when I got home and we could do some proper fishing together.

War news was pasted over one whole wall of the cabin now, but he hoped to start pasting peacetime stories soon. Momma said she couldn't wait till the war was over. She was gonna knock out that whole wall when the wartime shortages ended and get Waters to add on a room or two so they could have their own bedrooms.

Waters knew I was worried about Wiley, and he gave me some advice in one of the letters. "You two been through a lot together," he wrote. "You seen and done things I expect changed you some. But even when the world seem to swirl around your head, some things be the same. You and that girl Agnes help Wiley get back to himself when he come home. Love and friendship like anchors in the sea, something to hold onto. Good hearts put to the test come out strong."

I remembered Wiley saying he hoped the war wouldn't change him, how he just wanted to go back to being himself when it was over. I remembered my promise to keep him from going sideways.

One of Annie's letters really took me by surprise. Agnes' parents had finally heard from Jesse, and Annie passed on the full report. Wiley and I had been shocked when he showed up at the fleet rec center on Aore Island and clapped Wiley on the shoulder. I remembered how changed he seemed then and his vague comment about "a plan he was working on" and his "notion" that "things will work out."

Between what she found out from Agnes' parents and later, from Agnes herself, Annie knew about as much as anyone. "It's a wonderful story, Justin," Annie wrote. "I had no idea that Jesse could turn out to be so different than we thought."

As Annie told the story, Jesse had fallen for a nurse when

he was in the hospital in North Africa. She was part of a New Zealand unit treating the wounded. "A Kiwi girl," he calls her, Annie said. "They fell in love, but her unit was eventually sent home, and they got separated. Jesse promised he would find her, and he did."

I remembered that hint of a smile that crossed his face when he told us he had a plan he was working on—like there was a secret only he knew. He had been playing his cards close to the vest, for sure.

I didn't know what to think about it all. It had taken a war to beat that bully into a starry-eyed lover. Swords into plowshares, or something like that. Wiley and I knew Jesse had undergone a change. I guess maybe he had found out who he was.

"Oh, Justin, it's so romantic! He's followed her to the ends of the earth, and he found her! Her name's Elsie Taylor. Her parents have a big ranch on the south island, a 'sheep run,' they call it—thousands of sheep, from what I heard." I remembered all the lamb we'd eaten after we left New Zealand. Apparently we hadn't created a shortage.

Annie wrote that "it took a while for Elsie and Jesse to convince her parents that he wasn't part of the 'American invasion,' as they called it earlier in the war."

Apparently Jesse got her father's blessing when he showed he knew his way around number eight wire, the kind they used for sheep fencing and all kinds of improvised repairs. Jesse told him how American farmers did the same thing with baling wire. "Elsie may have had to go all the way to Africa to find a boy that would make her dad proud, but Jesse apparently passed muster with her folks."

Jesse turned out to have more smarts than everybody gave him credit for. He knew the army wasn't comfortable with people who had problems. Their usual solution was to just transfer them to someplace else and let somebody else deal with it. Jesse managed to travel halfway round the world on Uncle Sam's dime, getting shuffled from place to place as he "got his head on straight," and got himself discharged with a clean bill of health practically on the doorstep of his true love.

"They're getting married," Annie wrote, "but they will stay with Elsie's parents for a while. There's a lot of paperwork involved, rules about Kiwi girls marrying Americans, coming to America—I don't know what all. I can't wait to meet her."

Annie had a kind heart, always looking to see the good side of things. She got angry, sometimes, when mean people did bad things, but she walked on the sunny side of the street most of the time. She had pulled me out of the shadows when I was down and made me believe blue skies were always just ahead. Like Annie, I was glad Jesse had found his Elsie, a precious lamb among all those sheep. Jesse had forged a path through his own corner of hell and come out the other side a different man.

I wondered what Wiley and 'Leb were going through. Wiley's wounds would take time to heal. I hoped he would be good as new when he got home. 'Leb would be fine, I was pretty sure. His leg would heal.

He and Wiley had come a long way together. It was harder to see that chip on 'Leb's shoulder when Wiley was around. 'Leb had put himself in danger to save Wiley, maybe to save us all. But I thought Cubby was right. A lot of things would be different when the war was over—but some things would be the same, too.

It made me think about the people you thought you knew just by looking at them. Jesse was big. He was no good in school, so we put him in a box marked "dumb," and we didn't have to think about him anymore. Maybe we had to grow up a little to see the bigger picture. It was the same thing people did when they looked at Cubby or 'Leb and decided who they were because of the color of their skin. Everybody, it seemed, needed to grow up a little.

We were headed back to Eniwetok when President Truman dropped the bomb on Hiroshima. We heard his speech on the radio. He was telling Japan to "expect a rain of ruin from the air" if they didn't surrender. Three days later, a second bomb blew Nagasaki to bits.

Everyone on board the *Mintaka* had his own reaction to the news. A few doubting Thomases didn't believe it could have happened, said no one had a bomb that could create that much destruction. Most of the men cheered, slapped each other on the back, and wished they could celebrate with a drink in each hand. Some of the fresh faces aboard were downcast, complaining about missing their chance to fight.

Lots of guys, soldiers and sailors alike, got dewy-eyed and sentimental, thinking about loved ones far away, but closer now, as the war seemed to be coming to an end. Some sat on the deck, looking at well-worn photos and re-reading tattered letters from home. Many were writing new letters to post as soon as we arrived.

Opar and his boys made the rounds singing new tunes from his seemingly endless supply of novelty songs. His newest favorites were "You're a Sap, Mister Jap" and one called, "Hey Tojo, Count Yo' Men."

We had hardly dropped anchor in the lagoon at Eniwetok when sirens began to wail on shore and alarms blared on ships throughout the harbor. Everybody rushed to battle stations, but this was no ordinary drill. As we wondered what was going on, Captain Briggs' voice came through the loudspeakers announcing the "cessation of hostilities," as he put it. "Emperor Hirohito has agreed to surrender to the Allies. There will probably be some skirmishes yet and there's work to do before we get home, but the war is over, boys. God bless America."

When the excitement died down, I tracked down Cubby to find out what he thought about the news.

"Be plenty to do before they let us go home. When the party over, somebody always got to clean up."

I had been hoping the war would end for so long, I hadn't really thought about what would happen when it did. "You're probably right about that," I said. "How long d'you think it's gonna be?"

"I dunno. Couple months at least. Big wheels turn pretty slow sometimes." He turned toward me, punched me playfully in the shoulder. "Won't be too bad if they not shooting at us anymore."

Things settled down some after the news sank in. Everyone's spirits were floating high, but Eniwetok wasn't the place for a celebration. That would have to wait till we got somewhere else, some place like Ulithi's Mogmog or maybe Pearl Harbor, where the crew could spread out and blow off steam.

But Cubby and I had more to celebrate before we left Eniwetok. The mail caught up with us, bringing postcards from 'Leb and Wiley.

"Wiley says he's okay, says he's got a mean nurse who makes him walk all over the hospital for exercise. He says his shoulder hurts, but he's off the morphine. Can't get his arm to act like it's supposed to. The doctors say it will take a while for him to recover the use of his arm. Says he wrote to Agnes so she knows not to give up on him."

"Yeah," Cubby said, "'Leb say he know Wiley gonna be all right, 'cause he never heard of somebody about to die bitchin' that much."

"'Leb say his leg is pretty good now, walking with a cane

instead of a crutch like he was at first. He say he gettin' out pretty soon. Probably be sent home in a couple of weeks."

"I wish I could see him again, Cubby. We were just getting to know him. Hate to think the last time I'll ever see him was when they lowered him onto the rescue boat."

"I know what you mean, but that was prob'ly the last we see of 'Leb. He not the kind to make friends easy, no matter what they color. Took a liking to Wiley, though—calling him 'Whitey' and all. He called plenty of white folks by that name, I bet, but meant something different when he called Wiley that."

"Scared the shit out of Wiley the first time he said that. Took a while to see 'Leb was teasing him. But Wiley came around, knows that 'Leb's a good man."

The war was finally over. It was hard to believe after all this time. But I knew Cubby was right. There would a lot of clean up after this party. It would still be a while before we could go home.

Part III

33

Late in October the *Mintaka* touched at Pearl Harbor on her way home. A few thin clouds streaked across the blue sky above us. It was eighty degrees in the islands, still far from the turning leaves and November chill that would soon have folks in Glory looking for warmer coats and stocking woodsheds for the coming winter.

Just as we had seemingly followed the war around the Pacific, arriving after the battles were mostly won, we steamed into Pearl long after the three-day holiday that followed the Japanese surrender. The parades were over and the band had packed up the music. It was back to work for everyone, but hearts were light and eager for the good times ahead.

We refueled, took on supplies, and embarked veteran troops bound for home. Many of the crew, like Wiley and me, who had signed up "for the duration," would be discharged when we arrived in San Francisco. The career sailors, "lifers" and "duds," as some of the men called them, would stay on, joined by new crew members who would take our places as the *Mintaka* continued on to Portland.

The twelve-day voyage from Oahu to the Golden Gate seemed to take forever. The crew would have broken out paddles, if we'd had any, to help push the ship along. The soldiers passed the time swapping stories about where they'd been and where they would go. They complained about the food and the long chow lines. They played cards, compared tattoos, pitched pennies, and rolled dice. Some just stood at the rail, staring out at sea, watching the ship part the waves as we plodded along, the beating heart of the engine belowdecks pushing us homeward at a steady twelve knots.

Long before the *Mintaka* steamed into San Francisco Bay, I had packed my sea bag with all my things, which didn't amount to much, considering how long I'd been away. I put in all the letters I'd saved from Annie and Momma and Waters, the little Christmas tree Annie had sent me, the photos, and a little cloth bag with seashells I had collected for Rebecca. I made room for Wiley's war souvenirs, and carefully packed up his photos and letters along with my own.

When we finally reached the Golden Gate, the weather had turned chilly, and the towers of the bridge were shrouded in morning fog. I was dressed in my Crackerjack uniform with the collar of my peacoat turned up against the cold. I hadn't worn this many clothes in a long time, and it felt strange. As we passed under the bridge, Cubby and I stood at the rail with dozens of others, crewmen as well as the returning soldiers. When we entered the bay, the city spread out around us like welcoming arms, or so it seemed.

The *Mintaka* was "flying the broom" as we steamed toward Treasure Island. Our ship had splashed a Zero, earning a single battle star, and the broom lashed to the antenna mast above the bridge showed we had helped to sweep the enemy from the sea. I wished Wiley could have been with us to see that.

As the tugboat nudged us closer to the dock, the fog cleared, revealing cloudy skies that promised rain. When the mooring lines were fastened to the bollards and the gangway was swung out and lowered, those of us who were leaving shouldered our sea bags, impatient to get going. Captain Briggs and the other officers looked on from the bridge deck as we made our way down the steps. Everyone was in a good mood and most saluted the officers as they passed below them.

The men gathered in groups on the dock, waiting for the buses that would take them into the city. Some lucky ones would be met there by private cars. Others would make their way to the bus depot or the train station for the long journey home.

When the bus from Treasure Island let us off in the city, the men spilled out, full of good cheer, excited to be going home at last. Some parked their sea bags on the curb, gathering in groups of three or four to wish each other good luck. Cubby and I watched as they smiled and shook hands and parted company. Rex Morgan looked my way, gave me a silly salute, and headed off with Opar and his gang. It wasn't long before they all began to drift away, leaving the war behind as the bus pulled away from the curb.

As eager as I was to get home, I wasn't in a hurry to say good-bye to Cubby. I figured I wouldn't be seeing him again, and I felt bad about that.

"Want to get a beer before you shove off?"

Cubby looked at me as he pulled a cigarette pack from his pocket. "Sure, why not?" He snapped open his lighter, lit up, and exhaled, smoke drifting around him. "Probably won't get another chance, will we?"

We headed down the street, walking along under darkening clouds. It wouldn't be long until it started raining. I thought it was probably already raining where I was headed. We turned into the first place we came to, a tiny, narrow hole-in-the-wall called the Crow's Nest. It had a long bar on the left wall and a few small tables lined up on the right. It was early yet, and we were the only customers. An older man was lining up bottles on the back bar. As we entered, he picked up the empty case and disappeared into a back room.

Cubby and I took seats in the middle of the row of stools lined up at the bar. A skinny young guy behind the bar was wiping glasses with a cloth and stacking them in a pyramid on a towel spread out on the counter. His back was to us, but he was watching us in the mirror. He didn't seem in a hurry to take our order.

Still wiping a glass with the cloth, he finally turned and walked our way. He looked at me, and then he looked at Cubby, a kind of chickenshit grin on his face. "We don't serve your kind here. There's a colored bar around the corner."

I pushed off the stool as the older man came in from the back room. "What the hell are you talking about?" I said, my voice rising. Cubby put his hand on my arm.

The older man stepped behind the bar. He was a burly sort, with graying hair cut short and thick forearms, the right one sporting an anchor tattoo. He squinted at the young guy. "What's the matter, Earl?"

"I just told him we don't serve his kind here, boss. That's all."

The "boss" glanced toward us and then turned back to the kid. "What kind is that, Earl?"

He brushed his hand through his short wiry hair. "I don't know what you think you see here. You know what I see? I see two sailors looking to have a drink. Go polish your glasses.

"What'll you have?" he said then, smiling and shaking his head. "Welcome home, boys."

When the boss went to get our beer, Cubby looked at me, nodding his head toward the kid. "Yeah. We home for sure, ain't we?"

I looked over at the boss, who had put Earl in his place. "One brick at a time, Cubby?"

"Maybe…"

We stayed at the bar long enough to drink our beers and then left, heading toward the rest of our lives. I gave Cubby my address in Glory, told him to send me a postcard if he wanted to keep up. He was going to catch a train, see if Gussie was still waiting in Butterspring. I was on my way to the bus station for the long trip home to Glory. I wondered if I would ever see Cubby again.

I had time for a quick meal at the Post House restaurant in the Greyhound station. I ordered a grilled cheese sandwich, which came with a scoop of potato salad on a scrap of lettuce and a big pickle slice. I drank a Coke to wash it down. It reminded me of lunch with Uncle Hal at the Bon Ton in Glory. It was starting to get dark out by the time I finished eating and they announced that my bus was boarding. I tossed my sea bag on my shoulder and sprinted to the buses parked outside. I passed by several before I found the number above the windshield that matched the one on my ticket. The engine was idling, and the driver stood outside, collecting tickets. I handed him mine and swung aboard, moving down the aisle till I found an empty seat and stuffed my sea bag in the rack above.

There were quite a few people on this bus, including a couple of soldiers in uniform sitting in the long back seat. I was still wearing the Crackerjack uniform, and a few people looked up at me as I passed them, and most of them put on a friendly smile. The driver stepped up and took his seat behind the big steering wheel. He pulled the handle and the door flapped shut. There was a hiss when he released the brake, then a little clank and grind when he shifted into gear, and we headed off into the night.

The ride across the Golden Gate Bridge gave the folks on the bus a great view of the city lights and their shimmering rainbows reflected in the water below. North of the city, the lights disappeared, the road narrowed, and the trees grew closer, making up most of what little I could see out the windows. As we rolled on toward morning, I thought about those other dark nights on the beach with Jig at my side. I thought about Jack Moon and Lucy, his daughter. I thought about the boys in our company and wondered if we'd really meet again. I hoped so.

I thought about where I'd been, the places I'd seen, the people I'd known. I thought about Curt and Jesse, about how far away we'd gone and how close we'd come to not finding our way back. I thought about the *Wiilliam B. Allison*, the ship that got torpedoed while it was tied up beside us, and the men who had been killed. I thought about Wiley ripping the wing off that Jap Zero in time to save us all.

After a while it started to rain, and the rhythm of the wipers flapping back and forth and the hiss of the tires on the wet pavement made me relax. I thought about the first bus ride, the one that took me far from Glory. A lot of folks had gathered to see Wiley and me off. His mom and dad were there. Hal stood next to Momma with Waters beside her, holding up Rebecca so she could see. Annie's parents were next to them. Most of the other people we knew were there, too. Even Mr. Phillips had come to wish us luck.

Agnes had kissed Wiley like she knew what she was doing, told him she'd cry for him when he came home, and told him to get on the bus. Annie and Momma were teary, but trying to hold it together. Annie gave me a kiss to remember and hugged me for a long time before she would let me go. My cheek was wet from her tears when she pulled away and smiled, sniffing, "I love you, Justin. Be careful always."

When we finally got on the bus, we ran to the back, knelt on the back seat, and each of us looked out our half of the split rear window and waved as the people we loved waved back and grew smaller until the bus turned and they were gone.

I wasn't looking out the back window now. The view ahead was all I could think of. It was going to be a long ride, and the excitement had made me tired. I dozed as we rolled along, jerking awake once in a while, when the road was rough or the bus came to a stop.

I woke up suddenly, realizing that the bus had stopped. This bus was on a milk run, stopping in little towns that weren't quite worthy of the name, most of them not more than a wide spot in the road, but we seemed to be stopped in the middle of nowhere. It was light out, but I couldn't see any sign of life outside my window. Other people were mumbling to each other and craning their necks to see what was going on.

The bus driver got out of his seat, turned to face the passengers. "Sorry, folks, but the road up ahead is flooded. All this rain and the creek is out of its banks—happens once or twice a year. It's too deep to drive through—we'll have to turn back."

There was a lot of grumbling and complaining from the passengers. I couldn't believe it. I had come all this way, only to have to turn around. I wasn't having any of that. I got up, walked to the front of the bus, and looked through the windshield. The road ahead made a turn, and the creek beside it had gone out of its banks, covering about a hundred feet or so of the road. There was a car stopped on the other side, the driver standing beside it, looking at the water, too.

The bus driver looked at me, frowned, and shook his head. "Sorry, son. I can tell you want to get home, but we're going to have to go back."

I looked at the flooded road ahead. "Just give me a minute, sir. I'm no stranger to water. The water knows who I am." I made my way down the aisle, grabbed my sea bag and carried it back to the front of the bus. "Open the door for me, please."

"But you can't..."

"Oh, yes I can—just open the door!"

I was going home. A little water was the only thing in the way, and it wasn't going to stop me. I stripped down to my skivvies, stuffed my uniform in my sea bag, and tied my shoes together and hung them around my neck. I studied the road and the water for a minute or two. The creek ran to the left of the road, and the road curved to the left, following the creek. The turn was banked on the outside and the right side of the road was a little higher than the left. The current looked pretty swift on the left side. The water was deeper there. I tossed my sea bag on my shoulder and headed out into the stream. I must have looked a sight, but I didn't care —I was going home, come hell or high water, as they say.

I waded in, taking my time, trying to judge the current and get a feel for the pavement beneath my feet, balancing the bag on my shoulder. The water on the right side was shallower, I hoped, and I headed to that side of the road. The current was a lot weaker on that side, too. When I was about halfway and it was only up to my armpits, I knew I could make it without having to swim and get my things soaked. I kept on and finally felt the water getting shallower. The cold air hit my wet skin, my dog tags and Momma's St. Christopher medal, and I felt myself shivering. I finally sloshed through the shallows and made it to the pavement. I set my things down and looked back at the bus. The folks on the bus were all looking out the windows and waving at me. The bus driver was standing outside with the two soldiers and a few others who whistled and cheered. I waved back at them.

I picked up my gear and turned to head up the road. The driver who had been stopped on the other side stood there, holding out a blanket. "Need a ride, son?"

34

His name was Homer Rakestraw. He was in the wholesale hardware business, on his way to the city for a sales convention until the flooded road brought his trip to a halt. His car was a mud-spattered 1940 Ford sedan he'd been lucky enough to buy just before the war.

"Don't look so new anymore—put a lotta miles on this here puddle-jumper in my line of work—but she cleans up pretty good. Still runs like a top, too. Nice car—deluxe model. Didn't come with water wings, though."

I laughed at his jokes, trying to be polite. It was nice of him to give me a ride and a chance to dry out from my trip across the river. I didn't have much to say, but Homer never ran out of things to talk about. He had that "gift of gab" people talk about. If talk were religion, he'd be at least a deacon in the church. Must come in handy when you're trying to sell hardware to folks like he did.

Homer turned the car around, cranked up the heater so I could dry out, and headed back the way he'd come. After a few miles, we came to a wide spot in the road with a gas station and a café beside it. Homer pulled over. "You been on that bus all night. Your stomach probably thinks your throat's cut by now. Want to get some breakfast? Maybe a cup of coffee to warm you up? Place is just a greasy spoon like most others along the road, but breakfast is hard to mess up."

I didn't realize it till Homer brought it up, but I was really hungry. That Post House cheese sandwich was a long time ago. I told Homer it sounded great, but I'd have to throw some clothes on first. He headed into the café while I put my uniform back on, changing into some dry skivvies and socks from my sea bag first. When I was dressed, I sat on the seat with the car door open and laced up my shoes. I threw on my peacoat and headed into the café.

The price of breakfast and a hot cup of coffee was listening to Homer ramble on. He didn't have any trouble talking and eating at the same time, which kept me from having to say much at all. Homer asked me where I'd been during the war, and I told him enough to keep him from asking more questions, but he didn't seem too inquisitive. He was a "forward-thinking man," he said. "It don't pay to spend all your time looking back. Not with a bright future just around the corner."

Homer shared bits of his life story while he sprinkled Tabasco sauce on his eggs and mixed it all together with his hash browns. "My wife's a teacher up north," he said, pointing his fork toward the highway. "Fourth graders—she likes them best. Says they're old enough to wipe their own noses. Most of them able to sit still long enough to read a story."

He and his wife had two grown kids named Odie and Penny. "Never knew anyone else liked books as much as that woman. Told me if she was married to a man named Homer, those would be good names for his children." He looked over at me with a little grin on his face. "Comes from a story she knows. Told me all about it, but I'm not much for reading. I like to talk, though. By now you probably figured that out on your own."

Odie had gone off to the war like so many, but Homer expected him home soon. Homer couldn't wait for all the boys to get home, get "married up," and start making babies. Those new families were going to need new homes, and a building boom was sure to be good for the hardware business.

Homer and I parted company after breakfast. He was

going to stick around, maybe sleep in the car for a while, hoping the water would go down enough to get across the road. He said he hated to turn back if there was still a chance he could make it to the city.

I hoisted my sea bag and headed up the road. Water ran in the ditch beside the muddy highway, but the rain had stopped and there were patches of blue sky overhead. A rainbow stretched between the hills in the distance.

There was no traffic going my way since the road was blocked behind me. Once in a while a car came down the road toward me, tires hissing on the wet pavement, the driver looking over at me as he passed. One fellow nodded at me and waved when he drove by. I trudged along, shifting my load from one shoulder to the other, wishing like Homer that the water would go down and let some cars through so I could catch a ride.

The bus that had taken us away from Glory wouldn't bring me home. That had been a special, rounding up guys like Wiley and me who had joined up from little towns scattered across the northern parts of the state. The bus that was afraid to get its feet wet would have taken me up Highway 101, letting me off at Alton, a place where Highway 36 headed east along the Van Duzen River. It was a long way from there to Glory, and the bus would have saved me a lot of steps. I was on my own, but all the points on my compass led to home—and Annie.

Now and then I passed a country road leading off the highway, usually just a muddy track that probably led to somebody's ranch. One or two of those roads had cattle guards stretched across them. Late in the afternoon a fellow came up behind me, going my way. He was driving an old Model AA flatbed stacked high with firewood. A scruffy-looking dog with a gray muzzle swayed on top of the load.

When the truck pulled up beside me, it skidded to a stop, and the dog pitched forward, but recovered its balance quickly. Clearly, it wasn't his first time. I wasn't going to pass up a ride, and I hoisted my sea bag and walked over to the truck, climbing up on the running board to get a look at the driver.

The window was down, and an old guy squinted across the cab at me, asking me where I was headed. The inside of the cab smelled like the dog didn't always ride in back.

"Anywhere north of here. I'm headed for Glory."

The old guy chuckled like I'd just made a joke.

"We all go dere sooner or later. Climb in."

He was older than Uncle Hal, but still going strong if he'd split and loaded all that firewood by himself. He had a foul-smelling cigar stub clamped in the corner of his mouth, but it didn't appear to be lit, which was fine with me, especially after I noticed the sticks of dynamite poking out of the wooden box on the floor between us.

"Been blastin'-a stumps all day," he said when he saw me looking at the box. "Gotta speak-a louder for me to hear."

I tried again to explain where I was headed, but I might as well have been talking to the dog.

"Town-a called Glory? Never heard of it."

He threw the truck in gear, let out the clutch, and headed back onto the highway, the transmission protesting with a high-pitched whine when he shifted into second gear and mashed on the gas pedal.

As we bounced along, he told me about himself. His name was Matteo, but folks just called him Matt. He told me he was Italian, "here from da old country twenty-five years now." He had an accent still, but I didn't have any trouble understanding him. He talked really loud, loud enough to be heard over the noisy truck engine. If he spent much time blasting stumps, the noisy engine probably had nothing to do with how loud he talked. When he told me he'd never heard of Glory, I told him I wasn't surprised—most people hadn't. I settled back in the seat as we rolled along the highway.

Matt was headed toward Carlotta, a little place up Highway 36 that would take me a little further in the right direction. There was a hotel there that bought his firewood.

"I'm-a tell-a you, was nice-a place once. T'ree stories tall. Big-a fireplace on each end. Fancy people useta go in summer, ya know. But kinda slow in da hard times. New owners now, nice-a Italian family. Dey fix up, now da war over. People come back, be nice-a place again."

The hotel lived up to Matt's description. It was a big three-story affair with dormer windows on the roof and a wide covered porch on three sides. It was kind of in the middle of nowhere, but close to the river, and the countryside was probably pretty in the summer when the trees put on new clothes and the river washed clear over gravel beds with sandy spots beside them for swimmers and couples with picnic hampers. I could see how "fancy people" might like to "rough it" at a country inn. Something like life on the ranch, but they would go home to nice houses in their fancy cars while I would still be shoveling cow flop and pulling weeds in Hal's garden. Now, the alders and the willows along the river were bare, and the water was muddy and high. Redwood trees stood tall and dark on the hill behind the hotel. More grew on the distant hills further along the road.

Matt pulled his truck in behind the hotel, and I helped him unload and stack the firewood by the little kitchen annex out back. By the time we were done, it was nearly dark. Mr. Mazzeuchi, the owner, was a short, round man with a mop of curly black hair going gray around the edges. He couldn't help but notice my uniform right away when we arrived and offered to let me stay the night when he heard where I was headed. The kindness of strangers always surprised me when I hadn't done anything to earn it. I knew there were lots of guys making their way home after the war, and I was sure wearing the uniform helped, but it was nice to find helping hands when you needed them. I wondered if people would have been so kind if Cubby had been with me.

After we unloaded the firewood and stacked it beside the kitchen building, Mr. M. paid Matt for the wood and invited us into the kitchen. He poured us each a glass of homemade Chianti, and his wife set a plate of steaming ravioli in front of us. In the center of the table she put a basket with puffy, fresh-baked rolls she called pane rosetta. It was the best meal I'd tasted in ages.

Matt left for home when we finished eating, the dog riding inside the cab for the return trip. I thanked him for bringing me this far and waved as he disappeared down the road. Mr. M. gave me a place to stay and a chance to clean up, which I really appreciated.   Stacking firewood was a small price to pay. The next morning, after a big country breakfast and a round of thank yous and handshakes, I was on my way again.

The skies were clear. The weather seemed to be improving. I hoped the rain was over for now. Wisps of fog clung to the trees along the river. It was still chilly, but I didn't mind. A pair of mallards flew low over the water, beating their wings hard as they headed upriver. They flew in a straight line, like they knew where they're going and were in a hurry to get there. Watching them made me wish I could fly, too. In the distance an osprey wheeled above its nest in a burned-out redwood snag.

I had plenty of time to think as I walked along the road beside the river, and my mind wandered, crowded with all kinds of thoughts. I remembered a picnic beside another river with Momma and Daddy when I was little. Like Rebecca, I had tossed sticks and bits of bark into the water and watched them bob along on the current until they drifted out of sight. I remembered asking Momma where all the water went and her telling me how it went to the sea.

"'All the rivers run into the sea,' the Bible says, 'yet the sea is not full'." Momma had looked down at me, tousling my hair playfully. "Unto the place from whence the rivers come, thither they return again.'" I was too little then to understand all that. I hadn't yet seen the ocean. Cooper's Gulch, the logging camp where we lived, was closer to the coast than Glory, but still far from it.

But the little creek that ran along the Glory Road had made its way to the sea and taken me with it, and I was headed home now, going back upstream to the place "from whence the rivers come." The rivers or creeks that ran alongside the roads all seemed to grow smaller and smaller the further I went.

When I was alone on the ranch with just Waters and Uncle Hal for company, I used to go down below the barn and sit on that big rock by the creek and think things over, trying to sort out my troubles. Momma told me, "Some say they hear the voice of God in the sound the water makes when it goes tumblin' over the rocks. I don't know about all that," she said. "'Tis a soothin' sound, though." I had watched the water swirl around that rock, listening to the slurp and gurgle it made on its way to the sea. I don't know what God sounds like, but the sound of the water was always soothing.

Once in a while cars came along, going my way. Some just passed me by, but quite a few stopped to ask if I needed a lift. Most of the drivers weren't going far, some to a neighbor's ranch a ways up the road, some going a little further to the store or post office in some little spot along the road big enough to have a name. Most of those places were so small they made Glory seem big by comparison. Every once in a while I passed a sign pointing to a side road that led to some even smaller place with a name like Parson's Meadow or Stony Fork.

I got my first glimpse of Glory late that afternoon. My last ride had let me out when the driver turned off on one of those side roads from the highway. The road to Glory was only a few miles ahead, and I shouldered my bag, happy to be so close. A covey of quail scurried alongside the road ahead of me, whirring into flight when I got too near them. When the road turned off, it curved away from the highway, climbing a long hill through a forest of oak groves, big madrones with red, peeling bark, pine trees, and sharp-smelling pepperwoods. A gray squirrel leaped from branch to branch in a tree overhead, scolding me with his noisy chatter. Acorns scattered along the road crunched underfoot as I walked. A camp-robber jay with his black topknot landed in a nearby manzanita bush, adding his raucous insults. A woodpecker hammered in an oak tree below the road. It was the countryside I knew, its familiar sounds and smells in the air around me. I hoped I never saw another palm tree again.

When I crested the hill, I looked out over the valley below. The town lay before me, a picture postcard of home that I had carried with me in memory for so long. I dropped my sea bag and sat on a log beside the road, just taking it all in. I couldn't help wiping away a tear. It had been so long.

I had been to the other side of the earth, but this part of the world was mine, all the people I loved in one place, the future unrolling before me like the magic carpet in one of Mr. Phillips' stories. I remembered how nervous I'd been when Momma first came home, wondering how everything would turn out. I felt the same way now. I couldn't wait to read the rest of the story, but I was a little scared about turning the page.

35

The white clouds took on a rosy color as I sat looking at the town spread out below.   Everything looked newly washed by the recent storm, and the late afternoon sun cast a warm glow on the streets and houses in Glory. As I was sitting there, I heard a car coming up the hill behind me, its gears whining as it climbed the hill. When it came over the rise, I turned to look. It was a Chevy pickup, a faded green with black fenders, a '38 or '39 model I guessed from the look of its long narrow grille and the headlights on each side, above the fenders.

When the truck got nearer, it slowed, then came to a stop. I recognized the Shell emblem on the door and the words, "Al's Shell Service" painted below it. It was Al himself behind the wheel. He rolled down the window and looked me over. He had a grease-stained brimless cap on his head, the quilted kind mechanics wear, and a white three-day stubble on his chin. He leaned out the window and squinted at me with sharp blue eyes. One of the galluses on his overalls was missing its buckle and the bib hung down on that side.

"Hey, Justin," he said evenly.

Al was not on my list of favorite folks. When I drove the Model A to school every day, I stopped at his station to buy gas like everyone else in town. Al hardly ever made conservation with anyone I knew. Most of his sentences only had two or three words. "He'p you?" when you drove in beside the pumps and "Be eighty cents" when he finished pumping the gas and put the cap back on the tank. The only time he ever said anything more to me was after Momma came back home and brought Rebecca with her. When I stopped for gas one day, Al had called me in to his little office to tell me how he thought Momma didn't need to do what she'd done, how she should've left that "tar baby" wherever she had been keeping herself. We'd had words over that, and I'd told him off pretty good. Whenever I stopped for gas after that, Al'd had even less to say to me. I looked at him staring at me now.

"Get in the truck, son." A little hint of a smile appeared on his face. "Don't worry—I won't bite."

I was tired and didn't want to turn down a lift that would take me the rest of the way, but I couldn't quite shake the memory of our last conversation.

"Be dark soon—you gonna sit here all night? The war's over, you know."

I sensed a change when he said that about the war being over. Everybody knew the war was over, but I think he was telling me something else. I picked myself up, tossed my bag into the back of the truck and climbed into the cab.

We bounced along in Al's truck for a while, neither of us saying anything. I looked out the window, taking in the view as we rolled toward town. "War's changed a lot of things, seems like," Al said finally. "Town's pretty much the same. It's the people... been through a lot, you know. Miz Spencer lost her son. That Wheelock boy, Jesse, got hurt. Your friend Wiley, too."

Al took his eyes off the road for a second, glanced over at me. "Seems like the war brought the home folks closer together. Had something bigger than themselves to think about for a change."

I didn't know what to say, so I just rode along. I was afraid Al's thoughts might take a different turn, and I wasn't going to help him go there.

"You boys showed what you're made of, that's for sure," he said. "But the folks in Glory showed they had some grit, too. Made do—even with all the shortages and rationing. They gathered scrap, gave blood, had bond drives—did whatever they could to help."

We pulled into town, rolled up to the stop sign. There were streetlights on in Glory now. I looked down the street to Wiley's house, saw a light shining on the porch. I glanced over toward the school and the sheriff's office across the street. Al crossed the intersection, headed up the street between the stores, pulled into his station between the pumps and the office.

"Speaking of grit, your momma's got some sand in her craw for sure."

Here it comes, I thought, looking across the cab at him.

"I watched your momma that first day she brought the little girl to school. She and your girlfriend walking down the street while ever'body stared at 'em. Held her head up like it was an ever'day thing. Didn't pay no mind even when the other ladies wouldn't give 'em the time of day. I just leaned on the gas pump there, watching it all play out. Made me think what it was like for her."

Well, *that* wasn't what I expected. I just looked at him, nodded my head. I reached for the door handle to let myself out, but Al wasn't finished.

"I know I said some mean things to you before. You're prob'ly still mad at me about that. But I was wrong. I don't approve of what your mother did, but I can't put her sins on that little girl. I seen that fella Waters and your momma doing good things to help out just like ever'body else—pulled off that scrap metal drive all by themselves. Changed my thinking some, is all I'm saying."

"Okay, Al," I said. "Thanks for the ride." I got out then, retrieved my bag from the back, and headed down the street, thinking, *one brick at a time*, but I was pretty sure Al's brick needed to stay in the oven a little longer.

I headed down the street to Sadler's Market. The first thing I wanted to do was to see Annie. My heart raced a little, thinking about seeing her again. When I got to the store, the CLOSED sign hung crookedly in the window and the inside was dark, except for a little light above the counter. I stepped back and looked at the apartment windows above the store. They were dark, too. I tried the door to the stairway that led up to the apartment, but it was locked.

I turned around, looking up and down the street. Across the street the feed store and the Rexall were dark, as well. But down the block past the market, light poured out from the Bon Ton café. I walked down the street, curious about what was going on. When I peered through the front window, I saw several people moving about inside. They were moving the tables around, setting up for something. I saw Billie, the waitress, and Curt's mother, Mrs. Spencer. Carol Sadler, Annie's mom, was bustling about with the others. Wiley's mother was there, too, setting out plates of baked goods on a table in the corner. As I watched, the door to the back room swung open and Annie came in.

This was not at all the way I imagined it would be when I saw Annie again for the first time. I didn't exactly expect the angels to sigh as I swept her into my arms, but it wasn't like this—with a crowd looking on. I thought I'd walk into the market, setting off the little bell over the door. She'd look up from what she was doing, see me in the doorway, and drop whatever she was doing to rush up and put her arms around me.

I just stood there, watching her move easily among the other women. We had been just children, Annie and me, and I had left that girl behind. She was still small and dark and pretty, but she wasn't a girl anymore. We had put that all behind us when the war came. I wondered how different I would seem to her. I hoped she could still see the boy she knew so long ago when she looked into my eyes again.

When Annie went back to the storeroom, I tossed my bag onto my shoulder and rushed down to the end of the building and around behind it to the little alley that ran behind the stores. There was a light over the back door of the Bon Ton. The screen door was closed, but the inside door was open. Annie came in from the dining room and turned on the light. The screen door creaked as I pulled it open. She turned at the sound and saw me standing there. I dropped my bag on the floor as the screen door slammed against it.

We stood there for a long moment, just looking into each other's eyes. A tear ran down her cheek. "Oh, Justin," she said, and threw her arms around me. Who needs angels?

After some of the best kissing ever, we went out back and sat on a little bench outside. There was a lot more hugging and kissing, but when we finally came up for air, Annie told me what was going on. Wiley had made it home about three weeks ago. He was still recovering from the shrapnel wound to his shoulder. He didn't yet have full use of his left arm, but was expected to regain most of it over time. He was mostly mended, but that didn't keep his mother from smothering him.

"She hardly let him out of her sight," Annie said. "Waited on him hand and foot—even when he complained that he could do things for himself."

Agnes had come home last week, discharged from the Marines when the war ended. "Wiley seemed awfully quiet at first, but he really perked up when Agnes showed up at his door. She got him out of the house, and they walked all over town. Wiley's not quite ready to go riding yet, but they went out to the barn to check on Boots, saw how his daddy took good care of his horse while he was gone.

"Agnes told me Wiley's mom thought they were spending

too much time with that horse, but I have an idea Boots wasn't getting all the attention when they were in the barn. I think Wiley's mother knows what those two are up to. Agnes can't wait till they can get away by themselves."

Just then, the screen door spring creaked, and Carol, Annie's mom, stuck her head outside, looking around. "Annie, are you out here?"

"Wait till you see the surprise Agnes brought Wiley," Annie whispered, then turned toward the door. "I'm over here, Mom. Look who's here."

Carol looked toward the bench where we were sitting, squinting against the harsh light above the door. "Justin! Is it really you?"

We stood up and she stepped over toward us, reaching out to me. "Give me a hug, son. I can't tell you how glad I am to see you." She grabbed me and squeezed for all she was worth. "So handsome in that uniform, isn't he, Annie? And all in one piece, too." She finally let me go then, saying to Annie, "I just came outside to see where you had gotten to. You two stay here, spend a little time together before the party gets started."

As the screen door banged shut, I looked at Annie. "What party? " I asked.

"I'm sorry—seeing you standing in the door sort of took my breath away, I guess." She looked into my eyes, smiling. "Still feel like that," she said and kissed me again.

"The party was Agnes' idea. It's for Wiley—get him out of the house, get him back on his feet, let him know everybody's happy he's home. It's for Agnes, too, of course. Isn't it just like her to throw herself a party? Everybody's invited. Daddy drove out to your place to pick up your family. They should be here soon."

I didn't know what to say. It wasn't following the script I had written, but things were turning out just fine so far.

Annie put her arm in mine and steered me around to the street. "Let's go out front. Agnes and Wiley should be coming soon. "

We walked around to the front of the building. Annie leaned her head against my shoulder as we walked a little ways down the block. We hadn't gone very far when I saw Wiley and Agnes turn the corner and start up the street toward us. When they passed under the street light, I could see them clearly. I thought Wiley looked pretty good, considering what he'd been through. It was the first time I had seen him in civilian clothes since we left Glory. He had on a flannel shirt and black Ben Davis jeans that looked brand new. His left shoulder drooped a little, and Agnes had his good arm in hers, but he was walking along just fine.

They were wrapped up in themselves and hadn't seen us yet. They had only gone a little ways when Wiley stopped abruptly. He turned, looking behind him, and whistled. In a few seconds, a dog rounded the corner, and trotted up to Wiley, sitting at his feet. It was a big black and brown German shepherd.

I looked at Annie. She smiled, looking back at them as Wiley reached down to pet the dog. "That's Agnes' big surprise. She knew how much that dog meant to Wiley. She found him and brought him home with her."

I remembered how hard it had been for Wiley to give up Doc when they disbanded the beach patrol. That dog had saved his life, kept him from drowning when the boat capsized, tossing Wiley and the others overboard. It looked like Agnes was a lifesaver, too. Wiley would be all right.

"How'd she find out where Doc was? They just pulled us off the beach. We never heard anything more about the dogs."

"You know how smart Agnes is. That girl doesn't miss

a trick. She knew the military keeps records on everything. The dogs were donated to the service, given numbers, and their assignments documented. When the beach patrol didn't need them anymore, they were sent back to their original owners."

"She is smart, have to give her that. Used to annoy me sometimes when we were in school. But she must really love Wiley to go to all that trouble."

"Agnes wouldn't let it go," Annie said. "She did some digging, found out that some of the dogs had been sold, but managed to find Doc's people and get hold of them. When she told them about Wiley and how attached he'd been to the dog, they let her take him."

Annie gave me a questioning look. "You know that dog saved his life, don't you?"

"What do you mean?"

"When Wiley saw Doc for the first time, Agnes told me he just broke down and cried, told her the whole story about the men that drowned and how Doc had pulled him ashore. He was embarrassed, afraid she'd be mad at him, somehow. She said he made you promise not to tell anyone about it."

"You mad at me about that?"

"No, silly. You were just keeping a promise to a friend." She turned her head, looked into my eyes. "I like people who keep their promises."

I thought about all the places we'd been and some of the things we'd seen. I didn't feel much like talking about a lot of it. I wondered what Wiley'd had to say about shooting down that plane.

We walked a little further. When we got closer to them, Doc's ears perked up, alert, and Wiley looked to see what had caught his attention, noticing Annie and me for the first time. Doc's nose started twitching, catching our scent as we got closer. He looked at me, made a soft whining sound, then laid down and started scooching toward me on all fours.

"Remember Doc?" Wiley said. "Looks like he remembers you."

"I'm glad to see you too, kiddo," I said, shaking my head. We'd seen a lot of each other in the last two years, for sure, but I guess I came after Agnes and the dog now. I would have punched him in the shoulder, but it didn't seem like a good idea. "How are you, Agnes? I hear you've been taking good care of this guy."

We all hugged and chatted for a while. Doc took it all in, sitting at Wiley's feet, his tongue lolling, bright eyes sparkling. After a while, we headed back up the street to the Bon Ton.

Just as we reached the door of the café, a car came down the street toward us. It made a U-turn in the middle of the block, its headlights sweeping the street in front of us, and nosed in to the curb in front of the Bon Ton. Annie's dad waved out the window and tapped the horn as the car bumped against the curb and the doors flew open.

36

Annie's father stood, smiling, beside the car, taking in the scene as Momma rushed toward me, hugging the life out of me. Over her shoulder, I watched as Waters helped Uncle Hal out of the car and scooped Rebecca up in his arms.

"You're home at last," she said, pushing away to look at me, but still holding on tight. "'Tis a grand surprise, for sure. I'm so glad to see you safe and sound."

"I just got here a little while ago. Didn't know there was a party till I saw the lights on at the Bon Ton."

Waters stepped up beside Momma. Rebecca was decked out in a pretty pale blue dress, her hair tied back with a matching blue ribbon. She looked at me with an impish smile, then snatched my hat and plopped it on her own head. Waters put her down then, and she danced around on the sidewalk, holding my hat with both hands to keep it from falling off.

Waters put his strong arms around me then in a firm but gentle hug. "Welcome home, son." A lot of older people who didn't know me called me "son" when they talked to me, but when Waters said it, the difference wasn't lost on me.

Uncle Hal negotiated the curb with the help of his cane. He extended his arm, and we shook hands. He looked a little frail, but his grip was still strong. He held me in his gaze for a long moment. "Good to see you home, Justin." He nodded toward the others gathered on the sidewalk. "We all missed you."

We stood there on the sidewalk for a while, everybody gathered around Annie and me till all the attention kind of overwhelmed me. Several people came down the street, drifting toward the Bon Ton. I recognized Mr. McManus from the feed store and Mr. Babcock who owned the drugstore. I didn't want to pee on Wiley's party. Agnes had planned this for him, not me.

"Why don't you all go inside and get the party started?" I said. "Annie and I'll join you in a little while."

Momma corralled Rebecca, took her by the hand, and made her way to the door. Mr. Sadler walked along with Hal. Waters held back for a moment, looking at me and Annie.

"Been a long time coming, this day. And you two probably got a lot of catching up to do. Mr. Sadler say Wiley need a little help getting back on his feet. That girl Agnes on the right track, planned all this to get him back to himself. You go in there and prop him up, too."

I looked at Annie and then at Waters. "We don't want to take anything away from Wiley and Agnes. He'll come around."

"He's much better than when he first came home," Annie said. "Agnes is seeing to it."

"That girl know how to get things done for sure. Just look what she done about the dog."

We stood by the parked cars, out of the reach of the streetlights, watching as friends and neighbors drifted in to the Bon Ton. When no one came along for a while, we walked past the window of the café and looked in. Agnes still had a death grip on Wiley's good arm, and people were coming up to them, chatting and smiling. Agnes let go of Wiley long enough for a handshake or a gentle hug from a neighbor, and Wiley smiled, blushing once in a while from all the attention.

Annie and I went around to the back of the building again and went in the back door, hoping to slip in quietly without drawing the attention away from the crowd. We paused in the storeroom for another kiss and then went into the dining room.

We stood in the doorway for a moment, taking it all in. I wished I'd had time to change into some civvies, but it was too late for that. Mrs. Spencer was setting out some treats at a table by the door, and she spotted me in my uniform right away. She gave me a startled look that turned into a smile. She set down the tray she was carrying and stepped closer to Annie and me.

"Justin," she said. "You came home, too. I'm so glad to see you." She got a little teary, and I reached out to put my arms around her.

"Glad to see you, too, Mrs. Spencer. We're all so sorry about Curt. Wiley and I were in New Zealand when we got the news. It was a shock, for sure. I know how important he was to you."

She wilted a little in my arms, then pulled herself together, sniffing. "Thank you, Justin. Curt was gone a long time before he..." She wiped away a tear. "It's so hard knowing he's never coming home. People have been so nice, especially your momma. I'm glad you're home safe."

Mr. Phillips came in the front door, walked around the counter by the cash register, and looked around the dining room at the crowd. When he saw Wiley with Agnes, he walked over toward them. Doc Abernathy, the vet who had set Hal's broken leg, was chatting with Wiley and Agnes. Doc's wife, a sturdy, handsome woman, stood beside him, her arm looped through his. Mr. Phillips waited his turn to chat, looking down at Rebecca, who was still dancing around wearing my hat. He bent down to talk to her, pointing to the hat. He must have asked her where she got it, because she looked away from him, glanced around the room, and pointed in my direction.

Mr. Phillips looked across the room. When he spotted Annie and me, he headed our way, weaving between the tables, a big smile on his face. We shook hands. He pushed his glasses up on his nose and looked me up and down. "Good to see you home at last, Justin. All the students from my first year in Glory—a reunion of sorts, don't you think?"

"Sort of. The older ones, at least. Except for Jesse and Curt."

"Yes, of course. Curt's loss is a terrible blow, hit his mother hard, but I think you know what I meant. Agnes and Wiley together—you and Annie, too. Jesse had a rough time, from what I've heard, but Annie told me he's come out all right in the end—found someone to hold onto."

"Makes us the lucky ones, I guess," I said, looking into Annie's eyes. 'Just seems like a big waste, people all over the world bent on killing people they don't even know. Where's the glory in that?"

"Someone once said—Chesterton, I think—that 'a soldier fights not because he hates what is in front of him, but because he loves what is behind him.' Battles may make some men heroes, Justin, but you'll find your glory in the people around you. Think about that, won't you?"

Mr. Phillips left us then, making his way back across the room to speak with Wiley and Agnes.

Annie and I slipped into the room, gathered a few refreshments, and headed toward a table near the kitchen, where Momma and Waters sat with Rebecca. Billie came over to the table to have a word with Momma.

"Could you help me for a minute, Molly? I need to set out some more plates, more of those cookies you and Carol made. I shoulda known how popular they'd be."

Momma laughed. "Of course. I'm happy to help." She looked to see where Rebecca had wandered. "Can you mind Rebecca for a minute, Annie? Keep her from gettin' into things?"

Annie nodded, getting up and following Rebecca as she

pranced over to the refreshment tables.

I looked at Waters then, really looked at him for the first time. "How are things going?" I asked.

He looked at me for a moment, then smiled. "Well, it ain't all sweetness and light, exactly." His eyes swept across the room before he looked my way again. "These folks come around some, but plenty others not so much."

I watched Annie and Rebecca cross the room. They had stopped to talk to Doc and his wife. Annie held Rebecca's hand in hers. Rebecca had a big cookie in her other hand. Mrs. Abernathy leaned down to talk to Rebecca, smiling as Rebecca held up her prize.

"That girl could charm a snake out of his skin," Waters said, chuckling. "Don't know what'll happen when the cute wear off, but she got a way with folks, seem like."

I figured Rebecca's charm wouldn't work on everyone. It was hard to change minds once they were made up. Most of those gathered at the Bon Ton for Wiley were our friends, but even so, one or two gave Rebecca a frowny look as she stood holding Annie's hand.

I looked over at Wiley, standing with Agnes. He seemed a little embarrassed by all the fuss, but he was doing okay, I thought. I still wondered what all he'd told Agnes.

Waters followed my gaze. "Got some spark, that girl— and a heart of gold to go with it. Thinks her fella's a hero. Annie tol' me Wiley been pretty quiet since he come home. Folks ask him how he got hurt, he just say he forgot to duck."

Agnes didn't seem the type for hero worship, but it was pretty obvious she was in love with Wiley. I thought about 'Leb and his friend Toots, the one we met digging graves on Espiritu Santo. Mostly I thought they just showed they were brave when they had to be. Wiley had done the same. They had paid a price, but survived. Others hadn't been so lucky.

"Most folks be somebody's hero," Waters said, "the ones

who stand up for them when they need it."

I thought about what Waters said. I was just bothered by the word "hero," I guessed. It made me think of people in storybooks and legends. Courage under pressure might be the measure of a man. If so, they had all been tested and found worthy. In many ways, so had Waters. Mr. Phillips had said we'd find glory in the people around us. I knew he had the right idea.

37

It was hard to put everything that happened behind me. It was hard for others, too, I thought. It was easier to see where we'd been than to know what was ahead. The hardships of the Depression and the war had brought folks together in ways later generations would have no way of understanding. Neighbors who had little had been generous with neighbors who had less. We could laugh about lining worn-out tires with cardboard to grind out a few more miles and about chicory coffee and mock apple pies. Girls who drew seams on the backs of their legs with eyebrow pencils when they couldn't buy stockings could laugh about it now. Women who'd built ships and airplanes would come home to raise families, though some, like Agnes, would find it hard to stay on the farm. The camaraderie and the shared experiences of soldiers and sailors everywhere made for a bond that didn't need explanation.

When I returned to the ranch, I unpacked my gear. I packed away the uniforms and carefully assigned my letters from Annie to the safety of a bottom drawer, to be kept there forever. I gave the little bag of seashells to Rebecca, who was delighted by their shapes and colors. When I got to Wiley's things, I laid them out on my bed and looked at them. I thought his letters from Agnes would make a good wedding gift, love letters to treasure always. I looked at the Japanese soldier's knife and the piece I had cut from the Zero's wing. Those belonged to Wiley, too, but now was not the time for those. I packed them away in my sea bag and found a place for them in my closet. We would have to talk about that another time—maybe never.

As weeks passed, I came to think Homer was right. He was a forward-thinking man, he told me, looking ahead to brighter, prosperous times. The future's highway stretched before us, a long road of possibilities. We had fresh air in our new tires and we would race hell-bent toward the future as it receded before us, endless wonders just around the next corner. We didn't know where we were going, but we knew where we'd been, and we weren't going back.

Annie and Agnes were talking about a double wedding in the spring. Agnes was working on a cowgirl honeymoon, she and Wiley riding off into the sunset on their horses to spend some time in a cabin near the home ranch at Fowler's Rock. I figured they'd stay near her folks till Jesse returned, but I didn't think Agnes was the stay-at-home type. Maybe she'd take those flying lessons she'd told Wiley about in her letters. Whatever she had in mind, Wiley would trail along, faithful as Doc.

Since he had taken a magnanimous turn, I thought maybe I could talk Al into fixing up the Model A so it was drivable again. Hal and Waters had been looking at magazine ads for the 1946 models, scheming about how to get their hands on one. It was nice to see them working together on something. Maybe Annie and I would take a trip to the coast. I had seen enough ocean to last a lifetime, but it would be different with Annie beside me, dipping her toes in the Pacific for the first time. Maybe we could visit Jack and Lucy along the way.

We weren't thinking too far ahead, Annie and I. We were happy, for now. Waters once told me, "Tomorrow's a story ain't yet been told. You turn a new page each day. Don't worry how the story gonna turn out. Be happy with what you got today."

We talked about staying in one of the rooms above Babcock's Rexall. Annie and I could help out in her father's store. Waters and Hal would need help on the ranch, too.

Annie said she wouldn't mind having her own store, if the postwar prosperity made its way to Glory. She thought maybe a ladies' clothing store, something like Mode o'Day, would be just the ticket. Whatever was ahead of us, we would take up where we left off, a life new and improved. We would find our way to the end of the story, turning a new page each day. What had come before was behind us now, "in mem'ry time," as Waters would say. The possibilities were endless.

Author's Note

The real *Mintaka* was laid down as Liberty ship *SS Ansel Briggs* by California Shipbuilding Corporation in Los Angeles and launched 10 March 1943. She was renamed *Mintaka* (after a star in the Orion constellation) and delivered to the Navy. The USS *Mintaka* (AK-94) was manned by United States Coast Guard personnel and tasked with delivering troops, goods, and equipment to locations in the Asiatic Pacific Theater.

Following the war, the *Mintaka* was decommissioned on 12 February 1946 and laid up in the National Defense Reserve Fleet, Suisun Bay Group, Benicia, California. She was withdrawn from the fleet in 1968 and sold for scrap.

Far from Glory is a work of fiction, not history. I have generally followed the travels of the *Mintaka* during the war to provide a structure for the novel, though I have made necessary changes to suit the story's purposes. My father served with the Coast Guard, both on the Beach Patrol in Northern California and aboard the *Mintaka,* transporting troops and cargo in the Pacific. I hope my story will honor the memory of all those who kept our shores safe at home and fought for us abroad. All of the characters in the story are my own creations. Historical figures, places, and events, when mentioned, are treated fictionally.

Acknowledgments

I would like to thank those who have sailed with me on this voyage. They have helped keep me on course as the *Mintaka* steamed to distant shores and returned home safe. My thanks to Eileen Crowley, my brave first reader, for your continuing support; to Jim Nelson, my Navy expert, for looking over my manuscript from the viewpoint of a veteran sailor; to fellow writers John Cox, Kitty Fassett, and Davyd Morris, whose insights and suggestions have been most helpful and deeply appreciated. And to Tim Jollymore and *Finns Way Books* for the encouragement and critical guidance that have kept me afloat throughout this project.

www.ingramcontent.com/pod-product-compliance
Lightning Source LLC
Chambersburg PA
CBHW031215120726
47905CB00002B/347